About the

Janet Lee is a retired newspaper reporter and lectu[illegible] English/Creative Writing. She lives with Alex, her partner of thirty-six years, in Cannock, Staffordshire. Janet has a son, Kevin, and two grandchildren, Tom and Grace, aged fifteen and twelve. She works as a volunteer for the leukaemia charity, Paul's Fun Fund, in memory of her eldest son who lost his battle against the disease in 2011 at the age of thirty-seven. Janet's passion is rock music.

In Search of Dion

Janet Lee

In Search of Dion

Olympia Publishers

London

www.olympiapublishers.com
OLYMPIA PAPERBACK EDITION

A CIP catalogue record for this title is
available from the British Library.

ISBN: 978-1-78830-339-2

First Published in 2019

Olympia Publishers
60 Cannon Street
London
EC4N 6NP

Printed in Great Britain

Dedication

Dedicated to all those local rock bands who keep plugging away in the hope of one day hitting the big time.

Chapter One

Jo-Dan woke with a start and automatically reached for a cigarette in the semi-darkness. His shaking hand groped around the top of the bedside cabinet, knocking over a congealed, half-eaten pizza and an overflowing ash tray.

As he struggled to get his breath, he propped himself up, lit the cigarette and took a long draw, the warmth of the smoke filling his lungs and soul with comfort. His hand was still shaking and beads of sweat were running down his naked body as he propped himself upright.

It was that dream again – and it un-nerved him every time.

There was this extraordinarily beautiful young man: rock star looks, in his thirties, long blond hair cascading down his back. He stood right in front of Jo-Dan, repeatedly blowing smoke into his face, so hard and full-on that he found it increasingly difficult to breathe.

Even now, Jo-Dan could not understand why the first thing he did to get his breath back was to light up a fag. How did that make any sense? But it always seemed to calm him.

Something stirred next to him, something female and naked. Jo-Dan could just about make out her features as she rolled over towards him. He could see she was young, perhaps in her twenties. He looked at the clock on the bedside cabinet; it was five a.m.

"Who the fuck are you?" he asked, taking another long draw on the cigarette.

She grunted in response and went back to sleep.

Jo-Dan stubbed the cigarette out on the top of the cabinet and considered getting up to take a shower. He was hot and sweaty - and anxious. But eventually sleep took over again and it was ten a.m. before he finally emerged from his sweaty pit.

The shower was heavenly. God, he loved that shower. The bed-sit might have been a bit of a rat hole, but at least it had a functional shower. While cleanliness of his home was never a priority, personal hygiene was an absolute must.

He caught sight of himself as he got out of the shower – enraptured with his own image. What little money he had, he spent on expensive products to keep that shoulder-length, black hair shiny and glossy. He wrapped a towel round his waist, struck a pose and studied his reflection to make sure he looked hard-ass enough: arms raised in the air, fingers placed just so, in rock music salute.

The lean, tanned, toned body of a twenty-eight-year-old American singer glowered back at him. Perfect.

There was a half-full bottle of beer left somewhere in the mess of the bed-sit. That sufficed for breakfast. Jo-Dan made a quick phone call, then got dressed, returning to the mirror to check that the jeans were slung just low enough below the waist and the cut away T-shirt revealed enough of those toned upper arms.

He sat on the side of the only armchair in the room and nudged the girl with his foot.

"Time you went," he said as she looked bewildered at him. "I've called a cab. It'll be here in five minutes."

As the girl struggled sleepily to pull on her jeans and T-shirt, Jo-Dan turned on the TV to avoid any conversation. The only time he spoke to her again was to tell her "cab's here." He did not even look at her as she left.

"You're an ass-hole," she said, as she left the room.

Jo-Dan turned the TV up louder.

Chapter Two

In an English country house, thousands of miles away, seven people were holding a meeting which would change Jo-Dan's life forever.

Five members of an internationally known rock band and the two grown up sons of their former singer, Janine Freeman, were in sombre mood.

This was a meeting they had dreaded. It was a formal acceptance, if you like, that Janine and her iconic front man and husband had still not returned, a year after their "disappearing trick" – and it was looking unlikely that they ever would.

Not one word had been heard from them since that infamous night when the band's notorious stage effects seemed to have gone up a notch. It was the last night of the tour in Los Angeles. Jo-Dan had been there to witness it. He had been invited to perform a guest spot and had blown the audience away with his vocals. This had been his finest hour, the one and only time he had wowed a stadium audience and he had been prepared to make the most of it.

Jo-Dan had stood at the side of the stage with Janine's sons, watching the encore. They all laughed and applauded when a sphere of sparkling lights surrounded Janine and the love of her life, the extraordinary charismatic front man she shared vocals with.

The band had become famous, not just because their live shows were awesome, but because of the phenomenal special effects which accompanied a Son of Gabriel show. No one had yet established how the effects were produced – and that final show had topped all others.

Inside the electrifying sphere, Janine fought playfully with her husband, as she often did. And as the sparkles around them became denser the audience found it more and more difficult to see inside. But they did just make out the couple rising from the ground, then completely disappearing, as the sparkles fell on to the stage.

The boys' precious mum had gone and had not been seen since.

And the world had lost its most iconic front man: the irrepressible, demanding, impossible, self-centred, self-assured, funny and supremely talented Dion was gone.

"Thanks for letting us use your house for the meeting," Tommy said to Janine's sons, as they all gathered in the luxurious lounge.

"Still feels odd calling it 'our house'," Paul replied. "Came as a bit of a shock when we got back from the tour – and there was this letter from Dio (as the boys always affectionately called him) saying he'd signed the house over to us."

Paul's brother Lucas looked down at the carpet. It was still too raw, even a year later. Their mum had been their world – an extraordinarily beautiful, funny rock singer. And they adored their step-dad, who had educated, entertained and encouraged them since they were twelve and fifteen years old. Now Paul and Lucas were rich, very rich - but they would gladly have swapped their house and fortune to have their mum and Dion back.

They were nineteen and twenty-two, trying to find their own way in the world. The past year had been traumatic. Everyone had told them they should move on; that their mum and Dion had planned their vanishing trick so that they could escape the limelight and go off somewhere to live out their lives incognito.

But something didn't feel right.

There had been that conversation with Dion's mum and with the band's manager Miles, shortly after it happened. It gave them no answers, but it was enough to convince them all was not what it seemed. They still clung to a slim hope that they would be found – or would return. And that was why, here in this lounge today, the atmosphere was one of dreaded defeat. Where to go from here?

Everyone sprawled across the furniture, occasionally sipping their tea or coffee. Their heads were down and no one was making eye contact. Occasionally they would glance at the photo on the wall – a beautiful picture of Dion and Janine, not in rock star pose, but looking natural and happy at home, their long blond hair intermingling as if to reinforce how close they were. They were sitting in the garden with their fat, black mongrel Rolo – who, at the moment, was lying quietly, apart from huffing and puffing occasionally, on a rug in front of the fireplace.

It was Tommy, the drummer, who broke the silence.

"Look, we've put this off until now. We said we'd give it a year, then decide what to do," he said.

Still no one looked up.

"I loved them as much as all of you. I was their best man for goodness sake. Not a day goes by that I don't think about them and drive myself crazy trying to come up with an answer. But Dion would want the band to continue. He loved this band."

The backing singers, the beautiful twins, Eva and Lou, looked tearful. Dion had drilled them so hard, making them take a more up-front role before his departure, rehearsing them to the point of exhaustion. And they wondered now whether that hadn't been pre-planned.

Still no one spoke.

Tommy, for all his macho appearance, all shaved head and tattoos, suddenly looked vulnerable.

"I've never told you this before," he said quietly – and everyone looked up in anticipation.

"The first time Jo-Dan was given a guest slot – which ended up with him being dumped outside, after he kicked off, apparently - Dion came into the dressing room to talk to me before we went on stage. Even then I thought he sounded strange."

The atmosphere in the lounge was expectant and everyone held their breath, so desperate for answers, any shred of information.

"He told me he loved me – not in a 'come-on-to-me' kind of way. That wasn't his style. But he'd never said anything like that before in all the years I've known him. 'I love you man,' he said - then went on to say that, if anything happened to him, the band should carry on. It sounded like a goodbye to me, but I put it down to him being tired. It *had* been a long and gruelling tour."

"So did you ask him why he was coming out with this stuff?" Eva asked him. "That just doesn't sound like 'D' at all. Most times he was so energetic and enthusiastic I just wanted to strangle him, God love him."

"I said 'are you all right, mate?' or words to that effect," Tommy continued. "Then he seemed to snap out of it and he was back to normal."

Everyone continued to study the carpet, until Tommy continued.

"But there was one more thing."

All eyes bored into him – and they all looked desperate for this last piece of the puzzle.

"He gave me this," Tommy said, taking a small business card out of his jeans pocket. It was a bit crumpled and worse for wear, but the name and phone number were still visible.

Tommy put the card on the coffee table and everyone gathered round as if their lives depended on it.

"He made me promise, if ever anything happened to him, that we would recruit this new singer. He said that I should trust his judgement, that this singer would be a perfect replacement for him."

Tommy looked directly at the band members, one by one.

"And I promised him," he added.

The card sat on the table, challenging anyone to disagree.

"Jo-Dan Rox," the lead guitarist Rick scoffed. "That arsehole. Are you serious? Did you not hear about his sound-check tantrums and how Dion deliberately cut off his mic live on stage the first time he gave him a guest slot, because he was so obnoxious? Dion loathed him. I'm sorry mate, but I find it hard to believe…"

"Love him or loathe him, he was brilliant on that last night," Tommy reminded him. "He knew he'd been given a second chance. Why do you think Dion offered him a second guest slot? He'd made his point. He'd taught him a lesson.

"He *was* good," Lou said. "I remember 'D' was furious with him for coming on to us and Janine before the show, but he stormed it on the night."

The bass player Joey had looked thoughtful as he listened, before putting his word in. "Do you remember how Jo-Dan turned back as he was leaving the stage and actually shouted 'thank you' to Dion on that last night?" he said.

"That was the only time they looked as if they could get along," Rick chimed in. "Dion couldn't stand him. He hated that Jo-Dan couldn't even say his name right."

"Yeah, it came out something like 'Dee-arn'," the first twin said, in a mock American accent.

And the ice was broken. Everyone laughed for a few seconds, each with their own memory of how incensed Dion had looked every time Jo-Dan's name was mentioned.

"Anyway, how about we invite the dreaded Jo-Dan over to England, all expenses paid; we rehearse with him, then do a few trial low-key gigs?" Tommy suggested. "We needn't announce anything to the press yet. See if we can stand him first."

"I'm not hopeful," Rick said. "But if that's really what Dion wanted. He was never wrong about anything. He always negotiated everything for the band."

"So are we all agreed then? Tommy asked. "It's on the understanding that, if Dion and Janine come back, Jo-Dan will be out."

Everyone stared, unenthusiastically.

"Look, for all I know Jo-Dan might not accept, or he may have something else going on, or he may have changed his number and I won't be able to get hold of him," Tommy added.

"Or someone may have punched his lights out by now," Joey suggested.

There were a few smiles at *that* prospect.

"Paul and Lucas. You should have a say in this," Tommy added.

"If it's really what Dio wanted, then I'm OK with that," Paul said – but he looked sad at the finality of replacing his mum and step-dad. It felt like a betrayal and it felt too final.

"You go ahead," Lucas added. "This band was everything to them."

"So, is that settled then?" Tommy said, looking from one band member to another. The fact that no one disagreed he took as an acceptance.

"OK. I'll try the number later," he continued. "It'll be too early in the States to call him now."

Tommy took a deep breath and tried one last time to lift his band mates.

"Look, I don't like this any more than you do," he added.

Then he told them the awful truth.

"But you all know - Dion *always* got what he wanted - even now."

Chapter Three

It was late afternoon in L.A. when Jo-Dan got the call. It was hot, really hot and he was hungry and irritable. The air conditioning was noisy, so he turned up the radio station, which was tuned into the local rock channel, until it blasted a wall of sound.

He was stretched out on the couch, one hand idly banging the coffee table with a drumstick in time to the beat. When the phone rang, he only just managed to hear it and cursed that he had to drag himself off the couch to answer it.

"Yeah?" he shouted, the music still blaring, making a conversation impossible. "Hold on, will ya? Can't hear what you're sayin'."

He kept the caller on hold for an impossibly long time while he turned the TV down, lit up a cigarette, cracked open a cold beer from the fridge then settled next to the phone.

"Yeah?" he said disinterestedly.

"Hi. Is that Jo-Dan?"

"Who wants to know?"

"It's Tommy here. Drummer with Son of Gabriel in England. Dion gave me your number a while ago and made me promise I'd get in touch with you."

It was as if the very words 'Son of Gabriel' and 'Dion' had electrocuted Jo-Dan. He was immediately alert, scrambling to turn off the noisy aircon so that he could hear more clearly. He breathed out hard, drew on his cigarette, then forced himself into composure.

"You windin' me up?" he said, feigning disinterest.

"No. I'm serious. I need to talk to you."

"What about? You heard anything from Dion? Anyone found out where he is?"

"No. That's why I'm calling you."

There was something about Tommy's tone of voice that made Jo-Dan sit up straight. His tone was a mixture of sadness, foreboding and as if he was about to say something of immense importance.

"What's it to do with me?" Jo-Dan asked, doing his best to sound surly. In truth, Dion was his idol and he was as devastated and mystified by his disappearance as everyone else – but he wasn't about to admit that.

"Dion and Janine have been missing for a year now," Tommy continued. "We had a band discussion today and we agreed we'd like to try you out on Dion's lead vocals – if you're free."

Jo-Dan physically shook so much he could barely hold the phone. The rest of Tommy's words went over his head, as his brain struggled to unscramble that last sentence.

"Jo-Dan? You there?"

"Yeah, yeah. Sorry, the line wasn't very clear. What did you say about England?"

"We'd like you to come over, all expenses paid. We'll put you up here, get in lots of rehearsal time and get on the road with a few low-key gigs to start with. See how we get on. You available? You up for that?"

Jo-Dan covered the phone so Tommy could not hear him laugh almost to the point of hysteria. He was pacing around so much that he almost pulled the flex of the phone out of its socket. He was punching the air, breathing hard and whispering "yes, yes" to himself.

"When are you thinking? Got a few things lined up," Jo-Dan lied.

"As soon as you can," Tommy said, seeing through the lie.

And so it was arranged. In a month's time the dreaded Jo-Dan would be installed in a flat in Lichfield, Staffordshire, England, and launched on the unsuspecting public.

Chapter Four

Paul and Lucas were locking up for the night.

And with a house this size, it took some doing. So many windows to check, so many doors to lock, make sure Rolo is installed in his basket in the kitchen, switch on the security cameras.

Their girlfriends were staying overnight again and their presence had become a welcome distraction from that nagging ache that was always there. Where was mum? Why had she disappeared without a word? Why did none of this ring true?

They had discussed it over and over and over with their girlfriends. They had watched the video footage countless times together; they had watched the news reports, read the newspaper and magazine articles, dismissed the latest wild theories – and all that was left was an empty recording studio in the grounds of their Cannock Wood house. They had searched that studio down to the last inch, in the desperate hope of finding a clue, but to no avail.

Dion's and Janine's bedroom was left untouched. Rolo looked downcast and always looked up hopefully when anyone arrived at the house – only to return to his basket, huffing and puffing with disappointment.

The "boys", as Janine called them, could still see Dion careering around the huge garden - with Rolo in hot pursuit, trying to take the ball from him. Those had been happier times, when the house was full of people and laughter.

The boys knew that their mum would never voluntarily have left them. Dion's mum had talked to them the morning after the disappearance, when they had been in their hotel in L.A. She had been tearful, but had said she needed to reassure them. The band's manager Miles was with her and they said some pretty weird stuff.

It was obvious that they were struggling to find the right words.

"Dion and Janine were special people who loved each other very much," they had told the boys.

"Dion had told us – and sworn us to secrecy – that he never wanted to be forty. He wanted to be always remembered as a beautiful soul with a body to match.

"You know how vain he was," Dion's mum had said, trying to defuse their distress with humour. But her tears fell too as she spoke to them.

"And he would never have been able to leave your mum behind," she had told the boys.

"But mum would never have left us, especially not without telling us," Paul had insisted.

Miles had been less sympathetic. He was more matter of fact when he spoke to them.

"Your mum may not have gone voluntarily," he said.

"Gone where?" Lucas had cried out in frustration.

And now he looked back on that night with a sickening feeling in his stomach. The boys had watched as their mum fought Dion hard inside that sphere, as he held on to her tight. Now they wondered whether it had been play fighting at all. But they loved Dion. He would surely never take their mum anywhere against her will, would he? And he knew how close they were to her. He would never part them from her, surely?

"There are certain forces that people will not understand," Miles had said. "Many, many rock stars leave too soon – because they are given to the world gift-wrapped, for us to have for a while. But when their time comes – some of them go because they want to. Others…"

"You're talking mumbo-jumbo," Paul had screamed. "Where's my mum? What's happened to her? Did that – that – sphere thing kill them both? Why is there *nothing* left to find? Why is there no trace of them? And don't tell me it's one of your magic tricks. You're not a crazy or good enough magician to pull that off."

They had talked for an hour – but whatever the boys were told, it all sounded too nonsensical. They had gone to a "special place", they had been told.

"I'm sure they will do their best to visit you when they can."

But rather than comfort the boys, the words only added to their distress.

They resolved that their only option was to search for them. This was some stupid stunt. Dion and Janine would turn up somewhere – and they would follow up every lead, every sighting, no matter how implausible.

And the band members were right behind them. That final "special effect" had left a profound impact on the whole band. Not only were they constantly having to field questions from the press and public, they also missed their two stars. They had to constantly deny any knowledge of the whereabouts of Dion and Janine – or how the event came about.

They had even searched the stage: on it, below it, above it - for any sign of a trapdoor, a secret compartment, anything that could give them a clue. The police had left the case officially "open", though it was clear to the band and the boys that they, like the rest of world, saw the event as a massive publicity stunt for Son of Gabriel and a way out of the limelight for Dion and Janine. They were all tired of having to repeat the same old line, "I honestly don't know how it happened. None of us have any idea where they are."

Lying in bed that night, Paul was quiet.

"Can I help?" his girlfriend Stacy said.

"Not unless you can find mum and Dio," he said sadly.

Chapter Five

The band was all set up and ready as usual by the time Jo-Dan arrived at the small L.A. bar. There were a handful of customers and none looked like the type who would enjoy a rock gig; they were dressed more Country and Western.

But the band had been booked to perform, so perform they would. It was a paid gig and money was something that was in short supply for all of them.

Jo-Dan swaggered in, guitar slung over his shoulder, dishevelled except for the lustrous hair. The three band members looked up uninterestedly, acknowledged that he was there with nods of their heads, and carried on setting up the battered equipment; they had long since given up any hope that Jo-Dan would help.

Jo-Dan hovered around the guys, shuffling about aimlessly. He looked as if he wanted to say something, but couldn't find the words. He looked from one band member to another as they busied themselves and eventually the words just blurted out as if on their own accord.

"This will be my last gig with you guys," Jo-Dan announced as he plugged in his guitar.

"What do you mean?" his drummer said. "You givin' it up as a bad job? Can't say I blame you. I mean, this is 'nowhere land'."

"Got an offer," Jo-Dan said – feeling as if he would explode or spontaneously combust at any minute if he didn't share the news with someone.

The band members stopped what they were doing and actually paid attention.

"Going to England before the end of the month," Jo-Dan said, trying to sound as casual as possible. "Got a call from the Son of Gabriel drummer. The band wants me to try out for Dion's role (and he almost managed to pronounce the name properly, with a pretend English accent).

His words were greeted with a universal stare – one that told him that his band members were trying to process the information.

The drummer was the first who managed to speak.

"You mean THE Dion?"

"Yep."

"The one who's still missing – but could show up at any time?"

"Yep. If he turns up, I'll be back on the plane home I guess."

"But Jo – this is big. I mean, everyone knows that band. You sure this is not a wind-up?"

Jo-Dan let out a piercing riff on his lead guitar which made the small crowd cover their ears and pull faces at each other.

"Plane ticket's sorted and paid for by the band. Money's in my account for expenses," he said, glaring at the Country and Western dudes, daring them to say anything.

"Thought I'd play this last gig with you guys – you know – as a sort of farewell," Jo-Dan continued, looking embarrassed at letting his guard down.

"Well, fuck, we're gonna miss you man," his bass player told him. "Just hope it works out for ya."

"If I can get you guys over to England, I will," Jo-Dan said, suddenly feeling a lump in his throat.

He had known these guys since school days and they had scraped by in life together – and they all knew and understood Jo-Dan's background. They thought better of expressing their true feelings for now. Emotion or man love wasn't something any of them went in for, but they all felt a huge chapter in their lives was closing – and maybe, even, a new one was about to open.

"Anyway, beer's on me," Jo-Dan announced and suddenly everyone was cheerful. After a few beers, all their questions came flowing out and Jo-Dan found himself feeling suddenly apprehensive (not that he'd admit it).

"So what do you make of Dion's disappearance?" the bass player asked him. "You were there on the night."

"There was all sorts of stuff going on at that concert," Jo-Dan said, quietly serious. "Weird stuff, I mean seriously weird. I watched Dion and his wife disappear into thin air in this capsule thing made of sparkly stuff. I tell you, if I catch sight of any of that shit I'll be off. Scared the hell out of me. I was close enough to see his wife look seriously pissed when she couldn't get out. After that, it got harder and harder to see them. But if you ask me, it was no publicity stunt. Some heavy shit went down that night. The band members were really shaken…"

"OK, guys, if you wanna be paid you better get on that stage," the bar manager yelled snapping them out of their conversation. "Punters are getting restless."

"One last time. Let's make it a good 'un," Jo-Dan said, as they quickly downed the last of their beer.

And it was. It was a blistering set, which even won over the Country and Western dudes.

Chapter Six

It was the first Son of Gabriel rehearsal in over a year and the mood was sombre.

Members declined the boys' offer to rehearse in Dion's studio – that would have been just too painful. Instead, they hired a studio in the small town of Rugeley; it was relatively primitive, compared to the state-of-the- art facilities they were used to, but it sufficed for a practice session.

The intention was to give a quick blast through all the songs, for the musicians to get back into the groove and for the twins to take on Janine's role. The drummer and two guitarists would do their best to take on Dion's vocals, for now, between them. The band also wanted to be note perfect for when the dreaded Jo-Dan joined them in a week's time.

But it was worse than awful.

None of the magic was there, the songs sounded painful without Dion's vocals and it was immediately obvious that the fun factor was missing. They all realised they had taken Dion's huge personality and style for granted. He *was* Son of Gabriel. His laughter and energy had filled rehearsal rooms – and oh, how they missed him, even more, now.

And they had also taken for granted the harmonies Janine provided on lead vocals, the sexy persona that she brought to live performances, the sheer magnetism of her partnership with Dion and the full sound of three female vocalists.

The band stopped the songs every now and then to explore how they could get round certain parts of the vocals. No one had the range or ability to cover for Dion and when they stopped for a break, half-way through the rehearsal session the atmosphere was one of total despondence.

"We're finished," Rick said. "That was the worst rehearsal ever. There's no way we are going to be able to perform to a stadium audience."

"He's right," Joey said. "It's not the girls' fault. They did their best. But we sound like any other band."

"Well, at least the damn lights didn't implode or the studio didn't go up in flames," Tommy added. "I was expecting some disaster or freakin' hologram ghosts or a running man up the walls or sparkly bits flying around the place. Nothing. Nothing. And you know what? We used to worry about all that kind of stuff going on – but I'd give anything for spontaneous 'special effects' now. We're done for. We owe it to Jo-Dan – and to Dion – to give him a trial, but I think we all know this is the end of the road."

Joey took a swig of water from his bottle and looked at his band mates. No – they were more than band mates – his buddies, his family, but he was downcast and saw the end in sight. He let out a huge sigh.

"Let's crack on," he said trying to shake himself out of utter depression. "We at least need to get through the set then we can fuck off home."

So they continued with the set, in the same order that they had last performed it – that fateful night in L.A. - and it was a staid process to say the least. They got through it: they played the same notes, bashed out the same beats and sang the same lyrics, but, oh my God, this was not the band it used to be.

"Guess we won't even bother booking any gigs," Tommy said, as they packed away the equipment. "Good job we've not released any publicity about starting up again. I think, guys, I love you all, but we'll be going our separate ways. This is not how I want this band to sound. And it's certainly not how Dion would want it to be. What would be the point of re-launching Son of Gabriel if it sounds shit?

"I'll re-book the studio for a couple of days when Jo-Dan gets here. We'll give him a few days to get over his jet-lag, then we'll suffer him in the studio."

At least that comment made everyone laugh.

"We can then maybe even treat him to some sightseeing," Tommy added.

"Well, you can take him, then," Joey said. "Don't think you'll have any other volunteers."

The smiles had already faded.

"At least I'll have honoured my promise to Dion," Tommy added.

"But as far as rehearsals with the ridiculously named Jo-Dan go - don't hold your breath…"

Chapter Seven

Tommy scanned the hordes of passengers, as they filed towards him like a herd of cattle. Strange places, airports, he thought. People crossed the world, each with their own agenda: lovers meeting up, business deals to be made, holidays to enjoy – guitarists to meet.

He was tired. It had taken four hours to get to London Heathrow. He had been stuck in traffic, which had made him anxious that he would arrive late, and he still had the drive back home to look forward to. And where the hell was he?

Tommy leaned forward over the flimsy barrier and scrutinised the 'arrivals'. He feared he might have missed him – perhaps he'd walked by, maybe dressed in a smart suit for the journey. Maybe he had cut his hair, so he hadn't recognised him. After all, it had been over a year since he last saw him.

He started to look behind him at those who were already hugging long-lost relatives in case he'd gone through without him noticing. Only a few stragglers were now coming through and Tommy's mind started to wander. Maybe he had decided against coming at all. He felt a pang of guilt at feeling elated by that prospect. That would absolve him of any promise he had made to Dion and it would save the band from what was bound to be an excruciating rehearsal. Anyway, their mind had already been made up, but they felt duty bound to go through this charade of auditioning him.

Maybe he was hanging back, nervous at being in a foreign country for the first time; maybe he had quietened down this past year and was actually quite a nice guy when he wasn't trying to play rock star…

And then he heard a distinct American voice – and so did everyone else. There was clearly some argument going on and the decibels were going up.

Tommy raised his eyes to the heavens and said a silent prayer, "Please God, don't let that be him." No sooner were the words out than he saw him – arms flailing and almost coming to blows with some middle-aged guy in a suit.

"Get the fuck out of my way," Jo-Dan yelled, taking a swipe at him with his holdall. Holdall? Where was his suitcase? All eyes turned to watch the spectacle: Jo-Dan, dressed in baggy patched jeans and a cutaway T-shirt, was hauling his holdall back over his shoulder and clinging on to his guitar case protectively.

"You keep that fuckin' trolley thing under control," he was yelling at the guy who was clearly struggling with a luggage kart that had a mind of its own. "You bash my guitar again with that trolley and I swear to God I'll run you over with it. Just stay the fuck out of my way."

The trolley guy, an Englishman, was clearly someone not used to being railed at.

"I said I was sorry," he yelled back. "Who do you think you are, coming into my country with your foul language? And look at you, for God's sake, why should I take this from the likes of you?"

Jo-Dan pulled his arm back ready to take a swing at him but stopped just in time as he saw the security guys moving in.

"Don't touch my fuckin' guitar," he yelled as they manhandled him away.

"Hey! Hey!" Tommy yelled and the security guards looked around. "It's OK. He's with me. He gets a little over protective about his guitar. Just let me get him out of here, huh? Jo-Dan tell them you're sorry, there'll be no more trouble and we'll get out of their way."

Jo-Dan shrugged hard to throw off one of the guards. He straightened his T-shirt and put his bag down in front of him. "He bashed into my guitar," he protested, arms spread out as if to appeal to the two burly guards standing either side of him to understand.

"Is that all?" one of them said. "Have you finished making a scene? You stand here for a few minutes, until the gentleman has time to leave. And we'll be watching you on CCTV. Any more from you and you'll be on the next plane home, do you understand?"

Jo-Dan gave an exaggerated sigh as if he was the victim here and unzipped his guitar case to check on his precious instrument.

"It seems to be OK," he told the guards who were clearly not interested. Jo-Dan's face was still fuming. He took out a packet of cigarettes and went to light up.

"Sir, you can't smoke right here. Sir…"

Clearly rattled, Jo-Dan glared at Tommy and mouthed "what the f…?"

Tommy gestured back at him waving his arms downwards as if to say, "calm down."

The security guards kept him in check for a few minutes, which gave Tommy more time to take in the force of nature that was Jo-Dan. His hair had grown longer since he last saw him; it was now way past shoulder-length. He was tanned from the L.A. sun, and looked healthy and strong, with not an ounce of fat on him. But his features looked older than Tommy had remembered. He was, after all, approaching twenty-nine years old, and although he still had the smooth features of a teenager, there was a kind of care-worn look about him.

The last few stragglers had now passed through Arrivals, so the security guards saw fit to let him go with a final warning. "Sir, we would ask you to moderate your language while you are the airport."

Jo-Dan snatched his holdall from the floor, slung it back over his shoulder, clung on to his guitar for dear life and swaggered over to Tommy.

"Let's get out of this shit-hole," he said.

"Hi, Jo-Dan," Tommy replied, taking his holdall from him. "Welcome to England."

He had a feeling the journey home was going to feel very long.

"When do we get on to the freeway?"

"You're on it."

"When do we get off these narrow roads?"

"These are our A-roads."

"What's an A-road? Shit weather, ain't it?"

"Actually, this is quite a good day for us."

"Whoah. Watch out, you just pulled out on him."

"I had right of way."

"Whoah. There's a fuckin' great lorry about to hit us."

"No, he's just in the box junction waiting to turn right. Jo-Dan, will you just shut the fuck up and let me drive?"

"Where's the next gas station? I need a piss."

"We call it a *petrol* station or garage, Jo-Dan. We're on a freakin' motorway; just try and hang on."

"Pull over, I'll just go in those hedges."

"This is a hard shoulder Jo-Dan, for emergency stops only."

"This *is* an emergency. Hard shoulder? What a ridiculous expression. Got a fag? I've smoked all mine."

"Here, but open the window will ya? This car cost a lot of money. I don't want stinkin' fags discolouring the upholstery."

"Can't you find anything better than this shit on the radio? Try the rock channels."

"We don't have dedicated rock channels."

"What? What's the matter with this country? Where am I going to stay?"

"I got you a flat in Lichfield. It's a tourist city. I think you'll like it. It's the birthplace of Dr Johnson.

"What's a flat? You mean an apartment? Who's Dr Johnson when he's at home?"

"Never mind. Here, have a sandwich. Perhaps that'll keep you quiet for two minutes."

"Does this Litch-bitch place have lots of bars?"

"We call them pubs, Jo-Dan. Yea, there's a few but you'll need to be sober. The audition's in three days and you need to rest and rehearse. You'll be jet-lagged."

"It's not really an audition, is it, since you'll all give me the job anyway?"

"How can you be sure? You been practising the songs hard?"

"Nah. No need to practise. Already know them all. I'll be brilliant."

"You know *all* our songs?"

"Yeah. And I've written some new songs for the band. Thought it was time you released a new album, somethin' a bit more edgy with a ballad or two thrown in."

"You write your own songs?"

"'Course I do. What's those stupid red box things?"

"Phone boxes, Jo-Dan. Not many people have cell phones in England."

"Anyway, one of the songs is a sure-fire hit single."

"Jesus Christ, Jo-Dan. Do you ever give it a rest?"

"What about chicks in this Lich-bitch place?"

"It's 'Lichfield', Jo-Dan. You're not gonna have time for socialising."

"Wanna bet? How far is it now?

"Jo-Dan, for fuck's sake get your feet off my dashboard."

"You sure have small houses here don't you? It ain't Beverly Hills, is it?"

"No – and don't expect to find Sunset Strip in Lichfield either. It's a small, quaint city with a pool. It's where we used to rehearse and perform with Dion in the early days."

"I'm gonna find Dion."

"What…?"

"Might be shootin' myself in the foot if I find him, but I'm tellin' ya, I will."

"What makes you think *you* can find him, if no one else has been able to?"

"Don't underestimate me. And find Dion, you find Janine too. Quite fancied her. That pissed him off big time. Put the aircon on, will ya? It's warm now the sun's come out in this Godforsaken country."

"The car doesn't have aircon."

"Jesus Christ. Does my apartment have aircon?"

"No."

"Fuck me. It better have a shower."

"No. It has a bath."

"Fuck, no shower? How am I supposed to keep this hair looking good?"

"You'll just have to figure it out, Jo-Dan. Aren't you tired after that long flight? Don't you fancy a sleep until we get to Lichfield?"

"Are you married, Tom?"

"It's Tommy. No, I'm not. You ever been married?"

"You kiddin'? Why would anyone stay with one person?"

"No one special in your life?"

"No way. Anyway, when I'm front man for Son of Gabriel I'm gonna be able to take my pick every night, huh? We nearly there?"

"About another half hour."

"Your traffic lights are weird, ain't they? You can turn right now, your road's clear."

"No I can't, Jo-Dan. The lights have to be on green."

"But nothin's comin'."

"That's the law Jo-Dan. You wait for the light to go green, even if there's nothing coming."

"I'd just go anyway. Quite green, ain't it, round here?"

"Yea, it's green all right."

"Can't see much to do, though. You'll have to show me where the action is. And what am I going to do for money? Who's payin' me?"

"You should have some left from what I send you. And I've got five hundred pounds for you in an envelope. That should be enough for a couple of weeks."

"What's that in dollars?"

"I dunno. You figure it out, Jo-Dan."

"And what about when the five hundred runs out? I'll be here longer than two weeks."

"You'll be here longer than two weeks if we take you on as lead singer."

"Better get loads more cash out then. I'm starvin'. Where will I eat tonight?"

"Jo-Dan?"

"Yea?"

"Can you please just-shut-up-for-a-few-minutes?"

"Jeez, you sure are uptight, aren't ya?"

Chapter Eight

The little boy cowered under the bed and imagined that he saw shapes move slowly round the bedroom. He stuffed his battered teddy bear into his mouth so he wouldn't scream. He found this worked the best, except a lot of the fluff got stuck in his mouth and made him cough.

Still, it was better than the beating he would get from his mum and dad if he screamed again.

He was seven years old – far too old to be screaming or still clinging to a teddy they said. He was beaten for wetting the bed in fright, he was beaten for screaming when he had nightmares, then he'd be beaten again for clinging on to his teddy.

The worse day was when his dad ripped the head off the precious bear. How the little boy had wept as he tried in vain to make it stick on again.

And then the call from the school came - and that resulted in another beating, one of the worst yet. This time his dad took off his belt and the buckle really hurt when it bit into his flesh. Mum was high at the time, so she didn't interfere.

"Get in here," his dad had called. And he was already weeing himself as he walked into the squalid living room. The pee ran down his legs on to the beer-stained carpet. It mixed with the fag ash and drug paraphernalia on the floor. It wouldn't make it smell any worse; it already stank real bad.

"What have you been sayin' at school again?" his dad bellowed. Then with his grizzled face right next to the terrified youngster he shouted even louder.

"What have you been sayin' again? I told you, didn't I, about saying those things? What the hell's the matter with you?"

The little boy looked at his dad and the aura around him was black, really black. This was bad. He didn't know how he knew, but he was sure it wasn't a good sign. The one around his mum was dark grey.

"You're scarin' the other kids again," his dad shrieked. "Ann, tell 'im."

His mum stirred, but was clearly out of it.

The youngster's skinny belly rumbled, but he knew there was nothing in the house, as he'd looked as soon as he got home from school.

His dad's face was still pressed next to his and his breath smelt foul.

"There's no such thing as colours round people do you hear? You don't see stupid colours. Do you want the kids to think you're mad? Do you?"

"No sir," the youngster said. "But I only told the truth. Mikey's granddad had a brown colour all round him. I did see it, I did."

"And after you said that, the poor sod died," his dad screamed at him.

The youngster felt the lash of the belt across his back. Being of slight build, it knocked him across the room.

"No more colours do you hear? You're even scaring the teachers, drawing pictures of them surrounded in yellow or purple or whatever. You *ever* say or do anything like this to anyone *ever* again and you'll be locked away in an institution. You understand?"

"Yes, sir," he managed to say in between sobs.

Chapter Nine

By the time they approached Lichfield, Tommy was fit to throw Jo-Dan out of the car, but with extraordinary willpower he managed to keep his cool, figuring he would be back on that plane sooner rather than later.

"You see the three spires," he ventured. "Those are the cathedral spires: quite a famous landmark."

"Uh-huh. Do you get wild animals round here?"

"No, not much."

Tommy looked sideways at his passenger, wondering just how his head worked.

"Frog Lane. What a stupid name for a road," Jo-Dan ventured. "Hope you ain't got me an apartment in Frog Lane. No street cred in that. Street cred? You get it?"

Jo-Dan laughed at his own joke – and it was a real raucous laugh – one that Tommy couldn't help but smile at. If he hadn't been so tired, he might even have thought of a response.

"You're in Bird Street, just round the corner."

"Bird Street? Fuck me, that's hysterical," Jo-Dan said, his infectious laughter filling the car. "Couldn't be more appropriate."

Tommy parked the car at the rear of the 'apartment'. Jo-Dan retrieved his guitar from the "trunk", as he called it, and Tommy took his bag.

"Here's your key. Don't lose it. Come on, I'll show you inside, then I'll leave you to catch up on some sleep."

It was a two-bedroomed flat above a shop, quite smart and well equipped. Tommy had filled the fridge and cupboards with enough food to last a fortnight.

Jo-Dan went from room to room, looking ridiculously out of place.

"Where's the refrigerator?" he asked.

"That's it there, right in front of you."

"What, that farting little thing? Where I am gonna keep all the ice and beer and stuff?"

"Jo-Dan, it's autumn. It's usually wet and cold. You're not gonna need much ice at this time of year. Let me show you how the heating works…"

He turned round to show him, but Jo-Dan was already in another room, lying on his back on the double bed, testing its bounce.

"Where's the TV?" he asked surveying the room.

"It's in the lounge, Jo-Dan. You wanna unpack?" Tommy said, throwing his bag on the bed.

"Sure," came the reply. Jo Dan unzipped the bag and took out several folders bulging with paperwork. He up-ended the rest on to the bed: some electrical attachments for his guitar, a couple of pairs of jeans, four T-shirts and a few mismatched socks.

"What's with the folders?"

"Lyrics. I told you," Jo-Dan shouted back as he sauntered into the lounge and flicked through the channels on the TV.

"Summat wrong with this TV. Where's all the channels?"

"That's all we have in this country. You'll get used to it. Look, I'm bushed. If there's anything else you need, you've got my number. I'll leave you to relax. I'll call by tomorrow afternoon. I've got a key so I'll let myself in. Have a good sleep."

"Hey, Tommy!" Jo-Dan yelled after him as he walked down the stairs.

"Yeah?"

"Leave me some fags huh? And mind the frogs don't get ya. You'll croak it if they do."

Tommy left his packet of cigarettes on the stairs. He had never felt so weary in his life and he now realised why Dion was always so incensed after spending just minutes with Jo-Dan, in person or on the phone.

He got in his car, rested his head on the steering well and said a silent, sarcastic prayer to his best friend. "Thanks for that, mate."

Tommy went home to his mansion in nearby Abbots Bromley village. He was so relieved for his sanity that he had decided not to invite Jo-Dan to stay with him. In fact, none of the band had volunteered, so they had scoured estate agents for a flat to let, figuring they couldn't even trust him to stay at a local hotel.

As soon as his head hit the pillow, he was fast asleep. Tommy was still the one who got all the girls: beefy and shaven-headed, he was the epitome of masculinity, but tonight he was grateful that there was no one staying.

The following afternoon, feeling refreshed, he drove back to the flat and entered quietly, reasoning that even the dreaded Jo-Dan had to sleep sometimes.

"Hey. Heard the car pull up," Jo-Dan said as he appeared from the bedroom. He had slung on a tatty pair of jeans and plain black T-shirt – and his hair was immaculate.

"I used the bath," he said proudly. "Managed to wash my hair by ducking under the water." He pronounced it 'wadder'.

He stood there, combing his locks through with his fingers, bouncing with energy and looking pleased with himself.

"You sleep well?" Tommy asked, puzzled, as he could have sworn he had seen something move in the corner of his eye.

"Sure. Had a few beers, found a couple of chicks and – you know…"

The couple of chicks, Tommy discovered as he opened the bedroom door to see what had caught his eye, were stirring in the bed.

"You went out last night?" he asked incredulously.

"Yea, wanted to see what Litch-bitch had to offer. Found two as it turned out. Hey girls, time to split."

Tommy stood open mouthed as Jo-Dan hauled the naked girls out of bed, virtually threw their clothes at them and stood sentry-like as they marched past him out of the door.

"But I thought…" one of the girls started.

"Time to go home. I got work to do," Jo-Dan told her coldly.

The girls scrambled to get their stuff together out of the lounge and one of them looked hurt and tearful.

"But you said…" she started.

"I said a lot of stuff. Thank-you-for-the-ride," Jo-Dan said slowly and deliberately as he indicated for them to leave.

Tommy cringed at the use of the Son of Gabriel song title.

"Shithead," one of the girls shouted back, as they left the flat and slammed the door.

The comment had zero effect on Jo-Dan; and as soon as the girls left, it was as if they had never existed.

"So what we doin' today?" he asked Tommy.

"Well, I had planned to show you around the city, but I guess you already did that last night."

"Didn't see nuffin'. Was in the dark. Found some pub called the City Frog and stayed there. What a stupid name for a pub. Anyway, got chattin' to some of the locals…

Tommy cringed at the thought.

"Did you tell them why you are here?"

"Yea, told 'em I'm the next big rock star. Don't think they believed me."

"Well, if you like, I'll show you around in daylight then. Thought you might like to see Dion's home town, you know, the places he went and where he worked and stuff."

"Cool. Got a fag? Smoked that last lot you gave me."

Tommy handed over an almost complete packet, knowing he wouldn't see it again, and led the way to Tudor Row.

"Do you need a jacket?" Tommy asked.

"Nah. Don't feel the cold," Jo-Dan lied. "But I do need to buy some pants. Where can I get some decent pants?"

"Yea, I noticed you hadn't brought any with you when you 'unpacked'."

"I did. What d'you think I'm wearing?"

"I dunno. I can't see your underwear can I?"

"What you on about?"

"Your pants. I can't see if you've got pants on…"

And so the conversation went, until Tommy finally cottoned on that he had been talking about trousers. As far as the English version of "pants" was concerned Jo-Dan never wore any, he announced.

As they walked through the main shopping area, Tommy noticed that Jo-Dan had what he called the "Dion effect." Despite being in a major rock band, Tommy was able to walk through the city relatively un-noticed. But everywhere they went, heads turned – and they weren't looking at Tommy. He had to concede that there was something about this ball of energy. Scruffy he may have been, but he was a good-looking guy. But more than that, he had this charisma about him that attracted attention wherever he went.

"This is Tudor Café," Tommy told him. "You had any lunch? Silly question; bet you haven't even had breakfast."

And by the way Jo-Dan tucked into his meal, moaning about the lack of something called grits that he enjoyed "back home", he could tell he hadn't bothered to cook anything. He also moaned about the size of the coffee cup, finding it too fiddly to hold by the handle.

Jo-Dan waved the waitress over and asked for a refill of his coffee, which Tommy took money from his pocket to pay for.

"What you payin' again for?" Jo-Dan asked loudly so that everyone around them heard.

"You don't get free re-fills in this country," Tommy said quietly, indicating for him to hush.

"Fuck me. You payin' again for that fartin' little fiddly cup thing?"

Tommy cringed as the ladies doing lunch looked aghast. He could see they were about to complain.

"Drink up. Let's go. I'll show you where Dion worked," Tommy said, mouthing "sorry, American" to the ladies behind Jo-Dan. They nodded, as if that said it all.

Dion's ex-boss greeted them enthusiastically as they walked into the music shop in quaint Tudor Tow, which was little more than a passageway with cobbled stones. Dion's boss had met Jo-Dan at that last concert, but had never had a chance to get to know him. Here, Jo-Dan was in his element. This was where his idol had worked, this was his ex-boss and good friend, this was a music shop – a world he understood.

Tommy took a back seat, grateful for a break as Jo-Dan chatted animatedly with staff and customers. He was chuffed that Dion's boss had seen him perform on that last night of the tour.

"I thought you were great," he told Jo-Dan. "And so did Dion. That's why he invited you to perform in the first place. Just wish he was here today…"

"I'll find him," Jo-Dan said confidently. "I'll find him, however long it takes. Just you wait and see."

They spent a full two hours at the shop before Tommy showed off the local Garrick Theatre, the Arts Centre, the "crazy café" (as Jo-Dan called the café with the beams and uneven floors), the cathedral, St Mary's Church, the Guildhall (where Jo-Dan was captivated by the ancient dungeons) and the birthplace of Dr Johnson – which bored him rigid. In fact, apart from the dungeons, anything remotely historical bored him to death.

"It's good to get a feel of where Dion came from," Jo-Dan said in an unguarded moment as they sat by Minster Pool.

"Jo-Dan. Stop throwing stones, will ya? You're gonna hit the swans."

It was quiet where they sat, except for the sound of birds and the cathedral clock striking four.

"I've arranged for you to go and see Janine's boys for dinner, that OK with you?"

"Yea, I like those two," Jo-Dan said. "Least I'll be with some young people."

"Thanks," Tommy said, slightly offended. He'd never thought of himself as old, being only in his thirties.

"No offence," Jo-Dan said, playfully pointing to the side of his head. "Don't engage my brain sometimes. The words just sorta fall out."

"Yea, I gathered that," Tommy replied as Jo-Dan started chucking stones into the pool.

Chapter Ten

"Mum, wake up."

The kid shook his mum gently. She was laid out on the couch on her back, motionless.

"Mum, wake up. I gotta go to school." He shook her more determinedly, but there was no response and something liquid-y dribbled out of the side of her mouth.

He was seven years old, but looked five, being so undernourished. He went into his father's room, a stinking pit of a place, with discoloured bed sheets. He was terrified of his father, but more terrified of being with the dead body of his mum on his own.

"Dad… Dad… Something's wrong with mum. I think she's…"

His over-active imagination saw black shadows move around the room making him shudder. He opened the curtains and the light made them go away.

As the light came into the room, he could see his dad more clearly. He was kind of yellow and his eyes were wide open.

The child darted back into his bedroom and pulled the sheet over himself, breathing hard. He had always known this day would come, but he hadn't expected it to be both of them at the same time. He crouched over, pulling his skinny legs towards him, not knowing what to do.

And it was two days before anyone came to find him. He had darted from under the sheet to get drinks of water, careful not to look at his mum and dad, then darted back under it, falling asleep fitfully, his stomach growling with hunger.

Then his grandma came, lifted him up and took him away. For two years he felt loved and cared for, even curled round her warm back at night, when he had nightmares yet again.

When she passed away there were no more family members to care for him, so a succession of indifferent foster carers followed.

He escaped his shaky start by writing. Stories and lyrics poured out of him – and he found that, while he lay in bed dreaming up lyrics, the night terrors would leave him alone, at least until he fell asleep.

Sometimes he would dart into his foster parents' bedroom, much to their annoyance, or he would climb into bed with one of the other foster kids. As long as he slept with someone else he felt comforted; otherwise he would sleep with the lights on.

As he grew older, he wanted to put his lyrics to music, so he taught himself to play guitar. While he was lost in the music, he felt free so practicing never seemed like a chore to him. He poured his angst into singing and playing guitar, finding that, eventually, both came easily to him.

He would listen to rock music, especially British bands, whose lyrics and pent up aggression he could identify with. He filled his soul with the sounds and feel of the music, growing confident as he emulated his heroes.

Thrown out to fend for himself at the age of seventeen, he scraped a living by forming a band. The drummer Mikey and the two guitarists were not only band-mates, they were his dearest friends in a tough world. He would never tell them that, of course, always keeping his guard up, presenting a false bravado, but they knew it all the same.

In his twenties, he had surpassed being merely proficient on guitar and vocals, so his confidence and ego took over. Now, he didn't know where the bravado ended and the real Jo-Dan began.

Tired of couch-surfing at friends' houses, and having to make excuses about keeping the light on at night, he just about managed to afford his own bed-sit. Old habits died hard. He usually found someone to keep him company in bed, but if he found himself alone – Jo-Dan always slept with the lights on.

Chapter Eleven

The Son of Gabriel guitarists and the twins pulled into Tommy's sweeping driveway.

Tommy had called for a crunch meeting, worrying whether they should even go ahead with the audition.

"Honestly, guys, I know how Dion felt now. I tell you, I'd only been with Jo-Dan for a day and a half, and I was fit to kill him. I just wanted to warn you, there's no way we're gonna be able to work with him. I was wondering if we should cancel the audition, but I didn't want to make the decision on my own."

"I didn't really get chance to know him when he performed that one song with us in L.A.," Joey said. "Just what does he do that's so bad?"

Tommy took a deep breath.

"Where do I start? He's so... so... irritating. He's cocky, arrogant, self-centred, foul mouthed, embarrassing, a complete whore - and that's just for starters. This guy will be representing our band. I know Dion said to take him on but... I tell you – spend some time with him and you'll see what I mean."

It was quiet as they sat in the kitchen, staring down at the coffee cups and distractedly adding the milk and sugar. They all knew what Tommy was really saying: this was the end of the band.

"Where is he now?" Lou asked.

"He's with Janine's boys. Bless 'em, they offered to put him up until the audition. They seem to get on with him O.K, perhaps 'cos he's in his twenties; they're nearer his age than we are. They'll find they have more in common."

"They grew up with Dion; he was no angel," Rick pointed out, not unreasonably. "You say Jo-Dan's arrogant and self-centred. Who does that remind you of?"

Tommy looked annoyed. This was his best friend he was talking about, someone who he had missed every day for over a year now, but he didn't want to be confrontational.

"I understand what you're saying. Dion was those things. But he had more good qualities than bad – and he, and Janine, got us to the top. But this guy…"

"Does it matter if we don't like him," Eva said, "so long as he's good at what he does?"

"We don't even know that," Tommy countered. "We're giving him this massive chance on the back of him singing one song in L.A. with us. He's even told me he's not gonna bother rehearsing for the audition. Oh – and there's something else I need to tell you. Miles is coming all the way from London to watch the audition. I am mortified at the thought of him coming all that way for this fiasco. I know I promised Dion – but even he couldn't stand Jo-Dan. In my view, we should cancel: save Miles a wasted journey and save ourselves an awful lot of embarrassment."

Everyone looked thoughtful for a while, and it was Lou who broke the silence.

"Wish D was back…"

"Oh, Jo-Dan reckons he's gonna find him," Tommy said sarcastically. "Ha. Dunno how he thinks he can find him when the police and the world and his wife have been scratching their heads for the past year. And Lou – think on this – the cocky little shit left his flat on the first night he arrived in England and took two girls back home to his bed. Yes, two. God knows how he does it. You and Eva need to be on your guard around him, I'm telling you. Do we really need that in the band?"

The twins gave each other a look that said that the very thought made them want to vomit.

"So, what does everyone think?" Tommy persevered. "What do we do?"

"Let him down lightly, I suppose," Joey said. "Tell him we've decided not to continue. Treat him to a couple of weeks' holiday then send him back home."

"Only one thing bothers me," Rick said quietly. "Dion always knew what was best for the band. If he couldn't stand this Jo-Dan, why would he want to inflict him on us? This band meant everything to him."

Everyone went back to stirring their coffee self-consciously. All eyes were downcast. It was as if even mentioning the name "Dion" tore their hearts out.

"What have we got to lose by auditioning him?" Rick eventually continued. "OK. It'll be a total disaster and Miles will have wasted his time. But if we don't, we'll never know. And if he's such a goddamned pain in the arse, we can tell him to shut the fuck up and put him in his place. That's what Dion would've done. Tommy? It's your call. You're the one honouring a promise – but you're the one who's spent time with the yank."

Tommy thought hard for what felt like an eternity.

"OK. Here's what we'll do. We'll spend an hour or so at the studio chatting with him. We can tell him the band wants to get to know him first. That way, you'll see what I mean. Then we'll go through, what, three of four songs? Then we can tell him we'll let him know. In the meantime, we'll give him enough cash to take himself off round the country for two weeks to see the sights. Agreed?"

There were general nods all round.

"OK, let's decide which songs you'd like him to try."

Chapter Twelve

Back in Cannock Wood, Jo-Dan was having the time of his life. He had never in all his twenty-nine years stayed anywhere that came close to this, a virtual mansion in a leafy green village.

Paul and Lucas had taken him to the local Park Gate Inn, where they sat outside in the autumn sunshine looking down on the stunning views of Staffordshire.

The locals seemed to find Jo-Dan some kind of novelty amusement. They found him funny and sociable. They laughed at his claims that he was going to be the next big rock star and teased him mercilessly about his "girlie locks" and accent. But Jo-Dan was in a good mood. He had five pints of beer inside him, money in his pocket, good company and the audition of a lifetime virtually in the bag – or so he saw it.

They returned back to the house just before dark and Jo-Dan immediately romped around the garden with Rolo – chucking the ball and mostly fetching it back himself. He laughed and rolled over on the lawn with the fat mongrel, then threw sticks for him to catch and run away with instead of bringing them back. The whole garden echoed once more with laughter and the dog barking excitedly.

Paul and Lucas exchanged a glance. They didn't need to say anything about who this reminded them of. It was a delight for them to watch, it was so good to have the sound of laughter back in the garden – but it really hurt.

Jo-Dan fell at their feet with the dog – both panting, both covered in grass and bits of twigs.

When he'd got his breath back, Jo-Dan sat on the lawn with Rolo at his side.

"I remember your mum," he said, not looking at the boys. "Actually I fancied her and that really pissed off your step-dad."

Then Lucas started to laugh at the image in his head, the familiar sight of Dion ranting.

"It's a wonder he didn't punch your head in," he said.

"He nearly did," Jo-Dan replied – and that set Paul off laughing.

And the three of them laughed about all sorts of things until the sun went down.

Jo-Dan went up to his room and took a shower in the en-suite. When the boys had shown him his room he whooped with joy at having shower facilities for two nights.

The boys' girlfriends had arrived and they were staying the night too. The four of them laughed, at first, when they heard Jo-Dan singing in the shower.

"Hold on a minute," Paul said. "He's singing *Marathon Man*; one of Dio's songs. Bet he's gonna do that for the audition."

He shushed everybody so they could listen in.

"Bloody hell, he's good," Stacy said. "You wouldn't think that voice could come out of such a bonkers guy."

And sensing the sudden sadness that had come over the boys she added, "Do you think he sounds like Dio?"

"No," Lucas said. "Different, just different. He's good, but different."

The song came to an end and they all applauded, not loud enough for Jo-Dan to hear, not wishing to embarrass him, but it was heartfelt.

"Hey, you sounded good," Lucas said as Jo-Dan came downstairs, hair standing in all directions because it was still damp.

"What? Oh, you heard," he said. "Yea, well, I love that song."

He spent the next two hours outrageously flirting with the girls but getting nowhere, the boys taking it all in their stride, confident that they were all rock solid.

"Anyway, I'm turning in," Paul said. "What about the rest of you? C'mon, Stace."

Much as he liked Jo-Dan, he had no intention of leaving him downstairs with her.

They all decided they'd go to bed; it was midnight and it had been a long day.

"Hey, don't mind if I leave my light on do ya for a while?" Jo-Dan asked. "Got some lyrics and music buzzing round in my head. Gotta get them written down. You know how it is. Bet Dion was the same."

"Sure," Lucas said as he climbed the stairs. "No problem. Have a good sleep. Night."

And it was true. Jo-Dan did have lyrics begging to be written down before he forgot them – and he poured his heart and soul into a notebook, until the new song stopped buzzing in his head. "I'll play it through on one of Dion's Spanish guitars in the morning" was the last thing he thought before falling fully clothed into grateful sleep on top of the bed, the notebook still lying next to him.

It was some time later, when Stacy got up for a glass of water, that she noticed the light still on. The door was slightly ajar and she peeped in. 'Aahhh" she thought to herself affectionately. He looked quite sweet when he was asleep, quiet for once. She reached in and put the light out for him. He must be exhausted. He'd hardly had any chance to catch up on sleep since he arrived.

Dion, looking majestic and surreal, stood in front of Jo-Dan, just inches away. There were those stunning, iconic features – looking seriously pissed off. He was in Dion's house, the home he shared with the beautiful Janine and the boys – and he wasn't happy. His long blond hair was a haze in the strange lighting, almost like a stage spotlight. There must have been a smoke machine because the smoke was rising, almost obscuring the singer at times. But no, it was cigarette smoke; the distinct smell of cigarette smoke. And it was getting thicker and thicker, because the space they were in was so confined. There were no walls, but there was no way out either. Jo-Dan coughed and breathed in hard trying to get some air – but the smoke hurt his lungs. He coughed again and struggled to get oxygen into his lungs. Dion laughed then was still. He gave a stare with ice blue eyes that could have killed at ten paces. He blew more smoke directly into Jo-Dan's face. Every breath was a struggle and he knew he was going to die. He fumbled frantically for the bedside cabinet to find his cigarettes, but there was nothing there, only a vast empty space.

Jo-Dan tried to scream for help, but the air would not go in and sweat was running down his back now. Panicking, his hand groped around for a bedside light, but there was none there.

He was out of the bed, scrambling around the room, desperately trying to find the light switch, totally disorientated in the darkness. There were no street lights, no moonlight - and the leafy village was no longer an idyllic movie set. It was pitch black, a scene straight from a horror movie and all Jo-Dan could do was scream in absolute panic and anguish until one of the girls, alerted by his heartrending cries flung open the door and switched on the lights.

Chapter Thirteen

It was nearly midday by the time Jo-Dan eventually emerged with a croaky "mornin".

The boys had already eaten breakfast and were now preparing sandwiches for lunch.

"You OK?" Paul said.

"'Course," Jo-Dan replied. "O.K. if I get some coffee?"

The boys watched him as he fumbled around, still half asleep, then savouring the coffee as if it was the first time he had ever tasted it.

"You still OK to take me to this Bir-ming-ham place today?" Jo-Dan asked, struggling to say the town's name all in one. "Need to buy my pants. You say you can buy pretty edgy stuff there, yeah?"

The boys laughed and tried to get him to pronounce Birmingham without a slice of ham on the end. Their efforts failed; he just couldn't get it.

"Yeah, no problem," Paul said. "We can go in about an hour if you like."

He paused, not wishing to bring up the subject, but his curiosity got the better of him.

"That was some nightmare last night, huh?"

Jo-Dan shrugged and topped up his coffee. "Oh that. It's nothin'. Got a fag?"

End of conversation on that topic.

"Jo-Dan, help yourself to toast or something."

Jo-Dan, not the most domesticated of people, managed to negotiate his way round the intricacies of a toaster, found the butter and demolished four slices.

"Stacy says you're kinda cute," Paul said, in an effort to diffuse the awkward memory of the screams in the night - which resulted in a roar of laughter from Jo-Dan.

"Well, I've been called some things, but 'cute' isn't one of them. You mean she fancies me really don't ya? Well, y'know, if you've got it... Don't worry, I'll look and not touch."

Paul and Lucas quite liked his humour, but the fact remained that he had been really scared last night and was not going to talk about it. "Bravado" was the word that came to mind.

"D'you often have nightmares?" Lucas tried again, immediately feeling uncomfortable that he'd asked.

"Don't like talkin' about it. Freaks me out," was all that Jo-Dan was prepared to say. "I'll go get a shower. Then we'll go to Birm-ing-ham."

The boys were pleased to see Jo-Dan back to "normal", as he prattled away on the way to Brum, cursing the British weather and opening the car door to hurl sexist banter at any girl that caught his fancy. As they approached the city, Paul and Lucas amused themselves teaching Jo-Dan how to say Brummie expressions – with hilariously failed results.

Jo-Dan was like an over-excited puppy in the big city, especially as it was the birthplace of one his heroes, Ozzy Osbourne.

It was all Paul and Lucas could do to keep track of where he was, as he dived in and out of the Bull Ring shopping centre shops. Twice, he nearly got run over, by looking the wrong way crossing the road, as they made their way back to the car and they had to drag him back sharply. But – mission accomplished – he spent every penny that Tommy had given him and had bags full of edgy jeans and T-shirts. He had chosen anything that seemed to scream out 'I am a rock star'. Every pair of jeans had buckles, zips and rips and all the T-shirts were cutaway, to show off his muscular upper arms. Some had outrageous statements across them; others featured a skull or one finger salute or something similar.

He didn't tell the boys he had absolutely no money left, figuring he'd just ask Tommy for some more when he saw him at the audition tomorrow.

The boys dropped him back at his flat in Lichfield, so he could pick up his guitar and the rest of the evening passed by with a meal cooked by the girls, then Jo-Dan strumming and writing in his room, before he fell asleep with the light on.

Chapter Fourteen

"So what's this Ruggerley place like?" Jo-Dan asked as Tommy drove him to the audition. "Any action?"

"It's pronounced 'Rouge-ly', rouge, like a woman's make-up Jo-Dan."

"Whatever. Anyway I spent all my money. Had to buy loads of clothes. Gotta look the part. Could I have some more money? Got any fags? Fuckin' weather. Don't it ever stop rainin' in this country? Are we nearly there?

"Which fuckin' question do you want me to answer first Jo-Dan?"

"Jesus, you're prickly today ain't ya? Just give us a fag, Tom, that'll do."

"It's Tommy you prick. How many times do I have to tell you? And it's pronounced 'Tommy', not 'Tarmy'," he said, as he threw a packet of cigarettes into Jo-Dan's lap.

"Slitting Mill? Fancy saying you live in Slitting Mill. Sounds like a…"

"Just shut up for one minute will you? Listen, our tour manager will be there today. Everyone's gonna spend a while getting to know you before we start the rehearsal. Try not to piss anyone off."

"Well, I'd just rather get on with the rehearsal. That's what I'm here for."

"It's not just about the music, is it, Jo-Dan? When you take someone new into a band, it has to be someone we can all get along with."

"Should be fine, then," he replied confidently, then lit up the fag with his legs stretched out on the dashboard.

Tommy pulled into the car park and retrieved Jo-Dan's guitar and bag out of the boot. He slammed the boot shut with such force the car shook.

"This it? Ain't much of a place is it?" Jo-Dan said as he took his precious guitar off Tommy – but left him to carry his bag.

Tommy stormed ahead, leaving the door to swing back into Jo-Dan.

And in a throwback to his first arrival in England, the first thing the rest of the band and Miles heard from their future superstar was, "Hey, watch my fuckin' guitar."

They were all assembled in the studio, except the technicians, who were seated behind the glass window of the control room. The band and Miles noted Tommy's glowering face and surmised the journey hadn't gone well.

Jo-Dan swaggered in, even more confident than usual, safe in the knowledge he looked great in his new expensive jeans and T-shirt. They were just what he wanted - new but made to look well-worn.

"Hi, guys," Jo-Dan said cheerfully and there were handshakes and high fives all round. The band seemed genuinely intrigued by him and Jo-Dan obliged with the small talk about how he was finding life in England, how was his flight, etc.

Rather than take offence at his insults about pretty much anything English, he made them laugh at the absurdity of their own culture and way of life. Only Tommy failed to see the funny side.

Jo-Dan was in his element. He had a captive audience and played up to it, but it was Tommy who brought him back down to earth when he could get a word in edgeways.

"OK, well, you know the reason we're here. Like I said, it's not just about a performance it's whether we can all get along."

Everyone nodded, including Jo-Dan.

"Well, that's that sorted then," Jo-Dan announced. "I already love you guys."

Tommy put his head in his hands and was just about to say something about the band wanting to formally interview him for the job, but there was no stopping him.

"Anyway, the way I see it," Jo-Dan continued, "you're pretty much fucked without me. Ain't no one I know got the range to take on Dion's songs and ain't no one got my ability on lead guitar. I have a bigger range than Dion and I've already kicked his ass on stage with my guitar. Turn me down and you're screwed."

Tommy went to interrupt but on and on he continued while the rest of the band sat there pretty much dumbstruck.

"And we need to make some changes," Jo-Dan continued – as if he was interviewing the band, not the other way round.

"I ain't gonna keep rehearsing the same songs over and over. You're a great band, but sometimes you come across over-rehearsed, you know? You keep rehearsing stuff over and over and you get sick to death of the song – you forget why it was written in the first place. And Dion came up with some great songs. The audience ain't stupid. They know when you're just going through the motions. You can be note-perfect but it don't matter if there's no emotion there. That's what Dion was good at. He sang and played like he meant it. The new songs, yeah, we need to rehearse those.

"But better to make mistakes with the old ones and be honest when you perform."

"And another thing – that *Magic of Rock* – you need to ditch that as a ballad. I've re-worked it – and ramped it up. It sounds amazing."

Jo-Dan had taken his guitar out of its case and it was resting across his lap like a comfort blanket.

"And we don't need to start with any low-key gig, we need to get straight back in there or the public will think we're some shit ordinary band. Our first gig should be major, no small-scale try-out shit. We need to start as we mean to go on – big time.

"I've written some new stuff too, we can try it out before we hit the road."

He paused for breath so Tommy jumped in.

"Anything else you'd like us to work on, Jo-Dan?" but the sarcasm was totally lost on him.

"Yeah. The video shoots. I know Dion hated all that stuff and he'd never do anything out of the ordinary, so you've ended up with some pretty dull stuff to watch. I don't care what I do; I'll do anything for fun; I'll embarrass myself if I have to – anything to liven up that borin' shit you've done in the past.

"And girls..."

The twins shuffled and looked very uncomfortable.

Jo-Dan leant forward and looked them up and down from head to toe, which made them feel even worse.

"Now - you both know you want me – so that needs to come across on stage," he said.

Miles looked down, desperately trying to hide a smile.

Tommy stood up and looked ready to punch him, but Miles gave him a look that said 'let him finish'.

"I'm goin' for a piss," Tommy said. "I'll leave the rest of you to finish the *interview*."

Jo-Dan didn't flinch. He was on a mission.

"Anyway, the audience loves that stuff. Let's make the performance more sexy. Jesus, let's make 'em think we're desperate to get our hands on each other. It'll drive 'em crazy. We need to play up to each other on stage, act if you like, and you never know, you might even start to believe it…"

The girls darted looks at Joey and Rick as if to say 'help'.

"You sure do have a lot of ideas, Jo-Dan," Rick managed to jump in.

"Oh, there's loads more. Did I tell ya – I'm gonna find Dion? I know I'll be cuttin' my own throat, but I figure I'll give him back to you as a sort of thank you. Anyway, by the time I find him, I'll be a big enough star to start over on my own."

"Jo-Dan, you're takin' something for granted, aren't you?" Joey interjected.

"What? That I get the job?" and Jo-Dan laughed out loud, that raucous laugh that was so infectious it diffused a potential explosion from the band members. The laugh spoke volumes. It said "you really think you are gonna turn me down"?

"Hey, I figure you flew me thousands of miles for this audition. Who else you got that comes close to what I do?"

Tommy came back in and looked astounded to see that Jo-Dan was still in full flow.

"Oh yeah – and Tommy – there's a few parts in the songs where I got ideas for the drums. I'll show ya in a bit."

Tommy turned round and walked straight back out.

"And Rick – you know in *Thank You For the Ride*, there's this middle eight bit where you're really bashing out? Well, there's a perfect part in the song where we could do a complete full stop – then come back in – really powerful like – I'll show ya later.

"And Joey, sometimes the bass is a little over-complicated, particularly on the more up tempo songs. We could try making it more laid back, really in the groove while my lead is wailing over it. Makes it much more effective.

"And some of the songs, we'll need to change the key to accommodate my range."

Then he actually stopped for breath and the band members, except for Tommy who was bashing his head up the wall outside, looked at each other utterly gobsmacked.

Rick was about to say that English people, particularly well-established rock stars, don't take too kindly to criticism and what sounds like boasting but Jo-Dan was on his feet.

"Anyways – let's see what we can do," he said, taking up his place on the mic and fluffing out his hair from underneath. "How about we start with *Thank You for the Ride*? I love that song. Wanted to perform that last time I was with you but Dion used it for the encore."

"What- a- twat," Rick managed to say to Joey under his breath, as they crossed paths. He darted a look at Miles, who just nodded, as if to say, 'Give him a go'.

Joey opened the door to call Tommy in. He spotted him, kicking the wall and smoking furiously.

"We're ready to start, mate," he said.

Tommy hurled his cigarette up the wall sending small sparks flying.

With everyone in place, Miles joined the technicians and looked on in anticipation, as the three guitarists tuned up their instruments.

Jo-Dan looked around at the band, to make sure they were all in position, as if *he* was the one in control.

"Ready?" he said – and there were nods from all round.

He closed his eyes for a full minute, keeping everyone waiting until they started exchanging looks that said "is he all right?"

Then he took a deep breath, opened his eyes and was more focussed than he had ever been in his entire life.

He played the opening bars of *Thank you For the Ride* faultlessly. The two other guitars joined in, Tommy crashed into the song and Jo-Dan's voice meandered effortlessly through the lyrics. He had to concentrate hard not to choke up, desperately trying not to give second meaning to the song because he had his own views on that.

Somehow, in between singing and playing lead, he also managed to energise the room with his mock rock stances, playing up to the girls, making them laugh and rocking out with the other guitarists, his hair swishing from side to side.

This was no rehearsal; this was a performance. Even Tommy felt something inside.

Jo-Dan finished the song with a trademark Dion scream, but it was a note so high that the band wasn't even sure it existed.

The song came to a crashing sudden ending, true to the recording.

Jo-Dan had triumphed – and he knew it. He held his guitar aloft, closed his eyes and said a quiet, "thank you."

The session continued with song after song, all sounding fresh and energised. There was a positive buzz in the air and the atmosphere was almost tangible. Jo-Dan noticed a connecting thread of silver and blue meandering around the studio, flowing through each performer and joining onto the next. He saw it as a positive, comforting sign, but he had learned to keep quiet about such things. The others were totally oblivious to it, except for Miles, who saw it clear as day.

There was no doubt in anyone's mind that, despite being the most irritating, obnoxious individual they had ever met, Jo-Dan was the next front man for Son of Gabriel. Even Tommy reluctantly went up to him at the end of the session and managed a, "you did good."

"Told ya," Jo-Dan replied, accepting a bottle of water from Miles. "I'm in then, I presume?"

"You're in as far as I'm concerned," Miles said. "Just try not to be so damned annoying. Is everyone in agreement? I vote yes."

Everyone either nodded or said "yeah" – except for Tommy who stared ahead, clearly wrestling with his conscience. Eventually, with all eyes boring into him, he came out with, "It's what Dion wanted, so yeah."

With the last vote in place, Jo-Dan wasted no time in celebrating and everyone quickly regretted their decision.

"Whoaoooooo!" he screamed – kind of a cross between a rock scream and an excited child. "Where's the beer? Let's go celebrate. When do we announce this to the world? Fuckin' brilliant. Tommy, I'm gonna need a bigger apartment, something fancy. And you can't have a front man without a fancy car. How much you gonna pay me? When do we sort out all that stuff? Whaoooooo!"

Miles pulled him aside, before everyone told him they had changed their minds already.

"Let's go into one of the lounge areas and talk business," he said, leading Jo-Dan out of harm's way.

"Girls, we're gonna be spending a lot of quality time together," Jo-Dan shouted back at the twins as he exited. "Know what I mean?"

The instant they were in the lounge area, Miles' friendly exterior slipped.

"Shut up. Just shut up," he said, shoving Jo-Dan onto the sofa. "Don't say a word, or I swear I will tell them about the colours you see."

"What d'y…?" Jo-Dan started – but Miles stood up as if to go and tell the band his secret straight away.

"OK. OK," Jo-Dan said. "I dunno how you know, but…"

"You gonna shut up and listen?"

Jo-Dan managed a slight nod of his head – and Miles relaxed his glare.

"I'll say what I have to say first, then you get to go – but only when I've finished. Do you understand?"

Jo-Dan nodded humbly.

"This is not the Jo-Dan show. This is Son of Gabriel. Everything you do from now on will be for this band. Step out of line and I'll fire you, however good you are, and you will be straight back on the plane to L.A.

"Dion chose you as his replacement, so I want you to respect that.

"I deal with all the business side of stuff, so don't go bothering Tommy. You'll be paid a salary, a good salary, with the opportunity to earn plenty of bonuses, plus money from advertising and merchandise. And you'll be paid royalties *if* we use any of your songs. But you spend it all straight away and it's gone, that's it. There's no more. Do you understand?"

Jo-Dan nodded and had an internal struggle with his overactive brain to remain silent.

"My only interest in you is that you will make me lots of money. If we can get on that's just a bonus, but I don't really care if you like me or not. I will largely leave the band to get on with it when it comes to musicianship. That's not my forte. So do NOT cause any arguments within the band. You do that and you are out. I cannot afford to lose any band members because of you. Learn to be more respectful. That is an order. Is that clear?"

Jo-Dan nodded, feeling a cross between hurt and fearful. It was like asking him to change his personality, but he knew this guy wasn't messing and he also knew he could go through life without ever getting another chance like this. So he made a mental note to just get away with as much as he could, whenever he could, without crossing the invisible line.

"Now, do you have any questions?"

"Where's Dion?"

"What makes you think I know?"

"Come on. I've heard about your magic stuff. Paul and Lucas told me about your stupid card tricks. You were there that night. I watched him disappear in that capsule thing. I know you're some kind of illusionist. You create all those ridiculous "special effects" for the band somehow.

"How did ya pull it off? Where's Dion – and Janine?"

"I had nothing to do with those special effects – and Dion's where he wants to be."

"What's that supposed to mean?"

"He chose to leave," Miles said slowly and carefully.

"And Janine?"

"You're assuming I know all the answers," Miles said. "I don't."

"How do I know that I won't 'disappear'?" Jo-Dan said. "That sort of stuff scares the shit out of me."

"Dion chose to. I'm presuming you don't."

"I have nightmares about him," Jo-Dan confessed. "Why would he choose to quit on such a great life? He had everything: the band, a beautiful wife, two step sons."

"Dion loved life, but he also loved himself," Miles said. "Perhaps he had his reasons. Can you imagine an old, fat, bald Dion?"

Jo-Dan shook his head.

"No. Neither could he. I'm sure, if he wants to come back, he will choose really carefully when he returns and for how long – because he sure as hell won't want to leave Janine for any length of time."

"How can I find him?"

"Try finding him through his music; that's what he loves - that and the limelight. Maybe, if you create the right atmosphere for him, he'll come back. It could be all down to you, Jo-Dan. Think what a responsibility that is."

Jo-Dan took in a breath to ask more, but Miles raised his hand.

"Some people in this world are born gift-wrapped and you're one of them Jo-Dan. But those chosen few are lucky if they are blessed with one God-given talent. You're an amazing singer, guitarist – and you say you also write songs.

"You have it in spades – ace of spades."

And as if to prove his point, Miles plucked a card from thin air and handed it to a dumbstruck Jo-Dan – the ace of spades.

"That's one of my 'stupid magic tricks'," Miles said.

"Keep it with you in your pocket. It'll remind you of our conversation. If you feel you're about to go on one of your over exuberant outbursts, feel the card in your pocket. It'll remind you to shut the fuck up."

Jo-Dan examined the card, half expecting it to de-materialise in his hand or something. It seemed sturdy, plastic-y and he had no idea how Miles had plucked it from thin air.

"You know more than you're letting on," he said to Miles, but his manager's demeanour had already changed.

"And I know about you," Miles said seriously. "Tell on me and I'll tell the world that you see colours around people; that you're scared of being alone in the dark; that you sleep with the light on; and have nightmares that make you scream. You want the world to know that? You fancy having that released to the press? How's that for your precious rock-star street cred'?"

Jo-Dan visibly squirmed, feeling as if his soul had been exposed.

"How do you know…?"

"I'm like you – I see your aura – and I see what makes people tick."

There was a knock on the door of the lounge area and Tommy walked in.

"Miles? You done? You better come and listen to this tape."

It was a subdued Jo-Dan who walked out of the lounge area and back into the studio. Everyone was crowded round the sound guy and the mixing desk. Eva and Lou were in tears.

"Oh God, is the recording that bad?" Jo-Dan said. "I thought the rehearsal went OK."

"Dion's on the tape," Tommy said, visibly shaking "We're used to dealing with phenomena – but this…"

"Let me hear," Jo-Dan implored.

Jo-Dan leaned over the mixing desk as the recording was played back. The first thing that struck him was how awesome *his own* vocals sounded and he almost whooped in excitement, but he quickly remembered Miles's advice, felt for the card in his pocket, and managed to contain himself.

He had never heard a professional recording of his voice before and he was very impressed by himself: his range, tone and power.

And then, on the track called *Love Me Tonight* (which had little to do with "love") there was the harmony which had originally belonged to Janine – performed by Dion. It was unmistakeable, there was no doubt.

And on *When You Wake*, the beautiful ballad written by Janine when Dion was in a coma, there it was again – Janine's harmonies, replaced by Dion.

"You overlaid that track on to our recording right?" Jo-Dan asked the technician.

"No I didn't. I know for sure we have *never* had a recording of Dion singing Janine's parts," he answered.

"So what do we do with it?" Jo-Dan asked.

"We release it," Miles said without hesitation. "We include those two songs on the new album with the words, 'featuring Dion and remembering Janine'. We don't have to explain anything. Let the public think it's over-dubbed. They'll love it just because it's something new for them by Dion. Plus, having two male vocalists sounds awesome."

Everyone nodded in agreement but there was sadness all round. Even Jo-Dan picked up on it and managed to keep quiet.

"You sounded great," Tommy said to him quietly as they left the studio. "Dion was right - as usual."

Chapter Fifteen

With a week to go before the press conference, there was time for fun and celebration – and Jo-Dan wasted no time.

He was under strict instructions not to announce himself to the public before the press conference, so sitting on that news took every ounce of his non-existent self-control.

He partied like there was no tomorrow – and wrote a song about it, "Party Like There's No Tomorrow," which would be presented to the band at one of their rehearsal sessions, he decided.

For now, he divided his time between his flat and Paul and Lucas's house. Whilst the boys enjoyed his company, they understandably told him they didn't want him bringing a host of females back to their house, because it contained many precious and expensive items. Jo-Dan simply told the girls he was "a famous rock star" in his country, but they wouldn't have heard of him yet in England – and left it at that – then took them back to his flat. That solved another problem for him. He didn't have to keep the light on at night, so he slept like a baby, much to the girls' disappointment.

He had already received a sizeable advance payout and he was bursting to spend it. Ironically, it was his young friends Paul and

Lucas who acted as financial advisors and stopped him from blowing the lot.

A photo shoot had been arranged – a defining moment for Jo-Dan, who kept his promise to do anything asked of him. He posed, preened, larked about, made love to the camera and enjoyed every minute of being the centre of attention.

Countless shots were taken of him with and without guitar, posing in front of a mic, leaping from a platform into the air, strutting in front of various backdrops, laughing, singing or looking mean and serious. He did whatever he was asked to do; anything was game and the camera loved him back.

The night before the press conference Jo-Dan spent time with the boys and their girlfriends. He enjoyed being with them, feeling he could be himself and be accepted for who he was.

"Can I ask a favour?" he said, looking intently at the boys as they all sat in the lounge.

Paul and Lucas nodded and looked curious.

"Would you mind if I went into Dion's studio? I know it's a big ask but……it'd mean a lot to me. Say no if you want and I won't ask again."

The boys exchanged glances and nodded that it would be O.K.

"You wanna come in with me?" Jo-Dan asked, realising it would be a sensitive place to be.

Paul declined, saying it always made him feel too sad.

"Not been in there for months," he said. "We used to hold jamming sessions in there, practising Son of Gabriel songs with Dio when the band was on a break from touring. It was a really fun time."

But Lucas said he would go with Jo-Dan. He took the key off a hook in the kitchen and they made their way up the garden helped by the security lights showing them their way.

Jo-Dan gave a kind of impressed whistle as he entered the studio and took in the sheer amount of expensive equipment. Everything was in pristine condition, clean, organised and tidy.

"I come in here sometimes," Lucas said, "to air the place and clean it, just to stop it from feeling musty."

Then he went quiet and Jo-Dan thought he looked tearful so he avoided eye contact.

"Mind if I look around?" he said.

"That's fine," Lucas told him and he sat tuning one of the guitars while Jo-Dan walked slowly around the hallowed ground.

Lucas expected Jo-Dan to examine all the equipment, but that wasn't what he was in there for. He examined every inch of the place for any paperwork. There were some folders on a desk positively bulging with lyrics.

"Can I?" Jo-Dan asked.

When Lucas shrugged as if to say O.K. Jo-Dan found he was actually shaking. Here were Dion's lyrics, in his own handwriting, in his own studio. And there were so many, sheet after sheet of haunting words and scribbles and crossings out and refining notes. If he had ever felt a strong connection to his icon it was now.

Here was the original *Thank You For the Ride* in Dion's immaculate handwriting. Here was *Love Me Tonight* and *Marathon Man.* Oh, how he cried, standing there, cried so hard that he feared the tears would make the ink run on those pages.

"I'll leave you here for a while," Lucas said, finding it all too much.

Jo-Dan held one of the folders to his chest as if it was a baby.

"Come back," he said quietly to the amplifiers and speakers. "Come back – and I'll fuck off home to L.A. How could you leave this behind? How could you quit knowing so many people loved you?"

Jo-Dan started talking quietly, but his sadness gradually turned to anger as he thought of Janine and how much the boys missed her.

"It's the press conference tomorrow," he said, the tears still flowing. "What do I tell the world?"

Now he felt furious because there was no reply.

"What do I tell the world?" he shouted. He waited but there was no answer.

"Tell me," he screamed. "Where are you?"

The silence annoyed him even more.

"I'm in **your** studio Dion. O.K. you want me to beg, I'll beg."

Jo-Dan dropped to his knees and prayed like he had never prayed in his life.

"Talk to me. Tell me what I have to do," he shouted into the silence, his voice breaking with emotion. He waited listening to the sound of his own shuddering breathing."

"Let me see you," he screamed in frustration, so loud that he seriously worried he would damage his vocal chords and his career would be over before it started.

He knelt there, feeling pathetic, clinging onto a folder of lyrics as if it was the Holy Bible.

It was cold now and Jo-Dan could see his own breath hanging in the air.

He waited, dejected, beaten, then cursed himself for being such a fool. What did he really expect? Dion was probably sunning himself on some beach somewhere while he was on this self-imposed mission to find him, somehow, somewhere.

He locked the door of the studio, went back into the house and put the key back on its hook. He could hear the boys and their girlfriends in the lounge, quietly chatting as they watched T.V.

Jo-Dan walked straight upstairs to bed rather than have to pretend he was fine. He wasn't fine, but he was so cold and exhausted he quickly fell asleep under the warm duvet.

Dion was standing in front of him, surrounded by a distinct red aura.

"You still get on my nerves," Dion said matter of factly. "I'll keep this short because I don't intend ageing any more that I have to because of you.

"There's a new song if you look under the mixing desk, *Ice Blue*. It's my gift to you. Give that to the world. And give my love to the boys and Tommy. They won't believe you, but tell them anyway."

"Where's Janine?" Jo-Dan said, throwing down the gauntlet to Dion, who stood within touching distance.

"She's with me, she's fine, but you won't see her. We visit often but her boys don't see us."

Jo-Dan thought he looked kind of sad when he added, "I can't bear it when she cries for the boys. I'll make it right."

And he was gone.

Chapter Sixteen

"You O.K.?" Lucas asked as Jo-Dan came downstairs late the following morning. "I thought I'd leave you in the studio for a while last night, then I heard you come in and go straight upstairs. Want a coffee?"

He tried to sneak a look at Jo-Dan without making it obvious; he could tell there was something up.

"Bad night? I noticed you left the light on."

"I dreamt I saw him in the studio," Jo-Dan said quietly. "At least I think it was a dream. He said to tell you both he loves you and he'll make it right about your mum."

"What's that supposed to mean?" Lucas asked.

"Dunno," Jo-Dan said with a shrug.

"You left some of Dion's lyrics in the hall last night. I re-read some of them," Lucas said. "I read *Thank You For the Ride*. How stupid have we been? It's all there; it's all in the lyrics. That song is nothing to do with picking up a hitchhiker is it?"

"No, it ain't. I'd already twigged that," Jo-Dan said, unusually subdued."

Jo-Dan quietly sang the lyrics, word perfect, in a croaky 'just-got-up' sort of voice.

You hitched a ride and ran towards me
In my TVR sports car
I had started on my journey
And it seemed so long and far

As soon as my eyes saw you
And you sat right next to me
I knew just what I had to do
I couldn't set you free

We talked and laughed along the highway
We sang, you said you loved my eyes
We made out several times along the way
I should Thank **You** *for the Ride*

We had many, many miles to go
I planned it all along the way
But how could I ever let you know
I'd have to make you stay?

I promised that I'd take you home
But then I locked the door
I couldn't be without you, all alone
Wanted you forever more

Sorry to those who we left behind
I didn't know what else I could do
I was blessed with a determined mind
I'm going nowhere without you

Lucas was impressed by the vocals, but saddened at the same time as the words hit home.

"He knew he was going to take mum away," he said. "He even put it in a song, so we could figure it out when it was too late."

"We may never know what really happened," Jo-Dan said. "But whatever happened, Dion loved your mum and you guys."

"I know," Lucas said. "We just miss him and mum, that's all."

Jo-Dan sat staring into his coffee and it was as if a revelation suddenly hit him like a thunderbolt.

"Hang on – in my dream last night – he said… *Ice Blue*."

And he was on his feet.

Lucas looked at him as if he had suddenly gone mad.

"Ice blue? That's how mum always used to describe his eyes."

"I need to go back into the studio," Jo-Dan said urgently. Might be crazy but…"

Jo-Dan took the key from the hook and fled down the garden to the studio, with a confused Lucas running behind him. Rolo joined in, barking and running in between them with a stick, thinking it was all a game.

Inside the studio, Jo-Dan put the lights on.

"Here, help me lift this mixing desk," he said to Lucas, as if it was really urgent.

"But why? It weighs a ton."

"He said in my dream there was a new song under there, Ice Blue," Jo-Dan said as he strained to lift up the mixing desk and look underneath at the same time. Lucas held the desk up as best he could while Jo-Dan stretched his arm underneath.

Jo-Dan felt a lurch in his stomach when he spotted a sheet of paper tucked towards the back. "It's just a piece of paper, it's just a piece of paper, it's just a piece of paper", his brain was saying as he reached out trying to convince himself it was nothing.

They replaced the mixing desk carefully and Jo-Dan turned over the blank sheet hardly daring to breathe. On the other side were lyrics with chords and suggestions scrawled over them:

Ice Blue

You gave me the cold shoulder
Told me it was over
All I got from you
Was ice blue

You thought it was funny
When I pleaded with ya honey
Say, 'What's up with you
Ice blue?'

Chorus
You laughed as I cried
Tortured me inside
My blood ran cold right through
Ice blue

I saw it in your eyes
There was nothin' left inside
You left with someone new
Ice blue

And now you're on your own
Beggin' me to come back home
You know what you can do
Ice blue

"How could you have possibly known that?" Lucas said.

"I didn't, I swear. And this is a classic Dion-type song."

"So, what does this mean – that he visits you in your dreams? That would be crazy, huh? You sure you didn't see that song when you were in the studio last night?"

"Honestly, the only time I've ever heard the words 'ice blue' is in the song *When You Wake* – you know, the one that your mum wrote for Dion. Look, I know this all sounds crazy, but that's the truth."

He was aware the song sheet was quivering in his hand, because he was shaking so much.

"You know what?" Jo-Dan said. "The band can perform this song. I'll just tell them I found it in the studio. Looking at all the notes on it, I can see where Dion was going with it. I can already hear the audience shouting 'ice blue' at the end of each verse."

"Do I tell Paul about the dream?" Lucas asked.

"I'll leave that up to you. I don't want him to be mad with me if he thinks I'm makin' it up. You should tell him I found the song though – just not how. A bit sensitive, I'd say, wouldn't you?"

"Think it's you who's 'sensitive' in some way," Lucas said, which actually made Jo-Dan laugh.

"Sensitive? That's a new one," he said, misunderstanding what Lucas meant. "Usually I get called things like shithead or ass-hole."

Chapter Seventeen

"Gotta be at the press conference in a coupla hours. Been warned to try an' keep my mouth shut," Jo-Dan said, as he preened himself to get ready in the house at Cannock Wood.

"You? Keep your mouth shut? Well, how's that going to work at a press conference?" Lucas asked.

"Tommy's doin' all the talkin' – apparently. We'll see about that," Jo-Dan said with a mischievous grin. "He's pickin' me up on the way. Do I look like a rock star? Don't answer that. 'Course I do."

Miles had decided that the press conference would be held at a local venue and he would be there to keep an eye on how it went. The Garrick Theatre, in Lichfield, was chosen for a number of reasons: it was local for everyone, big enough to host the event and it was where Son of Gabriel had performed way back when, before they launched on to the international stage.

"You're quiet for once," Tommy said to Jo-Dan, as they drove to Lichfield. "Not that I'm complaining; makes a pleasant change."

"I'm trying," Jo-Dan said.

"Yeah – you are," Tommy replied.

In truth, Jo-Dan had no intention of keeping quiet; he was planning what he had to say at the press conference, going over it in his mind – and he had plenty to say.

Tommy managed to park in the multi-storey car park nearby. The film crews had already arrived and there was a buzz inside and outside the building. A small crowd had gathered outside, their antennae telling them that something was going on. The rear doors of the building were open for the TV and radio crews to get their equipment inside, so Tommy and Jo-Dan dived in rather than face questions from the crowd at the front of the building.

The rest of the band was already there and a line of tables and chairs was set up on the stage for them to face the media. They were pampered by a make-up girl and shown the press pack, which was to be issued to the media.

It was the first time Jo-Dan had seen the pictures which had been chosen from the photo shoot - and he was more than happy when he saw the results. He looked a 'proper' rock star, he thought: arrogant pose, toned body, guitar held high, long hair caught in mid-swirl from the wind machine. The lighting in the photo enhanced his features: big brown eyes and flawless complexion.

"Look at that tight ass," he said flashing a photo at Eva. "Now you can't tell me you wouldn't wanna get your hands on that."

"I just got engaged, Jo-Dan, remember?"

"So?"

"Are you nervous?" she said, desperately trying to change the subject.

"Why would I be? This is where I've always been meant to be."

The band kept out of the way until everything and everyone was in place. Jo-Dan was warned by Tommy about any swearing, as some of the broadcasts were going out live.

Miles took to the stage and gave some background on air about the mystery of Dion and Janine's appearance, how they had waited for a year, hoping they would return – and how they had found an extraordinary new front man.

"Ladies and gentlemen, members of the press, I give you – Son of Gabriel – with the force of nature that is Jo-Dan Rox," he announced.

There were about a hundred assembled journalists, broadcasters, press officers and hangers-on. The cameras flashed as the band members took their place with name cards placed in front of them.

There were cheers and whistles from the hangers-on.

The twins looked impossibly beautiful; the rest of the band looked really serious and instantly went into moody, rock star mode.

Tommy was to do all the talking, so he kicked off, thanking everyone for being there, outlined what a difficult decision it had been and referred the media to the dates and venues for the UK tour.

"We will also be taking time out to record a new album," he said. "And it will feature two tracks which have never been heard before, which feature Dion."

There was an instant buzz and mad scribbling from the journalists.

"Now I'm sure you have lots of questions," he said.

Jo-Dan felt for the ace of spades in his jeans pocket and felt the comforting touch of the plastic card, but the questions fired in like missiles.

"Jo-Dan (is that how you pronounce it?). What's your take on Dion? Were you a fan? What do you think happened?"

"I was, am, a huge fan. He's my idol – and I'm gonna bring him back."

Tommy said a "for fuck's sake" under his breath and gave Jo-Dan a kick from under the table.

The cameras flashed and became almost blinding. The colourful auras emanating from all those people intermingled and made Jo-Dan feel nauseous, but he stayed focussed. The questions came from all sides at once.

"What do you mean you'll bring him back? Do you know where he is? What about Janine? And won't that mean you'll be out of the band?"

"I'll gladly step aside if Dion wants to return," Jo-Dan said graciously.

(Cue mad scribbling from the journalists).

"I know he'll come back when he wants to. There's no way he would have given up such a great career permanently. Janine, I'm not so sure."

"You're from L.A., we understand. How come we've never heard of you before? What makes you think you can take on such a big role, '*Mr Rox*'?"

The media laughed at the absurdity of the surname, which was made to sound even more ridiculous by the deliberate emphasis which the journalist had placed on it.

"Well – er," Jo-Dan said, leaning forward so he could see the journalist's name badge, "well, Mr *Greyman*. I've never heard of you but I'm sure you're brilliant at your job. And I'm sure your surname reflects your personality, just as much as mine does."

Cue laughter from the media and furious expression from Greyman, who was already planning his hatchet job in the local paper.

Tommy leapt in, desperately trying to steer the focus away from the band's front man.

"Anyway, guys, perhaps you've got any questions you'd like to address to the rest of the band?"

"Jo-Dan. Is your name made up?"

"No more than Dee-arn," he said, emphasising his accent, the sarcasm and disrespect not going down well with the press.

"Jo-Dan. What makes you think you can take the place of such an iconic front man?"

Tommy cringed, knowing full well what was coming.

"I'm a better singer and a better guitarist."

Sitting at the back of the hall was a real Dion fan – the Garrick theatre's posh press officer, Victoria. She hadn't intended saying anything, as her role was purely to publicise the venue, but she was so incensed by that comment she stood up and moved further to the front.

"Jo-Dan, what if audiences decide they don't like you?" she said when she got chance to get a word in.

"She's a blue and pink aura," Jo-Dan noted to himself.

"I'm gonna blow them away. That'll win them over. Come and see for yourself. I'll arrange a guest ticket."

'When hell freezes over,' she thought to herself.

Tommy tried again to intervene.

"Anyone else got a question for the rest of the band?"

"Jo-Dan. You single or married?"

Jo-Dan laughed uproariously at the question. "Why would I be married? What would be the point in that?"

Cue scribbling from journalists.

"Jo-Dan. What do you think of Dion's home town?"

"Litch-bitch? It's a bit up its own arse if you ask me."

There was a collective gasp and frantic scribbling from journalists. Miles looked down, trying not to smile. He could already visualise the headlines, and he knew no publicity was bad publicity. Tommy wanted the floor to open up and swallow him. The rest of the band shuffled uncomfortably.

"Jo-Dan. Are you going to stick faithfully to Dion's songs or will you put your own take on them?"

"I've already started to improve them."

"Jo-Dan. Some people are saying you'll *never* live up to Dion. Have you got a message for Son of Gabriel fans?"

"Yea, I have," Jo-Dan said, clearly rattled by that last comment.

Tommy held his breath.

"You think Dion rocked. You ain't fuckin' seen nothin' yet."

And he walked off the stage, flinging the press pack into the crowd, the papers inside scattering all over the journalists.

"I'm so sorry," Tommy managed to say before all hell broke loose.

Jo-Dan made his way to a small dressing room which he had found earlier as he wandered around beneath the stage. He chose it because it was somewhere he could escape to for a cigarette. He could hear the furore going on upstairs and was aware of crowds outside, so there didn't seem anywhere else to escape to.

He sat, staring at himself in the mirrors, an air of defiance all around him.

Did he regret anything he'd said? No.

Should he have made it less of a Jo-Dan show? No.

Did he care if the band kicked him out? Yes.

It was a good hour or so before Tommy found him – and that was only because he smelled the smoke.

"Band meeting, next Monday, my house, two o'clock," he ordered coldly. "Make your own way home." And he was gone.

Jo-Dan never even turned to look at him. He could see him through the mirror – and furious didn't even come close to describe how Tommy looked. He could imagine the conversation he'd had with the rest of the band.

But Jo-Dan was mad too. Was it his fault all the questions were directed at him? What was he supposed to do, not answer them?

Had he said anything that wasn't true? No.

He lit up his last cigarette, figuring he'd make his way outside if the crowds had dispersed.

A female voice startled him out of his foul mood.

"Hello?" she called from the corridor outside.

"Hello? Anyone in there?"

It was Victoria, the snotty Garrick press officer.

She put her head round the open door, taking in the sad spectacle of Jo-Dan sitting alone, staring ahead, a fog of smoke surrounding him.

"We're locking up," she said simply.

Jo-Dan blew out more smoke to add to the fog and took his time before answering, which irritated the hell out of her. It wasn't her job to check the building was clear, but she often helped the overworked duty manager, to make sure.

"You're not supposed to be smoking in here."

Jo-Dan laughed, somehow finding that funny.

He could still see her pink and blue aura in the reflection.

"I'm sorry, I'm going to have to ask you to leave now," she tried politely.

What she wanted to say was, "Get out, you ass-hole. How DARE you disrespect Dion and my city." But Victoria never swore, that was far too unladylike. She only *thought* it.

Jo-Dan laughed to himself, but it seemed to Victoria as if he was laughing at her and taking no notice of her request, which made her even madder with him.

"What's funny?" she said, trying to maintain her composure and professionalism.

"Your accent," he replied. "What's your name?"

"Victoria," she said, trying to sound proud and defiant.

"You sound like the fucking queen – Queen Victoria." And Jo-Dan laughed all the more at his own joke.

He stubbed his last cigarette out on the expensive shiny counter.

"Don't suppose you've got any fags?"

"No," came the curt reply.

"Didn't think you would have."

He turned round to look at her and it suddenly occurred to Victoria that she was in the basement alone with this madman. The duty manager was probably on the top floor, checking the bar area, and she suddenly felt extremely vulnerable.

They were total opposites: Jo-Dan slouching in his jeans and T-shirt, long hair half covering his eyes; Victoria standing upright, doing her best to look authoritative in her smart suit and court shoes.

In fact the only thing they had in common was their age and dark, long hair – though Victoria's was pinned into a neat bob with a slide keeping it in place for work.

Jo-Dan stared at her, making her feel even more uncomfortable.

"Do you drive?" he said.

"What?"

"I can't very well walk across Lichfield can I?" he said, quite reasonably. "I'll probably get lynched."

"Well that's your problem," she said.

"Bitch," he countered.

Victoria was a milli-second from losing her composure when she heard the duty manager call 'Vicky'.

Jo-Dan sighed like a petulant child and moved towards the door. She stood back as he walked passed her.

"You aura's pretty," he said, though it came out as 'priddy'.

"What?"

"Never mind."

He made his way upstairs to the reception area and peeped outside. There were hordes of people.

"Looks like I'm gonna have to stay the night then," he said.

"Oh for goodness' sake," Victoria exploded, thinking she'd never get home at this rate. "Where do you need to go? I'll pull my car up to the back doors, but you'll have to get in as quick as you can – and get your head down. I'll put a blanket on the back seat."

"Got any fags?" Jo-Dan said to the duty manager who just glared back at him without even answering.

Victoria sneaked out of the back door, after checking there was no one hanging around. She fetched her car from the multi-storey and drove back to the rear entrance, where the duty manager was waiting with a moody Jo-Dan. The duty manager was cheerfully ready to throw him into that car.

Jo-Dan dived on to the back seat and covered himself with a blanket as Victoria pulled the car away calmly and expertly.

"Where to?" she said.

"Anywhere," Jo-Dan replied.

"Where do you live?"

"Bucking-ham Palace, Ma'am," he replied.

Victoria raised her eyes to the heavens, indicated left and pulled over into a lay-by.

"Look, I'm trying to do you a favour," she said in her posh accent. "You can tell me where to drop you off, or you can get out now."

She watched in her mirror as Jo-Dan sat up.

'What a shame he's such a twat,' she thought to herself. 'He has the most beautiful brown eyes'.

"Dunno where I live," Jo-Dan said. "Got a flat in Litch-bitch but it's probably under siege right now. Staying with friends in Cannock Wood but I don't know the way. Never take any notice when other people are driving."

"If I get you to Cannock Wood will you be able to find the house?" she said.

"Yeah. It's near a pub, the Park Gate Inn."

"I know it," she said, her eyes darting around nervously in case anyone noticed them and recognised Jo-Dan.

"Try not to look like a rock star if you're going to sit up, OK?"

Jo-Dan laughed. "Yes ma'am. I'll disappear up my own arse if you like," then he sat glaring out of the window in silence for the rest of the journey.

Victoria drove Jo-Dan to the Park Gate Inn and he directed her to the boys' house.

"Lovely house," she said politely as they pulled up outside.

"Wanna come in?" Jo-Dan said, leaning over from the back seat and suddenly feeling lonely. He figured Paul and Lucas could not possibly object to this type of girl in their home.

"Er… I think I'll just drop you off if you don't mind."

"I wasn't comin' on to ya; just sayin' thanks," Jo-Dan said.

"No, thank you," she said politely.

"Suit yourself. I'll have some concert tickets delivered to the theatre for ya. Don't suppose it's your kind of music though, huh? Can't picture you rockin' out," Jo-Dan said ungraciously.

"Actually you are wrong," Victoria said. "I love the band's music, especially the ballads. I met Dion a few times when he came to the theatre and I was there when he performed before going off on tour. He was really polite and funny – not with anyone who annoyed him – he didn't suffer fools; but he was always fair."

"Come to the Wolver-ham-pton gig then," Jo-Dan said. "See how I measure up to Dion."

Now it was Victoria's turn to laugh.

"What's so funny?"

"You. You can't say Wolverhampton or Dion."

They sat in the car for a moment awkwardly.

"I'll come to the concert," she said.

"I'll include backstage passes," Jo-Dan said. "You can come and tell me how crap I am compared to Dion then – that is, if I've still got the job of course."

"I'll be honest," she said.

"I'm sure you will, Queen Victoria," he replied as he got out of the car.

"See ya there. Give us a royal wave as you drive off."

Victoria did her best attempt at a "royal wave" as she pulled away and couldn't help but shake her head and smile to herself as she drove away.

Chapter Eighteen

The press conference had been broadcast on local TV later that same day and resulted in a storm of protest.

The newspapers followed over the next few days with screaming front page headlines such as:

JO-DAN: PUBLIC ENEMY NUMBER ONE
ROCK OFF
CITY SHOCKED BY YANK RANT
YANK GO HOME
DION 1: YANK 0
JO-DAN WHO?

Anything positive he had said at the press conference was ignored. Instead, they focussed on the cardinal sin of bragging and trampling on the sacred memory of Dion.

Only the more edgy music publications took a positive spin, branding him some kind of 'metal hero' for 'saying it as it is'.

"Well, everyone sure knows who you are now," Lucas told him, flicking through the newspaper – which was full of local comment – including plenty of "kiss and tell" stories from all the girls he had taken back to his flat. And they weren't complimentary.

"I don't give a stuff what anyone thinks," Jo-Dan said – and he meant it.

"What time have you gotta be at Tommy's?"

"Two o'clock."

"How you getting there?"

"I've ordered a cab."

"You mean a taxi?" Paul said, trying to lighten the mood – but they both knew Jo-Dan was in for the chop.

"Know what the worst thing is?" Jo-Dan said. "I was gonna bring my band over from L.A. See if I could get them some gigs, set them up – or even get them to crew for Son of Gabriel on the tour."

Paul looked down. In truth, he would be sorry to see his bizarre friend go.

The "cab" pulled up at the address Jo-Dan had been given – a sumptuous mansion, hidden away in the Staffordshire countryside. The driver buzzed the security gates, introduced himself and was allowed in.

"You have some pretty rich mates, huh?" he said as he dropped Jo-Dan off, taking in the expansive property and expensive cars parked outside.

"Not my mates any more," he replied without explanation. He paid the driver, took a breath and couldn't help but say "Thank You for the Ride" – which he instantly regretted because it made him feel tearful.

Tommy was on the doorstep, dressed like an off-duty, casual rock drummer in baggy tracksuit bottoms and black T-shirt, his tattoos snaking their way down his arms. He opened the huge oak front doors and Jo-Dan stepped inside onto the marble floor.

"This way," was all Tommy said. "They're all here."

Jo-Dan felt as if he was walking to the executioner's chair.

They were all sat around what looked like, to Jo-Dan, a banqueting table, but there was just a jug of water and glasses on it.

"What's this, the last supper?" he said as he swaggered in, full of false bravado.

"Just sit down," Tommy ordered.

"I ain't apologising. I was just answering their questions - so just say what you have to say and I'll fuck off."

"Jesus, don't you ever shut up?" Tommy said. "Miles? You update him."

Jo-Dan wasn't surprised to see Miles there; he was, after all, their manager. All the hiring and firing was down to him.

"You pissed us all off Jo-Dan," Miles said. "You have no respect and the general view is you should be fired."

Jo-Dan got up to leave, his eyes stinging with hurt, but he wasn't about to let them see that.

"I haven't finished," Miles said.

"I don't wanna hear it," Jo-Dan replied as he went to walk out of the room. "I'll call the cab driver back."

"The tour's a complete sell-out," Miles shouted from behind him. "Every venue is fully booked and there's a waiting list for tickets."

Jo-Dan stopped dead in his tracks and turned round – not sure what they were saying. Did that mean he was still "in" then, or were they just taunting him, letting him know what he was about to miss?

"You may be the most annoying person we've ever met," Miles told him, "but it's thanks to your tantrums and controversial comments that the media gave us such coverage. Not that I'm recommending you do that in future."

"You drive me crazy," Tommy said. "But we don't have time to find a replacement. We need to get in some serious rehearsals; the tour starts in one month."

Wanting to be a rock star performing before thousands of people is one thing: being about to do it is another.

For Jo-Dan, Tommy's words were an epiphany – a moment when he realised there could be no more messing. He had wanted this more than anything and unless Dion returned he wanted to be in it for the long haul.

What Tommy had actually said was 'we don't have time to find a replacement'.

But what if they 'found' time later, Jo-Dan thought. Were his days still numbered? Was he just standing in for now?

On the way back to Cannock Wood in the taxi, he reasoned there was no way they would want to get rid of him. He was always going to give the performance one hundred per cent; he always did, even with his old band back in L.A. Confident in his own ability, he figured that, if the audience supported him, so would the band.

They had talked long and hard at Tommy's house about the mechanics of the tour and a rehearsal was set for the following day.

They were short of crew members, so Jo-Dan was ecstatic when his suggestion of bringing his band members over was accepted – albeit he had to almost donate a kidney to convince everyone he wouldn't wreck the tour by misbehaving with them.

"No, they'll be crewing; they'll be working. I won't even be with them until we get breaks in between the shows," Jo-Dan argued. "They're all great guys. I promise you, on my life, I will not do anything that jeopardises the tour. I'll pay for their air fare out of my own money. They can have my apartment in Litch-b… Lichfield when they arrive and I'll stay with Paul and Lucas when we come back home."

Deep in thought, he relaxed into the comfortable leather seat in the taxi and almost fell asleep as he felt the stress leave him.

And then he spotted something that made his heart lurch.

"Stop the car," he yelled to the taxi driver. "Stop now."

The bemused driver screeched to a halt while Jo-Dan fled into a local shop shouting back 'wait there'.

The driver sat drumming his fingers on the dashboard staring at the shop front and eventually his eyes caught sight of the billboard outside which screamed *DION FOUND*.

It was front page news and Jo-Dan could hardly read the words fast enough as he stood outside of the shop.

Lichfield rock icon Dion has been spotted with his wife in Miami, USA.

The star, who has been missing for over a year, was seen strolling on a beach yesterday.

A British fan, on holiday in the area, took a photo of the star walking with his arm around his wife/ band member Janine.

The holidaymaker, who does not wish to be named, said the couple looked tanned and happy.

"They were unmistakeable, both with their long blond hair, wearing jeans and T-shirts. I wish I had approached them, but I was too awestruck," he said.

"I shouted 'Dion' and he turned around. I'm a real fan. I am sure it was him."

He claims the couple made their way to a busy local bar where he lost sight of them in the crowds.

**Dion and Janine have allegedly been spotted in Wales, Majorca, Boston, USA and Italy, but so far none of the sightings have been confirmed.*

Have you seen Dion and Janine?

Let us know and send us a picture.

There is a £1,000 reward for information leading to the real Dion.

The paper then went on to give background about the "on-stage disappearing illusion in a sphere of lights."

Jo-Dan could have cried in frustration. He scrutinised the picture, but it hadn't been taken close enough to be sure. Sure, it *looked* like them, he thought – but he wondered whether this couple were getting some kind of kick out of being mistaken for the stars – probably even wearing wigs.

And if someone had shouted "Dion" wouldn't the guy have turned round anyway, just out of curiosity, to see who was calling?

And if they were in hiding, why would they go into a busy bar, where the chances were that rock fans would recognise them?

He stood at the roadside, staring and staring at the picture. Could it be? He *wanted* it to be them – but so did half the world, hence the constant stream of lookalike photos which had appeared over the last year.

"You OK?" the taxi driver called.

"Yeah. It's nothing," Jo-Dan said, as he tossed the paper into a bin.

Paul and Lucas greeted Jo-Dan, as the taxi pulled into their drive in Cannock Wood.

"Well? How did it go?" Paul asked, surmising that Jo-Dan had been fired, because he looked so anxious.

"Oh, great," he said half-heartedly. "I still got the job. Start rehearsals tomorrow. The tour's a sell-out already."

"Then why so down?"

"See the newspaper today?" Jo-Dan asked.

"Yeah," Lucas said. "Another fake sighting; we're getting used to them. Maybe one of these days…"

And they all went into the house, each with their own thoughts.

Jo-Dan soon shook himself out of his melancholy, as news of the tour actually started to sink in. His spirits lifted even further when Paul and Lucas told him they would be crewing for the band. They didn't need the money; it was something they had always done and they had loved every minute of it; but this time it would be bitter-sweet.

By the time Jo-Dan had phoned Mikey in L.A. to tell him the good news, that he and the rest of the band could come to England, he was ecstatic and back to his impossible self.

"We're going out tomorrow for bonfire night, if you wanna join us," Paul said, now also in a better mood. "It's at the Park Gate."

"What do you mean, 'bonfire night'? Why would they have a bonfire there?" Jo-Dan asked, genuinely puzzled.

"It's November 5th tomorrow."

"So?"

"Bonfire night."

"Am I in the twilight zone or something?" Jo-Dan answered. "I'll ask again, what the fuck's bonfire night?"

And after ten minutes of trying to get Jo-Dan to understand about an attack on Parliament having been foiled, and why this merited lighting a bonfire each year, the boys felt exhausted.

"So let me get this straight," Jo-Dan said.

"You make an effigy of some guy."

"Yeah, Guy Fawkes. It's not really an effigy, it's sort of a home-made thing made out of stuffed trousers and a shirt, with a pretend head on."

"Then you put this poor guy on top of the bonfire and watch him burn. And there are kids there watchin' this spectacle, too."

"Yea, well – I know how that sounds – but…"

"Jesus. And you think I'm weird."

"It'll be fun, Jo-Dan. There'll be a firework display, have a few beers, meet some friends."

"OK. I'll come to your bonfire night, but it sounds kinda creepy to me. I'll make sure I sleep with the light on tonight."

The boys smiled, not saying anything, knowing that he always did anyway.

The following morning, Jo-Dan ordered the taxi driver, John, again. They were now on first-name terms. There hadn't been time to sort a car out for Jo-Dan yet and there didn't seem much point if they were off on tour soon - and anyway, John was at his beck and call. But getting a fancy car was definitely on the priority list for when the singer had a decent break.

Jo-Dan was up and out before midday, unusually for him. "See ya later at yer creepy bonfire," he shouted back at the boys – guitar in hand. The rehearsal was to start at two, but he had somewhere else he had to visit first.

"Just pull over here," he told John as they arrived at the Garrick theatre. "And guard my guitar with your life – I *mean* it. I shouldn't be too long."

Jo-Dan darted into the theatre foyer, hoping that the faster he moved, the less likely it would be that anyone noticed him. He was wrong, of course. All eyes were on him as soon as he entered.

The ladies who do lunch were seated in the café area near reception and Jo-Dan was something they did not see every day: red leather fringed jacket wide open, hair with a mind of its own way past shoulder length, scruffy torn jeans and a T-shirt with 'bitch' emblazoned on the front.

A lady in a smart uniform walked by and looked alarmed as Jo-Dan approached her.

"Quee – er – Victoria in at the moment?" Jo-Dan asked.

"I'll see," the lady said officiously. "Who shall I say is asking?"

"Jo-Dan."

"I'm sorry?"

"Jo-Dan. That's Joe and Dan together," he said, condescendingly.

"One moment Mr Dan."

"Hey," he called after her. It's not *Mr* Dan, just Jo-Dan. What the hell's wrong with you?"

His accent and tone were now attracting attention from the ladies who do lunch.

"Then it's Mr what?" the uniformed one said.

"Why do I have to be a Mr anything? Just tell her it's Jo-Dan for fuck's sake."

The manager came out of his office nearby and walked towards them.

"Is there a problem, Maureen?" he asked, looking the future rock star up and down as if he had just wiped him off his shoe.

"This 'gentleman' is asking to see Victoria."

"And you are?" the manager said.

"Oh for fuck's sake, I'm not going over that again," Jo-Dan replied, now clearly rattled. "What's the matter with you people?"

There were lots of tuts from the ladies who do lunch.

"Sir, sir, you can't go in there," the manager tried haplessly as Jo-Dan stormed into the main theatre area yelling 'Victoria'.

He ran up and down the stairs, calling into empty corridors with the manager trailing behind saying, "Sir, I am going to have to call the police if you…," his voice disappearing into the distance as Jo-Dan hurtled around the building shouting her name.

And there she was, just coming out of an office upstairs.

Victoria stopped dead as she saw this lunatic standing in front of her, the breathless manager trying to catch up, his arms flailing.

"I just had a phone call from reception downstairs," Victoria said. "Why is it there has to be a scene every time you come here?"

Jo-Dan stood in front of her like a scolded child.

"It's the staff here, they're all fuckin' mad – present company excepted."

"It's alright, Mr Bates, I know him," she said almost sympathetically indicating that it was safe for him to leave. "It's fine. I'll be fine."

"Get in here," Victoria ordered, opening the door of her office.

"You sound sexy when you're angry," Jo-Dan said as he started twirling in the office swivel chair and picking up and down everything within reach.

Victoria stared at the spectacle in front of her.

"So, what did you want exactly? Leave that alone. Please put those down."

"Just called to see you. Wanted to give you some news, Jo-Dan said messing with a box of paper clips."

"Oh?"

"I still have a job. They didn't fire me."

Victoria was genuinely pleased, but didn't want to sound overly excited.

"That's fantastic. I'm really pleased for you."

"So you still comin' to the gig?" Jo-Dan asked, making 'boing' noises with a ruler on the edge of the desk.

"Can you stop that? Of course I'll come."

"Of course I'll come," Jo-Dan said slowly mimicking her posh accent, thinking of its alternative meaning and holding her gaze with his brown eyes.

Victoria belatedly twigged what he meant and felt flustered.

"Well, let's just hope *I* still have a job after your dramatic entrance," she said, desperate to change the subject.

"It's my job to make a dramatic entrance," Jo-Dan said. "Your top button's undone. No – don't do it up."

Victoria felt herself flush as she did the button up.

"We should go," she said. "I'm not really allowed to have visitors in the office."

"I have a cab waiting outside so gotta go anyway. Got intensive rehearsals for the next four weeks. I just wanted to let you know."

"Victoria?" Mr Bates called from outside the door. "Is everything OK?"

Jo-Dan got up to leave the room and as he brushed past the hapless manager, he leant into him closely and said, "She's fine *Master*-Bates."

"It's *Mr* Bates, young man," he stressed angrily, unaware of Victoria's stifled laugh behind him.

"Whatever. See ya, Queen V."

Jo-Dan gave her a brooding look for a moment, knowing full well he was anything but her type, then ran down the stairs, hair bouncing around him.

The Garrick theatre returned to normal.

Chapter Nineteen

The rehearsal sessions were to take place at Tommy's, in a purpose-built separate facility, a brick building in the grounds of the mansion, fully equipped with the latest technology and equipment.

The band sat on the comfy sofas for a chat before the rehearsal started. All the talk was about performing the classic songs that the audiences would expect. Jo-Dan had to stifle comments about not wanting to rehearse the classics. He already knew them inside out and so did the band. He would rather have approached them fresh and raw, even if that meant performing them for the first time together live on stage. But the rest of the band members were having none of it. They saw the sessions as a way of ensuring that they were skin-tight when it came to performance. Outnumbered and outvoted, Jo-Dan resolved to grin and bear it, but he had every intention of introducing new ideas when it came to the performance. What would the band do then? Stop performing in front of thousands of people to insist he sang and played lead guitar "as rehearsed"? No, the band would just have to get used to his improvising, he reasoned.

While they were talking, Jo-Dan struggled to find the right time to introduce the subject of *Ice Blue*. Everyone was so focussed that twice he reached out for the song in his guitar case, touched it and left it alone, feeling the time wasn't right. He wasn't sure what effect the news would have on the band and he figured it was bound to disrupt the mood.

So he resolved to bring up the subject after they had at least got through most of the rehearsal.

The band performed eight classic hits one after another, Jo-Dan in his element, putting everything out of his head so he could concentrate fully on the job at hand. And he seemed to be getting away with slight changes, the band accepting that the songs did indeed sound better that way.

From the minute they started to perform, the colourful thread that joined the performers was back, albeit only Jo-Dan saw it. And he detected electricity in the air, but not as most people think of it – as an atmosphere - it was real electrical particles in the air. He could not understand why no one else seemed to notice. To Jo-Dan, the air was positively fizzing with particles. He could even see them occasionally sparkling. He could either be afraid or be thankful for the energy that was generated, he thought – so he resolved to be grateful, but at the back of his mind was the thought 'it was the sparkles that took Dion and Janine', and he prayed that he wouldn't suffer the same fate.

Everyone was upbeat. The band sounded great and the girls were really starting to gel with Jo-Dan's vocals.

The band took a short, well-earned break for drinks, some left for the "rest room" as Jo-Dan called it.

When they were all back in the rehearsal room, Jo-Dan felt he couldn't put it off any longer, but didn't know how to introduce Ice Blue. He didn't feel he could just blurt it out so he decided to just blather on and see what came out.

"Guys, I've tried not to piss you off since you told me I could stay – and apart from gettin' yelled at by Tommy for playin' his drums, I don't think I've got under yer skin much, huh?"

There was no reply. For the most part Jo-Dan was annoying just being himself, he didn't have to particularly do anything wrong.

"And I haven't even come on to the girls – not 'cos I don't fancy you both any more – cos I do. Jesus, I get aroused just looking at you in those low cut…"

"Jo-Dan, leave it," Rick said as the twins pulled the front of their T-shirts up to make their tops less revealing.

"Anyway, I'm tryin' not to be so much of a dick and I've got something really important I need to show you."

He took the sheet of paper from his guitar case and handed it to Tommy.

"Found this under the mixing desk in Dion's studio," he said. We could work on this. It's a Dion classic, with three-liner type verses and a killer fourth line."

"You found a new Dion song?" Tommy said, not convinced. "What? Just under the mixing desk? Why would you look under the mixing desk?"

"Dunno," Jo-Dan lied. "Just searching for anything that might give us a clue about… you know…"

Everyone gathered around Tommy as if they needed to see it for themselves to believe it.

"Oh my God," Tommy said. "We could really do something with this. He's even put the chords in and notes about how it should be played and sang. It's like a… like a gift… and to have it in his own handwriting… I'd recognise that anywhere… and it's classic Son of Gabriel stuff."

There was a general buzz about the room; it was as if Jo-Dan had found the Holy Grail.

But for Tommy it was all too much. He got up and left the room, taking the lyrics with him. The sight of the tattooed, shaven-headed drummer looking really distressed even tugged at Jo-Dan's heartstrings. After all, this was his best mate's handwriting.

Joey went out to see if he was OK, but not before saying, "Stay here" to Rick – as he looked from the girls to Jo-Dan. Rick knew what he meant, so stayed put.

It was a good twenty minutes before they came back in, Tommy looking an odd mixture of elated and upset at the same time.

"We'll work on this tomorrow," Tommy told the band. "I can't deal with it right now."

"He left it 'cos he loves ya mate," Jo-Dan said. He figured he could hardly tell Tommy that his best mate had visited him and asked him to pass on his love - so this was the only way he could think of to pass on Dion's message.

"I already got a feel for how it would go," Jo-Dan added, feeling a little more accepted by the band now. "Imagine introducing that – a new song by Dion."

"I guess we should thank you for finding it and bringing it to the rehearsal," Joey said and there were general nods of agreement.

"Jesus, I don't feel like rockin' out right now after that," Rick said and everyone stared ahead, each in their own thoughts.

Jo-Dan decided to seize the chance.

"I wondered, bein' as I'm not public enemy number one at the moment, that you'd cut me some slack and let me introduce a new song of my own."

"We don't have time to learn many new songs, Jo-Dan," Tommy said. "We've got our work cut out to get this show together – and now we've got Ice Blue to figure out."

"But it's a real easy, laid-back ballad. Dunno if you'll like it, but why not at least hear it?"

Glances were exchanged that spoke volumes. The "Jo-Dan show" was what they were thinking.

"I wrote it a few weeks back. Think it might have somethin'. You can tell me you think it's crap if you want. I like it; it's just a bonus if other people do. There's scope for harmonies and it's a gift of a song for power chords and sing-a-long chorus."

"OK, let's hear it," Tommy said wearily, not expecting much; then, with a hint of sarcasm which went over Jo-Dan's head, he added, "Entertain us."

Everyone found somewhere to chill out on the sofas as Jo-Dan set himself up in front of the mics, seated on a stool with his guitar. Everyone felt irritated already because he was doing his usual "give me a minute" as he focussed and kept everyone waiting.

"It's called *Someone Out There Somewhere*," he said eventually – and he played the opening bars of a beautiful and complex chord progression which grabbed everyone's attention straight away. Like him or not, he was a damned good guitarist.

After a couple of bars he came in with the lyrics and almost immediately he was aware of sparkles in the room, which he could see in his peripheral vision.

Somewhere out there is a special girl
Living life so aimlessly
Searching for someone throughout the world
She just doesn't know it's me

Chorus

Someone out there needs to find me
But doesn't know that I'm around
Someone out there's hiding from me

I'm right here – waiting to be found

She feels so near, yet she's so far away
Almost touching distance now
Could it be that we will meet today?
I'll find my soul mate soon somehow

Repeat chorus

Does she feel the same way that I do?
Is she waiting to be mine?
I promise faithfully I'll find you
Somehow, somewhere, some day, some time

Jo-Dan slowed down the last line so that the words really hit home. And, as the saying goes, you could have heard a pin drop.

Jo-Dan opened his eyes slowly after the final line of the song and brought himself back to reality. He had sung his heart out, his heart was on his sleeve, his guard had not just fallen but crashed down to earth.

But he couldn't tell what the silence from the band meant and it seemed to go on for a long time. The sparkles were fizzling out, but no one seemed to have even noticed them.

Eva was the first to speak. "Oh, my God, Jo-Dan, where the hell did that come from? I didn't know you had it in you."

"That was absolutely beautiful," Lou added. "You really wrote that song?"

"I write loads of songs," he said defensively. "It's just one of many."

"You've really shocked me, Jo-Dan," Lou continued. "You sang it as if it was really heartfelt."

"It's just a song," Jo-Dan said dismissively, trying to get the heart off his sleeve.

"It's not 'just a song'," Tommy said. "You have a sure-fire hit single with that. I vote we work on that now this minute."

And within an hour, *Someone Out There Somewhere* was a full blown ballad with harmonies, power chords and powerful drumming – just aching to wrench the hearts out of the public during the tour. And the sparkles were back with a vengeance.

Chapter Twenty

"So how did the rehearsal go?" Paul asked, as they walked along the dark country lane to the Park Gate Inn with Lucas and the girls.

"Brilliant," Jo-Dan said. "Really good – and they're actually gonna record one of my songs, a ballad."

"Wow; that really is something. And Lucas told me about *Ice Blue*."

"Oh yeah," Jo-Dan said, struggling to know what to say next, as he wasn't sure how much Lucas had told him. "We start work on that tomorrow. Can't wait."

"How amazing that you found the song. We thought we'd found everything we could in that studio. And it was under the mixing desk all the time? What made you look under there?"

"Dunno. A bit of paper just caught my eye," Jo-Dan lied. "Thought I'd check it out."

"Glad you did," Paul said. "A new song by Dio – priceless."

"Anyway, what's with this creepy bonfire? Are there gonna be many chicks there?"

"Why? You gettin' desperate?"

"Well, you know how it is. You won't have me bring girls back to the house – I understand that – but I've been kinda busy lately so haven't had much time for..."

"Yeah, I get it. Look, it might be better if you try to look less rock star, or you're gonna cause a scene as usual."

"So how am I gonna look less rock star?"

"I dunno. Maybe get rid of some hair or something. Tuck it down the back of your jacket. And try and keep your head down."

Paul asked the others to help, as they tried to make Jo-Dan somehow blend into the darkness, but even with his hair shoved down his jacket, he still looked impossibly different.

"Your jacket's gonna stink of smoke, you do realise?" Stacy said.

"Will make a change from cigarette smoke I suppose," Jo-Dan said. "You'll have to get real close to me later, then you can tell me if I stink or not."

Stacy shoved him away playfully, then walked arm-in-arm between Paul and Jo-Dan for the rest of the way, shivering in the cold.

"Gonna have to get someone to snuggle me when we get there. I'm freakin' freezin'," Jo-Dan said.

"I'm sure you'll manage to find someone in the crowd," Lucas said, pulling his girlfriend close.

"Probably more than one," Paul added, pulling *his* girlfriend close.

"You know, it's a nice village an' all, but it really creeps me out at night. This place here's got a real bad feel to it; makes me really uncomfortable."

"What, Castle Ring?" Paul said.

"See – that's what I mean?" Jo-Dan answered. "Even the name sounds weird."

"We could go a walk around Castle Ring tomorrow if you like; it's really pretty with some great views."

"No thanks, rather have a leg off," Jo-Dan said, hopping along the road, clinging on to his friends.

They arrived at seven p.m., just in time to watch the bonfire being lit. There was a huge crowd at the popular event and Jo-Dan got as close as he could to the bonfire, as he was now really shivering with the cold.

"Is this supposed to be fun?" he asked Paul.

"I'll get you a beer. That'll stop you complaining."

"Yea, a cold beer; that'll warm me up won't it?" Jo-Dan said, dithering.

Then he leapt sideways, yelling something that sounded like a shocked "ha!" as if he had been stung.

"What the hell's the matter with you?" Lucas said.

He watched Jo-Dan looking all around the crowd, obviously seriously spooked, his eyes looking terrified in the light from the bonfire.

"Can you see them?" Jo-Dan asked, clearly scared out of his wits.

"What?"

"The sparkles. They're back. They're all over the place."

"What are you talking about?"

And Jo-Dan leapt away again, yelling, as a child with a sparkler came near him.

"They're sparklers Jo-Dan."

"What? I know they're sparkles."

"No. Sparklers – harmless kids' sparklers. Kids like holding them and making swirling patterns with them. Nothing to do with our sparkle stage effects."

"Jesus, they scared me to death; I really hate those things."

"Wanna hold one?"

"No I fuckin' don't. Get them away from me. Oh my God, now they're tossing a man on to the bonfire."

"Are you Jo-Dan?" a young female voice from behind said.

Jo-Dan turned round to find a gaggle of excited, giggling teenage girls behind him.

"Yes, I am," he said, pulling his hair back out of his jacket so it was in full flow.

Cue giggles and screams.

"Look. Keep quiet," he said in hushed tones. "Shhhh. Don't attract attention or everyone will want me. As soon as my beer arrives you can get me away from here. Take me somewhere private where I can keep warm, if you know what I mean."

Cue more giggles and screams.

As soon as Paul returned with his beer Jo-Dan disappeared into a nearby field with the girls in the darkness, and didn't return until about two hours later, when the fire was just a smouldering ember.

The boys watched as he emerged from the darkness, dishevelled and adjusting his clothing, bits of twigs and grass stuck in his hair, with five girls hanging onto whatever part of him they could grab.

"Gotta go girls," he said. "Maybe another time…" The false promise left them jumping up and down with excitement and they ran off, desperate to tell their friends.

"You enjoy the fireworks, Jo-Dan?" Paul said, knowing full well he wouldn't even have noticed.

"Oh yeah. I really enjoyed all that banging…"

"So you like bonfire night, then, after all?"

"Yea. Found a good way of keeping warm. Could do with a few more beers now; worked up quite a thirst."

Chapter Twenty-One

At the Bird Street police station in Lichfield, the lead officer in the case was addressing his subordinates in one of the conference rooms, as they all hunched around the computer.

"So. You know where we're at? The case has remained open for over a year and there is still no sign of Dion or Janine. Now – with enhanced technology – I want you to review this tape again.

"Our expert here is going to show us what he's found. He's spent countless hours trying to clean up the tape and zone in on the couple.

"See here. See how she appears to be struggling. She's actually trying to kick him and he's holding her tight. We could just make that out when we reviewed the tape over a year ago, but everyone thought they were larking about.

"Look, now, if we enhance this bit – see how it looks as if he's taking something out of his pocket. Can we zoom in on this section some more?"

"Looks like a bit of rope or twine or something to me," one of the officers said.

"And – it's not very clear now – it gets a bit dense with that clever illusion thing going on – but if you look here… can we enhance that some more?"

"Looks like she's collapsing," another officer said, straining his eyes to look closer, "but it's difficult to say, unless we can get a clearer picture."

"I think we have enough new evidence now to at least have a warrant of arrest issued, so he can be taken in for questioning.

"I don't think he just took her away somewhere. In my view, he killed her, then went into hiding and may even have planned it all along. He was a multi-millionaire, so could have stashed enough cash away. He's smart, so wouldn't use credit or debit cards, knowing they could be traced. Did you complete those other enquiries I asked you to?" he asked one of the officers.

"Yes sir. I spoke to all her associates, including her former partner, Alex. He says he has always been convinced Dion killed her. Says he was really possessive; wouldn't have her alone with any other man; would follow her if she went anywhere without him, even to a local café. In fact, he said he warned Janine when she first got together with Dion. He says he told her one day he'd make her choose: him or her kids.

"He was so worried about Janine he even went as far as attacking Dion, you remember? He admits to wishing he'd finished him off, then Janine would be here now… We can't condone that of course, but it looks as if he may have been proved right.

"And Dion's ex, Lucy, she told me how he demanded everything his way, only wanted her for sex and treated her really badly; says she feels lucky; lucky she got out alive.

"Spoke to Janine's brother and sister. They were of the opinion Dion was completely mad anyway, before all this happened.

"I even spoke to loads of technical staff and the media. They all said the same. He was a nightmare: what he said went; it was his way or not at all. They also said he was clever, manipulative. They're the worst kind.

"Maybe Janine had told Dion she was leaving. It's only a theory but, from everything I'm told about his controlling personality, he wouldn't allow her to leave him. If you ask me, he's one of those guys who would think 'if I can't have her…'

"And then there are Janine's bank cards and credit cards. None of them have ever been used since that day.

"The only people I didn't interview are those who have publicly supported him and called for him to return: his band, his parents, former boss and Janine's sons. Even the new singer the band has recruited to replace him has gone public to say he'll find him and bring him back."

"Where's he most likely to turn up do you think?" one of the officers said.

"He's an ego-maniac. My bet is he'll turn up on stage in another dramatic 'special effect'. That's his cover. He can get the glory, all the adoration from his fans, then escape again in a shower of sparkly bits or whatever other elaborate illusion he has planned. His sort will not be able to stay out of the limelight for long.

"And when he does – we'll be waiting. Get the tour dates. Make sure we have a presence at every gig for the foreseeable future. If he shows up, we'll have him, however long it takes."

"God, that means some poor buggers in the force have got to attend every Son of Gabriel rock show."

"And if there are any more 'Dion found' press reports, we'll follow them up – just in case. He can't have changed appearance much in over a year."

"Do we tell the press about the warrant?"

"No. Don't want him or his mates and family tipped off, or he'll stay in hiding."

"When we get him, if he's innocent, he'll tell us where to find Janine.

"If not, the rock world's precious Dion will spend thirty years in a cell. Wonder how he'll take to that?"

Chapter Twenty-Two

Weeks of rehearsals at Tommy's house resulted in a blistering set for the upcoming tour.

The band agreed to introduce two new songs into the show: Dion's *Ice Blue* and Jo-Dan's *Someone Out There Somewhere.*

What Jo-Dan lacked in people skills and restraint off stage, he more than made up for with prolific song-writing, musical ability and on-stage presence. And he tried, really tried, not to throw away his once in a lifetime opportunity. He thrived on rehearsals and could not wait for the live performances.

But a couple of things were bothering him; they probably bothered the others, too, but no one was saying anything about the elephants in the room – until Jo-Dan brought them up during a break in rehearsals.

"I wanna talk about how we keep Dion in the show," he said, as they all sprawled on the sofas, having a drink.

That got everyone's attention. They had assumed that Jo-Dan would be the ego-maniac from hell once the live shows started.

"I have been thinking along the same lines," Tommy said. "But if we're gonna do this, it's a difficult balance getting the audience to accept you and remember Dion.

"I'm wondering how the audience is gonna take to you Jo-Dan. Yeah, you're good, but we have to consider the possibility that this might not work."

"I don't much care whether they take to me or not," Jo-Dan said. "I'll batter them into submission; but what I do care about is that we honour Dion in some way. I know I get… got… on his tits and we never really hit it off, but I still respect him as a performer and songwriter. And it's down to him that I got this job. I know you guys had your doubts, probably still do, but I'm being serious for once.

"I've been thinkin' – you know that huge backdrop that was used right at the end of the last show?"

"The one with his picture and his arse showing the 'kiss my ass' tattoo on it?" Rick asked.

"Yea," Jo-Dan continued. "Everyone loved that final bow, that final defiant message from Dion. I vote we use that backdrop every night as our tribute to him. I'm not trying to replace him; I want to honour his memory, make it clear to the audience I *want* him to return – and show respect for what he achieved. I'll even get on my knees and bow down to that picture every night."

"Wow Jo-Dan, I never guessed you could be so humble," Lou said. "I wasn't expecting that, but I love the idea. What do the rest of you think?"

The band members were unanimous: the backdrop would be used for every show.

"And I need to talk about somethin' else," Jo-Dan continued.

"Now what?" Tommy said.

"Those fuckin' sparkly things. They've been in this room while we rehearsed. Not many, but I've noticed them out of the corner of my eye. Has anyone else?"

Blank and puzzled looks from the others told Jo-Dan they hadn't.

"But how come you see them and we don't?" Eva said.

"Look, I'm probably bonkers..."

"Yea, that's true," Joey interjected.

"But I don't mind admitting I'm scared that those bloody sparkly things will be back when we perform. Nobody's mentioned all the stage effects. Are we gonna have special effects or what? Has Miles sorted something out?"

"Miles has never had anything to do with the stage effects," Tommy said. "They just kind of happened."

"Bullshit," Jo-Dan said. "They don't 'just happen'. If we don't sort some kind of effects out, it's gonna look a pretty bland show. People are gonna expect something to happen."

"Something *will* happen," Tommy said. "We don't need to arrange anything. The magic is back; we can all feel it. Whatever happens we'll just have to embrace it. And if the sparkles show up, what you gonna do? Run off stage? Yea, that'll look rock 'n' roll. You'll just have to man up and go with it.

"Listen, I'll tell you something," Tommy continued. "When I look back on conversations I had with Dion and the way he was behaving, he knew something was going on. And I know he *wanted* to go wherever it is he went that night. He never explained it to me in so many words; but he had sorted everything out, put everything in place, for when he'd no longer be here – even down to leaving his house to the boys and making me promise to contact you, Jo-Dan. I don't pretend to understand it, but I know one thing, if anyone can come back, Dion can."

"I'm gonna make damn sure I will create such a show that he *will* want to come back," Jo-Dan said. "The way I see it, I'm only the caretaker of his role. "We'll make the show so good that he will want to return. And it's all here waiting for him.

"As for special effects, fine, we'll see – but don't expect me to be walking into some weird capsule thing and disappearing into the ether. That's not happenin'."

And with that, all fired up, he got up, grabbed his guitar in mock anger and launched into the opening bars of Dion's up tempo song *Love Me Tonight*, quickly followed by the rest of the band, who felt inspired by his attacking style.

Band members could already see the potential of fast-paced *Love Me Tonight*, its suggestive lyrics giving Jo-Dan ample opportunity to torment females in the audience - and males of a certain persuasion.

He acted out the words suggestively and with humour, taking full advantage of the second meaning in some of the lyrics, singing as if he meant them.

And that was just in rehearsal; the band members could only imagine how it would come across on stage.

Love Me Tonight by Dion

It's been comin' for a while
We'll go our separate ways
You no longer make me smile
And neither wants to stay

One more time and then we're through,
A distant memory
There'll be no more me and you
We're over and out, we're free.

Chorus
So love me tonight,
One for the road, oh yes.
Use me and

Abuse me now
Then we'll have a rest

We're in and out of love
It's so hard to sustain
Believe me, lord above
No way I can refrain

And when we've said goodbye,
Our sweaty souls at rest
We don't have to live a lie
Time to see who's next - whoah.

Repeat chorus

Before everyone left the rehearsal to go their separate ways, Jo-Dan had one final request.

"Been talkin' to Paul and Lucas about the Rock For Dion charity," Jo-Dan said. "They tell me thousands of pounds are still coming in to support bands across the country."

"That's right," Tommy said. "The girls in the charity office tell me they have requests from all over the country from bands desperate for funding for rehearsal and recording costs."

"Well, I think it'd be great if we could hold collections at every show to boost the fund. Maybe if Dion gets to hear about that, he might be even more inclined to meet his fans again."

"Great idea," Tommy said and the rest of the band nodded in approval. "We'll arrange for collections as people enter and leave the stadium. You've surprised me today, Jo-Dan. You're not completely self-centred after all, are you?"

"See girls?" Jo-Dan said to the twins. "See how fuckin' sensitive I am? See what you're missin'?"

Chapter Twenty-Three

"Hi. Can I speak to Victoria?"

"Who shall I say is calling?"

"Joe Dexter."

"One moment sir."

"Hello? Mr Dexter?" Victoria said, swivelling in her office chair and preparing to write notes, curious as to who it might be.

"Hi. It's me."

There was a silence at Victoria's end of the phone. He had only spoken three words, but there was no disguising the American accent.

"Er… Joe Dexter? Where did that come from?

"My dad's name. Didn't think they'd put me through if they realised it was me."

"Oh, so you're *Mr Dexter*, then, are you? That actually makes you sound like a normal person," Victoria said, laughing, and struggling to match the surname with the image of this crazy guy she had in her head.

"Yea, well just don't tell anyone, huh? You'll ruin my street cred. I changed my name legally but figured the least I could do was keep the 'r' and 'x' in my new name."

"What can I do for you, Jo-Dan?"

There were a lot of visual images he wanted to pass on to her in answer to that question, but he took a deep breath instead.

"I'm free tonight. You doin' anything?"

"Are you asking me on a date?"

"A date? That sounds quaint. Don't think I've ever been on a date. You'll have to decide where we could go. I don't know the area and it needs to be somewhere quiet or I'll be mobbed – by those who hate me or by those who love me."

"I think you're taking something rather for granted, aren't you?" Victoria said, in that posh voice that went right to Jo-Dan's groin. "What could you possibly want with someone like me? I'm not your type at all."

"How do you know what's my type?"

"I can imagine your type, Jo-Dan."

Jo-Dan was imagining too and the image in his head was not unpleasant.

"How many women have you had since arriving in England?"

Jo-Dan squirmed at the direct question and was grateful she couldn't see his expression right now. He could have said, 'how about the five in one night?' but figured that wasn't an option.

"You haven't answered me, Jo-Dan."

In truth, he didn't have an answer and didn't want to come up with a lie.

"The silence speaks volumes," Victoria said.

"Look, I know I ain't no saint, but I really would like to get to know you better, Queen V."

"In what way, Jo-Dan? I lead a very dull life compared to what you do. I work nine till five, for goodness' sake."

"I could work nine at night till five in the mornin'," Jo-Dan said. "See? We do have somethin' in common.

"I've never been out with someone whose hair was longer than his shirt collar – and certainly never with anyone whose hair was longer than mine. I can't imagine…" Victoria replied.

"Well, first of all I can't imagine wearing a fuckin' shirt. And as for the hair, well, I could tuck it down my T-shirt or somethin'."

"You're on another planet, Jo-Dan. I don't want to be with a guy who sleeps around; that's nasty. And I don't like it when women go out with a guy and try to change who he is – so I don't think there's much point, do you?"

For once in his life Jo-Dan was lost for words. They had reached an impasse.

"But you'll still come to the gig? You got the tickets and backstage passes I sent?"

"Yes. Thank you. I'm looking forward to it."

"I'll see you there, then."

He thought of pleading some more, but his pride wouldn't let him, so he simply said, "Bye, hon'."

'Hon'? Who on earth says 'hon'?' Victoria thought to herself and she put the phone down very slowly.

The conversation left her distracted for the rest of the afternoon and she was annoyed with herself for allowing this foul mouthed womaniser into her head. There was no way on earth…he might have nice eyes, but that's where it ended.

Still feeling unsettled, Victoria left the building as usual at five p.m. and made her way to the multi storey car park. It was dark and cold, so she was glad of the ceiling lights which made her feel secure. But her pulse rate quickened when she saw a man leap out of a taxi and run towards her car.

"Hi, V," Jo-Dan said. "Bought myself a shirt. Like it?" And he draped himself across her bonnet as if he was posing for a photo shoot. It was a plain white shirt, which, on anyone else, might have looked smart; but the top two buttons were undone and it was still creased where it had obviously been folded in the packet. And coupled with light blue jeans, covered in chains, it didn't exactly create a smart overall appearance, especially as it wasn't even tucked in.

And Jo-Dan had tucked his hair down the back of the shirt, so the whole overall appearance was bizarre.

"What? What are you doing here? And get off my car. Now you've got dirty marks all over the back of your shirt. Why are you wearing a shirt, anyway?"

"Wearing it for you – here I am – a guy in a shirt without long hair. Now d'you fancy going out tonight?"

"Oh, for goodness' sake."

"Give us an answer, eh? I'm fuckin' freezin'. And my cab driver's gettin' hacked off. We've been waitin' for you for half an hour."

"Now you're making me feel guilty if I say 'no'. And I've just finished work; I can't go out anywhere dressed like this."

"Well, I can wait for you if you wanna get a shower, get changed…"

"I live at home, Jo-Dan," Victoria said exasperated. "Do you seriously expect me to take you home and just announce 'mum, this is Jo-Dan, can he just wait with you while I get ready to go out?' I couldn't even trust you for half an hour. I'd come downstairs and there'd be chaos. My mum would freak if she saw you – you look ridiculous."

"Well, I got an idea. How about we just chill out at a local hotel. You could just slip into a dressing gown or something…"

"Are you completely mad? Do you really think I would go to a hotel room with you and swan around in a dressing gown? I hardly know you."

"OK. So you come up with an idea. I'm a bit stuffed for places to go, what with having to keep a low profile an' all. Come on, Queen Victoria. I only want to get to know you better. I can be a complete gentleman you know."

Victoria laughed at that prospect and started to get into her car.

"Tell you what," Jo-Dan tried in a last desperate attempt. "John will take us to my flat. We can go there now things have calmed down a bit. We can order a pizza or something. You hungry? I got wine and stuff. What d'ya say? And I swear to you, if you're not happy, I'll call John and he'll bring you back here."

Victoria was in her car and was about to close the door when Jo-Dan knelt on the ground next to her.

"When you marry me, we are going to have the most amazing babies," he said, his eyes searching her face.

Victoria didn't know whether to laugh, cry, hit him or shove him over.

"Now I know, you are completely insane," she said, looking at him directly in the eyes, something she had tried to avoid previously. "You are most definitely not the marrying kind – you said so yourself at the press conference."

But as he knelt there, his big brown eyes looking hurt, she felt as if she had kicked a cute puppy.

"Come to my flat," he said pleadingly, still kneeling on the cold floor. "And please decide soon, 'cos I'm fuckin' freezin' and I'm kneelin' on a nail or somethin'."

Victoria gave the biggest sigh, leaned her head on the steering wheel and felt battered into submission.

"I'll come for an hour and I'll have pizza with you – and that's it," she said.

"Yes, brilliant!" Jo-Dan said, standing up and rubbing his knee.

"Let me help you out of your carriage, Queen V," he said and took her hand. It was the first time they had touched so he prolonged the moment as long as possible as she groped with her other hand for her handbag.

Victoria was aware of a tingling sensation inside. She knew it was not attraction; she still found him impossible, irritating, foul mouthed and pushy. And she hated all that hair, but there was something that stirred inside her.

He was not unattractive, she had to concede – just not right for her.

John drove them to the Bird Street flat, Victoria sitting next to him with Jo-Dan in the back. John did his best to reassure her that his bizarre friend was 'OK, really'. Jo-Dan took a quick look outside to make sure no fans or haters were hanging around the flat, then took her hand and led her to the door, his heart pounding so hard he could barely breathe.

"Thanks John," he shouted. "Call you later."

John smiled to himself, doubting very much that the call would come.

"Hey. Hang on a minute," Jo-Dan said as he opened the door. "Gotta carry you over the threshold."

And before she knew it, Victoria had been swept up into his arms and plonked the other side of the door.

"You daft bugger," she said as he placed her back down gently at the bottom of the stairs.

"Oh my God V; that's the first time I've heard you swear. Fuck me."

Jo-Dan switched the light on and turned to her, marvelling at her delicate features and warm eyes.

"It ain't much, but it's clean and warm," he said. "Come on. I'll get you a drink."

He took her hand and led her upstairs to the flat.

"I ain't gonna be here much longer," he explained as he led her to the lounge. "Here, I'll put the lamp on, sit down. My mates from L.A. are moving in. They're coming from the States in a coupla days, ready to crew for the band. What do you like to drink?"

"White wine please, just one. I'll be driving later."

Victoria was surprised to find how clean and organised the flat was. What she didn't know was that Jo-Dan had spent the weekend tidying in the hope that…

He busied himself going in and out of the kitchen, fetching wine, beer, glasses.

"I'll pour it for you like a proper gentleman," he said, the formality of it all killing him already.

"Thank you," Victoria said, studying him closely in the half light. His hair had already fought its way out of the back of the shirt and seemed to have a life of its own as he moved.

"I'll go and get this ridiculous shirt off," Jo-Dan said aware of her scrutinising him. "Can't stand it any more. You want me to find you something less formal?"

"Like what?"

"I'll bring you something suitable," he said as he disappeared into the bedroom.

Victoria winced at the prospect of what he had in that bedroom and started to feel a little uneasy. She downed the rest of the wine, which made her feel more settled, then poured some more, reasoning she could call for the taxi driver if needs be.

"Mind if I use the phone?" she called. "Just to let my mum know I'll be later than usual."

"Fine," Jo-Dan shouted from the bedroom.

He returned as she was finishing her conversation, which to him sounded completely alien.

"Bye, mummy. See you later. Yes I will. Love you."

She turned to see Jo-Dan looking more like his usual self, wearing a ripped T-shirt with a lightning strike down the front.

"Here. Thought you'd look great in this," he said, proudly displaying a blue T-shirt with the words 'I Rock' on it.

Victoria laughed and kicked off her shoes.

"Alright you crazy guy, I'll wear your T-shirt, but turn around while I put it on."

Jo-Dan did as he was told, desperately searching for some reflection somewhere, but not finding it.

"OK." she said. "Do I look casual now?"

"Nearly," Jo-Dan said. "Let me try one thing."

Victoria looked momentarily fearful as he came towards her so he stopped a couple of feet in front of her.

"Could you just let your hair down – I mean literally and metaphorically?"

Victoria unfastened the clip in her hair and her hair tumbled down. It was longer than Jo-Dan expected, almost as long as his, straight with a slight twist at the end.

"How's that? Now do I look crazy like you?"

Jo-Dan felt as if he had been punched in the chest. He had never seen her look so beautiful.

"One more thing. Hitch up that skirt a bit."

"Now you're pushing your luck," she said.

And he held his arms up as if to say 'I won't touch'.

Victoria turned the top of her skirt over, raising it a few inches, then struck a pose.

"You look amazing," Jo-Dan said. "I knew I was right. Now you look like a crazy rock chick."

And he ached to touch her, but knew that was off limits.

"I'll put some music on. What would you like? Anything - except Son of Gabriel."

"You choose," she said.

Jo-Dan put Journey on in the background, then cracked open another beer and sat opposite her.

"Why am I here, Jo-Dan?"

"Because I know there's more to you than meets the eye," he said, enraptured by the colours around her.

"You're weird, you know that?" she said as she watched his eyes take in every part of her.

She shifted her legs slightly, aware that her skirt was riding up.

"Blue suits you," Jo-Dan said. "It mingles with your aura."

"I don't know what you mean."

"I see colours around people. You are surrounded by a really nice pale pink and blue, same as me."

Victoria thought of laughing at him, but he looked so intense and serious.

"Like I said, you're weird. I'm not having sex with you, Jo-Dan."

"I know. I'll wait."

"I'm not *ever* having sex with you Jo-Dan."

"Then it'll be kind of difficult making our babies won't it?"

Victoria shook her head, wondering what on earth made him tick, and poured another glass of wine as Jo-Dan cracked open another beer.

"Are you weird like this all the time?"

"Pretty much."

"Priddy much," she said, mocking his accent to get her own back.

Jo-Dan smiled at her attempt at an American accent – and his appealing smile did not go unnoticed.

"People don't understand me, so they underestimate me," he added.

"Well, at least you're not dull I suppose."

Victoria felt a little safer, a little more relaxed. After all, he had honoured his promise to be a 'gentleman' so far.

"Can I sit near you?" Jo-Dan asked.

"Why?"

"Just wanna be near you. Jesus, don't be so suspicious. Let's chill out; dunno about you but I'm tired as well as hungry."

He didn't wait for an answer; he moved to sit on the floor next to her leaning against her legs with his back to her. Victoria could not see the expression of complete euphoria on his face. It took her a few minutes to relax, but as she felt the warmth of his body touching hers, she found herself looking at him closely from behind.

"You know, you do actually have beautiful hair," Victoria said. "It's clean and shiny. A mess, but clean and shiny."

"Would you do me the honour Queen Victoria of combing my hair with your fingers?"Jo-Dan said in mock English accent.

Victoria ran her fingers through his hair, trying to tame it into some kind of order.

Jo-Dan leant into her and could feel desire rising with every tiny touch of her fingers.

He reached behind him and took her hand, pulled it in front of him and kissed her fingers gently.

Electricity ran through her at the touch of him and she could not understand why. She would never in a million years have chosen someone like him.

Jo-Dan turned round and knelt in front of her, for the second time that night.

"I am a complete twat, that's true," he said kissing her fingers, placing one of them just a little into his mouth, which aroused feelings in her she had not known existed. "But, I wish you could really see what **else** I am."

Victoria could have pulled her hand away, but found she didn't want to. As he kissed her right hand she stroked his hair with her left hand and smiled at him.

"Are you trying to seduce me, Mr Dexter?"

"Only if you want me to, Victoria."

"I would never go to bed with someone on the first night."

"What if it was just to sleep?"

"Do you really think I'm that stupid?"

"I'm scared of the dark. That's why I don't sleep alone."

Victoria laughed at the very idea of a rock star being afraid of the dark and at the pathetic excuse for sleeping with women, but Jo-Dan looked so deadly serious, she suddenly felt ashamed, as if she was mocking him.

"You really *are* scared of the dark?"

"Yes I am. Stay with me; ring your mum and tell her you'll be back tomorrow. I promise I will hold you and nothing else. I won't even kiss you if you don't want me to."

As the night wore on they began to feel easier in each other's company, getting to know each other, sharing stories, alcohol, music, laughter and pizza.

Victoria found Jo-Dan hilarious, even when he was not trying to be - and sad in lots of other ways. They had both lost their mum at an early age, but at least Victoria had her step-mum, who treated her as her own. She also still had her dad, so she couldn't imagine how it must feel to have lost both.

By midnight, both feeling genuinely tired, Jo-Dan stood up, took Victoria's hand and led her slowly into his bedroom. Inside his head, he was shrieking 'Yes' at the top of his voice as she made no objection.

"We are just sleeping Jo-Dan," she whispered as they entered the room.

"I know, hon'," he said.

She lay on top of the duvet fully clothed.

Jo-Dan ached to kiss her, but sensed that if he broke his promise, the progress he had made tonight would have all been for nothing.

He fetched a blanket from a cupboard, covered her over gently, then huddled beneath it, curled around her back. He put an arm around her and buried his face into her hair, breathing in her smell. Lying there in total darkness, still wearing jeans and T-shirt, stroking her hand, he felt happier and more content than he had ever been in his entire life. The good company, wine and food began to take their toll and within minutes they were both fast asleep.

Chapter Twenty-Four

Victoria woke with a start and could see it was just gone eight a.m. according to the clock on the wall. It took her a minute to take in where she was – and who with. She felt sweaty beneath the warm blanket and there was a very hot body still lying next to hers. 'Very hot' indeed she thought, as she turned to have a proper look at the sleeping Jo-Dan, surprising herself that she found him even the slightest bit attractive. His hair and T-shirt were slightly damp with sweat so she peeled back the blanket to cool him down. He stirred slightly but fell back into a deep sleep.

"Obviously way too early for a rock dude to emerge," she surmised. But she was glad of the opportunity to have a good look at him without his returning her gaze with those heart-melting eyes.

She was relieved to find that she was still fully clothed, but had to pull back the blanket fully to check he was too. His T-shirt was scrunched up revealing most of his back and the button on his jeans was undone, but otherwise his clothing was intact. She studied his toned body while she had the chance and felt the urge to run her hand over his tanned back and flat stomach, but felt she should quit while they were ahead.

Half of his face was obscured by all that hair so she gently moved it away from his eyes. 'What beautiful long eyelashes!' she thought. 'Wasted on a man; women would give anything for those lashes.'

She moved off the bed slowly, as he sleepily reached out for her, so she pushed a pillow underneath his arm for comfort, physical and emotional.

Victoria had to be at work for nine a.m., so there was no time to wake him. And anyway, she hadn't the heart to disturb him, as he looked so peaceful.

She needed to rush across the city to the car park, drive home, quickly get washed and changed, then back to work. So Victoria rummaged around the lounge for pen and paper and left a note on the table next to the bed.

Thank you for a surprisingly pleasant evening.
Didn't want to wake you, as it's the first time I've seen you quiet.
Got to be at work for nine, so let myself out.
See you at the concert.
V – x

When he found the note four hours later, a sleepy Jo-Dan stuffed it in his jeans pocket, savouring the little 'x' after her 'V'. That was a kiss wasn't it? His first kiss from Victoria. Next mission: to translate that little x into a real one.

But he was now so busy that "Mr Dexter" only had time to ring Victoria when she was at work. Even then, she sometimes wasn't in the building or unable to talk because people were in the office.

Intensive rehearsals now took up most afternoons and evenings; his band was due to arrive from L.A. soon, so he had to leave time free to spend with them – and the one afternoon he did have free, Paul and Lucas had arranged a meeting with someone he desperately wanted to see: Dion's mum. He had so many questions he wanted to ask her and hoped that she would be able to give him clues about how he could find her son.

Paul and Lucas told Jo-Dan that she was home from Spain for a couple of months and had arranged to visit them at Cannock Wood. The boys had some misgivings about seeing her, as the last time they had spoken to Dion's mum was over a year ago - and they had been less than polite because of their own distress.

"Where's the girls?" Jo-Dan asked, as they waited for Dion's mum to arrive.

"They thought we needed space to talk to her on our own," Paul said.

"You sure you're OK with me listening in?"

"If you can get anything from her that helps us find Dio and mum, we're more than happy for you to meet her," Lucas said. "Just don't come on to her or anything."

"How did you get on the other night, dare I ask?" Lucas continued. "You didn't come home. You spend the night at the flat?"

"Yeah, I did – with the beautiful Victoria," Jo-Dan said.

"How did you manage that?" Paul asked.

"Battered her into submission; was just persistent."

"You seeing her again?"

"Would like to, but haven't got a minute. She's comin' to the Wolver-hamp-ton gig though."

"So – are you and her an 'item'?" Paul asked. "Thought you said she didn't fancy you. Bet you scared her to death, taking her back to your place."

"Actually, I was the perfect gentleman, I'll have you know," Jo-Dan said in his best attempt at an English accent.

The boys snorted with laughter at the very concept.

"No – I *was* – seriously."

"She stay the night?" Paul asked.

"She did. And I didn't touch her."

The boys laughed even louder.

"Fine. Don't believe me. I'm not always a complete asshole, you know."

"She's here," Lucas said as he looked out of the lounge window. Be polite for Christ's sake."

"Hey, this is Dion's mum – mother of a rock star," Jo-Dan said. "I'm sure she's heard some choice language from her own son."

Lucas went to the door and welcomed Dion's mum. As he brought her into the lounge, she lit up the room. She was prettily dressed in light-coloured trousers and a flowery blouse and looked immaculate with her long blonde hair and fit body, tanned from the Spanish sun.

Paul darted a glance at Jo-Dan, as if to say 'don't even think about it'.

There were hugs all round and casual chat about her flight, the weather, how long she was staying etc. She hugged Jo-Dan and her expensive perfume and soft hair did not go unnoticed.

Dion was like her, he thought to himself: beautiful, confident, intelligent; here were his genes.

Gradually, over coffee, the talk turned to the matter at hand.

"We didn't treat you very well last time we saw you," Paul said. "We're sorry."

"You were upset," she said. "So was I. It was the day after…"

"How have you been?" Lucas said. "How do you rationalise what happened? We're still struggling, I don't mind telling you."

She looked at Jo-Dan, as if unsure whether to say what was on her mind, then she smiled at him quite tenderly, he thought.

"Dion told me all about you," she said.

"Oh," Jo-Dan squirmed. "It's OK; I know he couldn't stand me."

"He thought you were supremely talented. He also told me you drove him crazy after even a few seconds."

"We can identify with that," Lucas said laughing. "We've kind of got used to him now."

"It's lovely that the three of you are close," she said. "I think it was meant to be."

"Where is he? And where's Janine?" Jo-Dan asked directly.

The boys looked embarrassed by his blunt approach.

"It's OK," she said, picking up on the boys' reaction. "I'll do my best to explain, but I don't think I can give you all the answers. I did try to tell you before, but it was too soon, and I'm aware how it must have sounded to you at the time."

Everyone was very quiet and concentrated. Here was the one person who knew Dion better than anyone. Jo-Dan and the boys were listening intently.

"Dion was always different," she said with a sad smile. "Even as a child, he was different; and as an adult, he was the vainest person I have ever known. I know I'm biassed, because I'm his mum, but he was also one of the most talented and spiritual people you could meet."

Jo-Dan nodded in agreement.

"And you are like him in lots of ways," she said to Jo-Dan. "I think that's what he recognised in you. Things happened around Dion and I expect things happen around you, being gift-wrapped, don't they?"

"Gift-wrapped. That's what Miles said to me," Jo-Dan answered, intrigued. "What are you saying – that gifted people attract stuff that other people might consider weird?"

"It happens to you, doesn't it?" she said.

"Cards on the table: I see stuff that others don't. I see colours around people; I know things – without understanding how. But what has this to do with Dion and Janine disappearing?"

Paul and Lucas looked at him, as if to say, "I knew you were weird, but I didn't know all that."

Dion's mum took a deep breath, as if she was about to impart the most important thing she had ever said in her life.

"Dion always told me he did not want to become old; he did not want to see his fortieth birthday. I was almost hysterical when he first told me, because I thought he was talking about suicide. In fact, that's why I moved to Spain because I never knew when…

"But he meant something else – and he explained it more to me after the attack that left him in a coma. He said he had been somewhere, to 'a place'. He said he always knew it existed, but now he had actually seen it and lived it."

She breathed hard and thought how best to express what she wanted to say.

"Let me ask you a question, Jo-Dan. If you thought a special creative place existed – somewhere where you would be constantly inspired and happy, would you not want to be there? But – it would mean giving up your life and leaving those you love behind. But you are not dead, you are 'somewhere else'."

Jo-Dan looked as if he was considering the prospect, but found it impossible to answer.

"Dion explained it to me as an 'irresistible pull' to this place," she continued. "He absolutely knew he would be there before he was forty, but wasn't sure exactly how. But equally, he believed he would know when the right time came.

"Dion made me promise I would try and explain things to you as best as I can – and that's what I'm trying to do again now."

She leant out to the boys and touched each of them on the hand. Time hung in the air as they waited for every word.

"He explained it to me as somewhere he felt 'invited' to go; somewhere where talented people could continue nurturing their craft with those they love. He did not have to die in order to go there, but neither could he live in this world. He could come back if he chose to – but he knew in his heart that this special place was where he belonged.

"Being forty was never an option for him; it was not what he wanted. This was a way of cheating death and cheating growing old. The thought of being old, fat, grey, with aches and pains, was absolutely abhorrent to him.

"Imagine, Jo-Dan, if you could be there too and never age. You could write and make music and perform and stay just as you are. Can you understand why he would want that?"

Jo-Dan tried to grasp the concept, and, although he could understand why it might be right for someone else, he wasn't sure it was for him.

"I am the last person to want him to leave," Dion's mum continued. "But, because I love him so much, I am also the last person to want him to stay against his will."

"But if this 'special place' exists, why wouldn't everyone want to go there and stay young?" Paul asked, surprising himself that he was even considering it even existed.

"Everyone would," she replied. "This is how Dion explained it to me: that it was not open to all – otherwise there would be no one on the planet over the age of forty, would there? And it exists for talented people, who, as we know, we often lose too soon."

"So, you think all those icons we have lost at an early age are in this place?" Jo-Dan asked intrigued.

"Perhaps not all; but Dion believed many of them are," she said.

"Will he come back?" Jo-Dan asked, already knowing the answer.

"If he comes back, he ages like the rest of us, and knowing my son, he will not want to do that. He could return for very short visits; but he was thirty-nine when he left – and that's the age he wants to stay."

"Has he visited you?" Jo-Dan said.

"Once," she replied. "Just to let me know he is fine and OK. You've seen him too, haven't you?"

"I have," Jo-Dan admitted – for the first time in front of Paul. "The world needs to see him once more. Miles said if I create the right moment he will come back."

"I think he will," Dion's mum replied with a smile, "but not for long."

There was a silence and everyone knew what was coming next.

"Where's mum?" Lucas said.

Dion's mum lost her composure.

"This is where I have difficulty," she answered. "I love my son and I am trying to defend the indefensible.

"We all know he adored your mum; I know he would never have gone without her. He told me he had tried to explain all this to her when he was thirty-three years old – and you can imagine her reaction. She adored him and was terrified of losing him. I know your mum hoped he would change his mind. She knew she made him happy and he had achieved all he wanted; she reasoned he wouldn't want to leave all that behind.

"But I know my son. I know how determined he is once his mind is made up. But there were two problems: Dion was not going to go without her and she was never going to leave her boys."

“So he took her,” Paul said. “She was talented and gifted, so she could go to this ‘place’ too?”

“Yes,” Dion’s mum replied seriously. “But – as I understand it you don’t *have* to go – you have to *want* to go.”

“And if she couldn’t make her mind up?” Jo-Dan asked.

“I fear that Dion made her mind up for her,” she replied. “And I’m sorry, but I think if the only way of taking her with him meant taking her life, he was prepared and determined enough to do that. Dion tried to mitigate what he had done by leaving everything to you both.”

Paul and Lucas looked furious with her for even saying what they feared – even though none of this was her fault. Their minds went back to that night when they had watched their mum struggling with Dion in the capsule and they had been laughing, thinking that he was playing about with her. To think that they actually laughed as they watched their mum die was the worst part to deal with. Neither of them could even bear to ask how he had killed her, though, unfortunately, they could imagine.

Paul stood up and began to pace angrily. “So you are saying he killed her as the only means of getting her there, but he knew she would be alive in this ‘special place’? So he can come back to our reality but she can’t? And he can come back without being in this sparkly capsule thing.”

“That’s how I understand it,” she replied. “I’m not trying to defend his actions; I’m just explaining as best as I can – as he asked me to do,” she said, looking down at the carpet, but seeing nothing really.

“Selfish, selfish bastard,” Lucas said. “And you know what’s even worse? We can’t even tell anyone this; they will think we are completely mad. I can’t even believe we’re considering it might be true. I’d prefer to think they disappeared in some kind of magician’s illusion.”

“So would I, sweetheart, so would I,” Dion’s mum said.

"So what did he say when he visited you?" Paul asked Jo-Dan.

"He told me to send his love to you, Lucas and Tommy; said he couldn't bear it when your mum cried for her boys and that he'd make it right."

"Dio always did what he said he would," Paul said, desperately trying to salvage some semblance of belief in his step-father. "He'll find a way to bring mum back."

Chapter Twenty-Five

The day Jo-Dan's band mates arrived from L.A., he was ecstatic.

He had paid for John to pick them up from the airport in his "cab"; then they had all planned to meet up at his flat.

Paul and Lucas were with Jo-Dan at the flat, as he paced in anticipation. He was adamant that Paul and Lucas should meet his L.A. mates straight away - and he was so hoping they would all get along. To Jo-Dan, his two friends from Cannock Wood and three mates from the USA were the most important people in his life, people who had been good to him, befriended him, took care of him, put up with him.

Jo-Dan had tried to ring Victoria to share his excitement, but was told she was away at some press conference for the day.

"Where can we all go for a guys' night out?" Jo-Dan asked the boys. "I can't really take them around Litch B – er – Lichfield; that'll attract too much attention. You just know I'd end up with my head kicked in by the end of the night. Where else can we go? Bir-ming-ham?"

"You could go to Stafford I suppose," Lucas suggested. "There's a nightclub there. You've not insulted Stafford, as far as I know."

"How far's this Stafford place?" Jo-Dan said.

"About twelve miles away, I guess," Lucas replied. "When you thinking of going?"

"Tomorrow night, maybe – don't suppose they'll wanna go out tonight; we'll just have some beers. I could get John to drop us off at this – what did you say – Stafford – place? You two coming with us?"

"Probably not," Paul said. "Don't think the girls would take too kindly to it. Remember, you promised Tommy there'd be no trouble when your mates arrive."

"What do you think I am?" Jo-Dan said pretending to take offence. "Can't a guy go out and just have a good time?"

A non-committal "hmmm" was all Paul could say; Jo-Dan looked out of the window, as he heard a car pull up outside.

"They're here. They're here," Jo-Dan hollered and thundered down the stairs to meet his mates. Paul and Lucas exchanged looks as if to say 'here comes trouble'. They had only just got used to one crazy American; now there would be four.

Soon, the small flat looked extremely full. Jo-Dan didn't say so, but he was so comforted to hear people talking in his own accent. There were man hugs and handshakes all round and the conversation flowed easily - when anyone could get a word in edgeways. Jo-Dan was in full flow, like an over-excited puppy, except that puppies don't chain smoke.

Paul and Lucas instantly liked their new crew members, finding them far less manic than Jo-Dan; and they all hit it off immediately as they sat sharing beer, cigarettes and laughter.

Jo-Dan gave the guys a mini-tour of their new home, occasionally stopping to give yet another man hug with shouts of "fuckin' brilliant; I still can't believe you're here."

When he came back into the lounge, with everyone around him, he picked up a bottle of beer and announced, "I have something to say."

"Oh God. Now what?" Paul said.

Jo-Dan came over to the sofa where Paul and Lucas sat and squeezed himself in between them, putting an arm around their shoulders and spilling beer over them.

"I want to say – you guys have all been amazing to me. I know I'm sometimes a pain in the ass…"

There was laughter and nods from everyone present.

"But Paul and Luke here, Dion's stepsons, have become my dearest friends; just like you guys were to me in L.A. They even let me live at their wonderful house, for Christ's sake. I wanna thank all of you for what you've done for me and for believin' in me. I am so happy that you are all here together. I love you guys, all of you."

And Jo-Dan actually looked tearful. Paul gave him an enormous hug and kissed the top of his head.

"Fuck off, I don't love you that much," Jo-Dan said – and the beer and laughter went on well into the night, until John, faithful as ever, picked Paul, Lucas and Jo-Dan up to take them back to Cannock Wood.

As John dropped them off, a hopelessly drunk Jo-Dan took him aside.

"Find out where Victoria lives," he said. "Follow her car home tomorrow but don't let her see you. I've tried to get in touch with her at work but she's always out or on another call or something. Find out where she lives. I need to see her before the start of the tour."

Chapter Twenty-Six

The beat was throbbing so loud that Jo-Dan and his mates could feel it in their chest as they approached the nightclub entrance. They were already up for whatever the night would bring, having downed bottles of vodka even before John picked them up.

"You find out where she lives?" was Jo-Dan's first question as he fell into the taxi.

"Boley Park," John said.

"What? She lives in a park like a hermit crab? Why does everywhere round here have to have ridiculous names John, tell me, huh? What's Bogey Park like?"

"Quite refined, Jo-Dan."

"Refined," he mocked in an English accent. "I'll fit in there then," and he laughed at himself. "Stop the car a minute; I forgot to take a piss."

His mates, equally inebriated, laughed until they were almost sick, as Jo-Dan peed into a bush at the roadside near the Bowling Green pub, fell forward and nearly disappeared completely into the foliage.

John had to get out of the taxi to help extricate an unsteady Jo-Dan from the bush, as his mates almost peed themselves laughing on the back seat. He placed his passenger in the front seat and fastened his seat belt for him.

"So can you take me to this posh Bogey Park place tomorrow, then?" Jo-Dan said – and laughed his infectious laugh at his own joke.

"OK. I'd advise that you sober up first, though," he said, but his words were lost, as Jo-Dan was trying to make up some nonsense joke about snotty swings and roundabouts in Bogey Park – while his mates were doubled up by his infectious laughter.

"You need me to pick you up in the early hours, Jo-Dan?"

"I'll ring you if I need you. If I don't ring, I am in a bed or on a sidewalk somewhere."

"That's what I'm afraid of," John said, as he hauled Jo-Dan out of the front seat. "Try not to look inebriated, or they won't let you in." He drove away leaving the four of them outside the club swaying together on the 'sidewalk'.

"O.K. guys, shenshible," Mikey said, steadying himself and they all clung onto each other laughing at his mistake. He tried again. "Look senshible, shensible…"

The four of them looked anything but sensible.

Suddenly a crowd of lads on a stag night turned up, so Jo-Dan hustled his little group in with them. He fished out a wad of notes from his pocket to pay entrance for himself and his mates.

"What's with the playing card?" Mikey said as it fell from Jo-Dan's pocket.

"Oh that? It's there to remind me to be shenshible," he said, leaving it lying on the pavement in the rain, and they all fell about helplessly again.

The four of them propped each other up and the more they tried not to laugh the worse the urge to laugh became. But buoyed up by the crowd, they managed to get through the nightclub doors without incident.

Jo-Dan was already wealthy, thanks to an advance payment for the tour, so he had plenty of cash to throw around. The vodka shots came thick and fast, the guys were soon separated and the girls, oh the girls.

Jo-Dan had been recognised and he was in his element, lapping up the attention and accepting the girls literally throwing themselves at him. They seemed to love his accent and hair, which massaged his already over inflated ego. Occasionally he would spot the other guys dancing, kissing, staggering and they would give a thumbs-up sign to each other, but the whole evening passed in a haze, a drunken fog of lights and scented smells and women who looked as if they had gone out in their underwear.

As the night wore on Jo-Dan was vaguely aware several times of having sex, but had no idea where he was or who he was with.

And then Dion was there – all in white – surrounded by sparkly things fizzing and cracking. And he was smoking and blowing the smoke into Jo-Dan's face. And Jo-Dan couldn't breathe and he tried to smash his way out of the capsule but he was trapped. Every time he touched a sparkle it burnt his hand. Dion laughed enjoying the moment. He took a long drag on the cigarette and blew more smoke into the air. The capsule filled up with smoke and now Jo-Dan was seriously in trouble, gasping, trying to breathe air into his lungs. Dion's eyes watched without compassion. *Ice blue.* Ice blue eyes. Then everything was black, pitch black, frighteningly, scarily black.

If only Jo-Dan could have reached out and turned on the light. He was back in his L.A. apartment; the lamp was right next to the bed; but it had disappeared and nothing was where it should be. His hand groped for the lamp, but now his chest hurt, hurt really bad.

He tried to cough but couldn't take in a breath to cough; and Dion's red aura was getting stronger. And Jo-Dan was wet, soaking wet, screaming for Dion to let him out of the capsule. Dion was disappearing in a haze of cigarette smoke and he could feel him pulling away.

Then there was a blinding light, so bright it hurt his eyes and oxygen poured into his lungs. He vomited so hard it hurt his head and he could feel another projectile on its way up, then another, then another.

There was a scream nearby.

"Oh, you dirty bastard. Oh, Jesus Christ, it's all over me."

Jo-Dan tried to open his eyes but the slightest flicker hurt his head. Someone was shaking him.

"Is he OK?" a woman's voice said. "God, what a state. I thought he was gonna die."

Jo-Dan opened his eyes and they became accustomed to the light but he threw up all over the carpet again.

"You need to go," the woman said, pulling on her knickers. Di, pass me his jeans and T-shirt. If he's gonna keep throwing up he can do it outside."

It took three of the women to get him to stand; two held him up while one opened the door.

The fresh air hit him straight in the face as he tried to comprehend what was going on.

"Where am I?" he said, feeling his stomach lurch again.

"Nowhere," the woman said. "Nowhere. That's where you are and that's where you're going. All that talk about being a rock star, and I fell for it. A rock star would not be screaming and crying in the dark – and he'd be able to keep it up for more than ten seconds."

She wasn't very attractive in the early morning light, black circles under her eyes where her mascara had run; and she was no spring chicken.

"Where's my mates?"

"No idea," she said and he was unceremoniously dumped outside.

Jo-Dan's trainers were thrown out of the door after him, on to the wet pavement, where he sat trying to breathe and clear his head.

He threw up into the gutter, hoping that one would be the last. The cold air and rain were refreshing but his addled brain could not comprehend whether he was wet with sweat, rain or both. He tried to stand, but the buildings opposite were moving around in circles, so he sat on the pavement and curled into a ball next to the roadside; he managed to put on his trainers, but couldn't tie the laces and prayed for the nausea to pass.

About an hour later a police car arrived, after being alerted by a local resident. It was winter after all and she actually thought someone was lying dead in the street, frozen.

Jo-Dan stirred as the car pulled up next to him.

"Sir, you OK? You need to move on."

"Sorry, yea, "Jo-Dan said, vaguely aware of his predicament, but his words came out more croaky than he expected. "Where's the nearest place I can get a cab?"

"Couple of miles that way," the policeman indicated and watched as Jo-Dan struggled to stand. Taking in the spectacle, the policeman doubted whether he would be able to walk a couple of miles so he decided to take pity.

"You need a lift?"

"Please."

Jo-Dan was now acutely aware of his precious hair stinking of sick and all he could think of was standing in the shower.

"Good night out?"

"Dunno. Can't find my mates. Can you stop the car…?"

And from the urgency of his voice, the policeman realised he was about to throw up yet again so he pulled over. The policeman tossed him some tissues.

"American?"

"Rock star," Jo-Dan said almost apologetically.

"Oh," the cop replied. "They always are."

"What time is it?"

"Five twenty."

The policeman pulled over into a taxi rank and helped Jo-Dan out of the car.

"Thank you. What's your name?"

"Dave."

"Thank you Dave. I'll write a song for you," Jo-Dan said, aware that his words were still slurring."

"Yea, you do that, rock star. Take care."

A few days later, a letter arrived at Stafford police station. On the envelope it said "For PC DAVE WHO WAS ON DUTY IN STAFFORD, NOVEMBER 20, five a.m."

All the local bobbies saw the following pinned on to their notice board marked 'FOR THE ATTENTION OF DAVE'.

Rock Star Rescue

Throwin' up on the sidewalk is no way to behave
Dunno where I'd be if it hadn't been for Dave
He took me to the taxi rank even though I stank of sick
He helped me out, he didn't shout, even though I'd been a dick.

Thank you to the anonymous cop who saved me one cold night

Was late November in Stafford town in early morning light
A pissed up rock star freezing cold before you came along
I promised when you dropped me off that I'd write you a song.

Chorus
Here's to Dave, my saviour guy,
What a PC, what a man
Here's 50 quid to get some drinks
With love and thanks – Jo-Dan.

A £50 note was attached.

Dave was to tell his story for years to come when Jo-Dan hit it big.

Chapter Twenty-Seven

Breaking news: reports are coming in that Lichfield rock star Dion has been found dead.

The star, who has been missing for over a year, was found washed up on a beach in Cornwall in the early hours of this morning. There was no sign of his missing wife Janine Lee.

The body was spotted by a coastguard who said he instantly recognised the man, believed to be about forty years old, by his distinctive long, blond hair.

Police are travelling from Dion's home town and will be waiting for the man's identity to be confirmed.

The news on the TV had reached Jo-Dan's ears, but not his addled brain. He was sprawled out on the sofa at Cannock Wood. The boys had fetched him in after they had heard the bell ringing, some time after six a.m.

Paul and Lucas were standing in the doorway of the lounge, listening to the lunch time news.

"Why aren't we feeling anything?" Paul said.

"Because we know it's yet another mistaken identity," Lucas answered. "What's the point in getting upset until we know for sure?"

Jo-Dan stirred and threw up again into the bowl they had placed on the floor.

"Better get him some more water and something for his hangover. He's got a rehearsal at two," Paul said.

"You had any words out of him yet?" his brother asked.

"No. One of his mates rang to see if he was here. They all found their way back to their flat somehow. He didn't sound too good."

"They obviously had a great night then…" Paul replied. "God, he stinks. Let's get him in the shower. Think we'd better give him a lift to the rehearsal; make sure he gets there in time or Tommy won't be impressed."

It was a very pale Jo-Dan who turned up for the rehearsal dead on two p.m. The boys had tried in vain to get him to eat something but he was afraid that if he ate anything he would throw it up at rehearsal.

"Not feeling too good," was all he said. "But I'll be fine. Let's just do it."

Somehow he sang and played for the next two hours on autopilot, drinking copious amounts of water and looking like death – but at least he was quiet in between songs. No one asked and he didn't offer any explanation.

Everything had to be right, because there were just days to go before the start of the tour. Jo-Dan made a mental note never, never to drink vodka again; well, except perhaps on special occasions; well, maybe just for the first night of the tour; or on the last night of the tour; or for Christmas or his birthday in March.

By the time John picked him up in the taxi, he was starting to feel a little more alive, apart from the thumping headache.

"You look like shit," John said as Jo-Dan fell onto the back seat so he could lie down.

He looked even more crumpled than usual and still had no idea how he had got dressed at all. He had a vague recollection of someone struggling to get his boots on and someone else tugging at his wet hair trying to get the knots out, but that was it. He didn't stink any more. In fact he smelled of deodorant spray, so must have had a shower, he thought.

"Take me to Victoria's," Jo-Dan ordered. John was doing very nicely financially out of all this running around and waiting with the engine running, so he never once objected. And anyway, it was none of his business what his passenger got up to, he reasoned.

Jo-Dan was startled out of a deep sleep when John shouted "we're here" at him. It was the third time he had told him, but the first two didn't register. John hadn't parked right outside the house, not wishing to alert Victoria in advance and also because he didn't want to take the blame for following her and bringing Jo-Dan here. It was pouring with rain and Jo-Dan had no coat as usual, so he would just have to get wet.

Sleepy Jo-Dan sat up, hair a dishevelled mess.

"Which house?" he asked John.

"Over there. See her car?"

"Oh yea, posh area, Bogey Park, ain't it?"

"You need me to wait for you?"

"Can you wait for a bit? If I'm not back in an hour you can go. You never know, she might be pleased to see me."

John smiled to himself, doubting that very much, but said nothing.

"Here, take a swig of water," he said handing Jo-Dan a plastic bottle then watched from a distance as he trampled over the neat lawn leading to the large detached property, slipped on the wet grass and knocked over a plant pot en route.

Jo-Dan rang the doorbell, under which there was a sign that said 'The Kennedy-Huff household'. The rain was dripping from the porch and ran down the back of his neck.

It was late afternoon, about five thirty p.m., and already dark and cold. Right at that moment, Jo-Dan ached for the California sunshine and started singing *California Dreamin'* out loud as he waited.

The door opened as he got to "and the sky is grey" at the top of his voice. The irony was not lost on him as he suddenly found himself singing to a rotund lady with grey hair. The hair was set severely in place with curls which had been ordered to do as they were told.

She was wearing a floral frock and a chain of pearls hung over her red neck and ample bosom. He could see into the hallway which smelt of expensive carpet and there were pretty little ornaments precisely placed onto lacy mat things which sat on polished little side tables.

Victoria's car was one of four cars on the block-paved drive so it must be the right place, he thought.

"Is Victoria here?" he said, doing his best to sound polite.

The lady in pearls stared for a moment trying to take in the sodden spectacle that stood almost upright before her and for the life of her she could not understand why he was singing on her doorstep.

"And who might you be?"

Jo-Dan resisted the urge to laugh at "and who might you be?" Whoever said "who might you be"? And whoever said it in that ridiculously posh accent? But with a supreme effort he managed to keep a straight face.

"It's Jo-Dan," he said. "Can you tell her it's Jo-Dan?"

"And may I ask what you require of my daughter, young man?"

This time Jo-Dan couldn't keep his face straight, so had to look down at his boots.

"Erm…" he said, biding his time and trying to stop smirking, "I would require to see her, ma'am."

He didn't think that came out quite right, but didn't know how else to answer such a strangely constructed question – and he had at least managed to look her in the eye when he said it.

"One moment," the lady in pearls said condescendingly – and shut the door on the dithering Jo-Dan.

He scrunched himself as far under the overhang of the porch as he could to get out of the rain, so being right up against the door he could hear a muffled conversation inside but couldn't make out the words. He could just make out a young woman hurrying down the stairs.

What the lady in pearls was actually saying was, "There is *something* on the doorstep asking for you Victoria."

"What do you mean *something*?" she said, and she could just about see the outline of a figure on the doorstep.

"A young man is asking to see you. He looks very unsavoury, Victoria. I don't know what he could possibly want with you."

"Well, whoever it is, it's pouring with rain out there mummy. Did he give a name?"

"A mister Dan I believe."

The lady in pearls noted her daughter's shocked expression.

"Shall I send him away, dear?"

Victoria could hear the rain intensifying, splattering up the pane of glass in the front door.

Jo-Dan, now thoroughly soaked, rang the doorbell again.

"Mummy, just give me a minute, I'll…I can't believe this…he wouldn't…surely not…please wait in the lounge; I'll deal with this. I'll have to bring him into the hallway. It's pouring with rain."

The lady in pearls padded in her pink slippers to the lounge, but left the door open so that she could hear any conversation in the hallway.

Victoria opened the door to find a drowned rat on the doorstep – no – a drowned rat would have looked less a spectacle than a drowned Jo-Dan.

"What on earth are you doing here? Get in a minute, you're soaked through. How did you know I live here? Stand there on the rug; you're dripping all over the place."

The water was now running off Jo-Dan's straggled hair and off his nose. His T-shirt was completely soaked through and his boots were already leaving mud on the pink carpet. He stood there, dithering, looking completely pathetic.

"Does it never stop raining in this fucking country? Jesus, let me hog the radiator a minute…"

Victoria's efforts to shush him fell on deaf ears as she darted a look at the lounge door, aware of a pearled presence on the other side of it.

"I'm fuckin' freezin'. You look gorgeous. Nice house."

"Stay there, I'll get you a towel," she said.

Jo-Dan watched her intently and his heart lurched. He scrutinised her pert behind in an expensive pair of jeans. Her hair was tumbled over her shoulders, still damp from the shower and she was wearing a flowery T-shirt.

"It's all right, mummy," she said to the sour face that greeted her. "I'll just get him dried off and warmed up, then he can get a taxi home. I'll take him into the kitchen.

"He's a musician," she added, as if that explained everything. "And he's American," she said apologetically, as if that explained even more.

"Victoria, I'm not happy," she said. "I'm not happy at all. I've already heard his foul language. I want that young man out of my house as soon as possible."

"Hey V, where's the John? Think I'm gonna throw up," Jo-Dan hollered from the hallway.

"Oh, Jesus," Victoria said as she hurtled back into the hallway.

"Language Victoria, language," her mummy said.

Victoria manhandled Jo-Dan into the downstairs 'bathroom facilities', then ran to fetch cleaning materials, to try and get rid of the trail of mud on the carpet before mummy saw it.

The lady in pearls went to fetch her husband from the conservatory – but not before she had heard loud retching from her spotless bathroom, which made her feel extremely stressed and unwell.

Victoria waited outside the bathroom door, but Jo-Dan did not emerge and it had gone very quiet.

"Jo-Dan?" she whispered through the door. "Are you all right?"

A kind of 'urgh' noise answered her.

Fortunately, he hadn't locked the door, but he had clearly passed out and was semi-conscious on the floor making it difficult for anyone to get in. Victoria managed to crawl into the bathroom to reach him and did her best to clean him up with towels.

She removed his boots so that he didn't make any more mess, then helped him to his feet and managed to sit him down in the kitchen.

"Went out last night V," he said by way of explanation.

"Oh," was all she said.

"Then rehearsed this afternoon. Bit tired."

"When did you last eat?"

"Dunno."

"I'll get you some toast. See if that will help. I really need to get you out of those wet clothes. Wait a minute."

She disappeared upstairs and came down with one of her more baggy T-shirts hoping it would fit and hoping it wouldn't look too ridiculous, being plain blue.

Mummy came into the kitchen with Mr Kennedy-Huff just as she was removing his wet T-shirt, revealing his soaking, tanned and deeply scratched back.

Mrs Kennedy-Huff visibly gasped.

"Victoria, what on earth are you doing?"

"Mummy, he's soaked – and he's not well. I'll just sort him out then he'll be on his way."

"First time you've undressed me, V," Jo-Dan said. "Never thought I'd see the day."

"Young man," Mr Pearls said. "We are not accustomed to having strange young men in the house, especially without their clothes on. I want to make it clear we are not happy, not happy at all."

"Daddy, it's fine. I'll take care of it. He'll be gone as soon as he feels better. Just give me a few minutes with him please."

Victoria could see Jo-Dan was about to say something crass about that prospect so she put a finger over his lips. Jo-Dan took the finger into his mouth and sucked it suggestively looking directly at her with bloodshot brown eyes.

Victoria pulled her finger away sharply as her shocked parents looked on.

"Some coffee would be great with that toast," he said. "Your daughter's beautiful. Got a nice aura. Sorry about throwin' up. Was a bit pissed last night."

Victoria raised her eyes to the ceiling as she pulled the warm dry T-shirt over his head. She noticed the scratches on his back and thought 'don't ask'.

She got his soggy wild hair from down the back of the T-shirt, rubbed it with a towel, stood back and looked at him and decided that whatever she did would not make any improvement. He was beyond help.

Her dumbstruck parents stood by as Victoria's shaking hands made coffee and toast.

Jo-Dan had somehow got through the previous night and today's rehearsal, but, having eaten nothing for over twenty-four hours he was light-headed and rambling.

"I'm gonna marry your daughter and we're gonna have babies. I've already carried her over the threshold at my apartment. She's my Queen Victoria... Your T-shirt smells nice V, smells like you."

"Jo-Dan, please shut up," Victoria tried, but there was no stopping him.

"I'm a rock star. She loves me really. She just don't know it, do you, V?"

"Her name is Victoria," Mrs Pearls said.

"Whatever. She ain't much like you, is she? She's comin' to see me on stage. Nice house you got here in Bogey Park."

Victoria's shoulders hunched over as she visibly cringed.

"Young man, how well do you know my daughter exactly?" Mr Pearls said.

"Not as well as I'd like, Mr V, but I'm workin' on it."

"Well!" Mrs Pearls exploded. "Victoria you have five minutes and then I want this... this... abomination out of my house. Come on, dear. We will be speaking to Victoria in due course."

Jo-Dan laughed uproariously as she padded out of the kitchen.

"Oh, God," he said, struggling to speak and hurting with laughter. "'Abomination'; that's a good one. Hilarious."

"Coffee, toast, drink, eat," Victoria said bossily placing everything in front of him.

"Thanks, V. I like it when you're assertive. They don't much like me do they?" he said with a mouthful of toast.

"They don't like you at all, Jo-Dan."

"That's a pity. It's always best if you can get on with your in-laws."

"What makes you think I would possibly…?"

Then she could not help herself; she had to ask.

"Those scratches on your back. How did you get those?"

"I'm obviously such a great lover," he said.

"Is John waiting for you?" she said coldly. Is that how you found me? You had him follow me?"

"He's over the road."

"I'll go and get him," she said. "Sit there, don't move. Finish your coffee and toast and then I want you out of here as soon as possible."

John confirmed her worst fears when she challenged him about following her home, said he was sorry, and pointed out that he had only been doing as he was asked.

Jo-Dan was waiting at her front door, the last piece of toast in hand, as she ran back to her house in the rain.

"How dare you have the taxi driver follow me home?" she said angrily. "And how dare you tell my parents I have been to your flat?"

Jo-Dan shrugged and wiped the crumbs off his face with his wet T-shirt.

"Your mum looks like she's got a stick up her ass," he said.

Victoria was aware of the neighbours' twitching curtains, something that would have bothered her mummy immensely.

"If you ever come here again I will ring the police. I will not have you stalking me."

Jo-Dan smirked. "Oh I would very much like to stalk you - perhaps after the Wolver-hamp-ton gig."

"Go away," Victoria said angrily. "I won't be coming to your concert, not after this fiasco.

"Victoria," her father's voice called. "Victoria, we need you to come inside now."

Jo-Dan fixed her a mischievous gaze, leaned towards her and whispered, "Oh I would really like to come inside now."

"You're disgusting," she said and slammed the door with such force that the glass shook in the frame. Something else was also shaken – Victoria.

"I'll sleep with your T-shirt - for now," Jo-Dan shouted through the letterbox. And as he opened the taxi door he waved to all the twitchers behind the curtains.

He could only imagine the holy hell that was about to kick off in the Kennedy-Huff household.

Chapter Twenty-Eight

Reports are coming in that the body washed up on a beach in Cornwall is not that of rock icon Dion – repeat not Dion.

The man, believed to be about forty years old, has been identified as a windsurfer on holiday from Sweden…

And as the news reporter continued on the car radio, there were no whoops of joy or celebrations from the passengers. This was about the seventh report of Dion having been found in the last month alone.

"Scared?" Lucas said, as he and Paul accompanied Jo-Dan to Wolverhampton Civic Hall.

"No," Jo-Dan replied. "This is what I've always wanted, and, if anything, we're over rehearsed. Can't wait to get on that stage and put my own take on the songs."

But his bravado evaporated when they reached the stage door of the building. There were already hordes of Son of Gabriel fans snaking around the building, even though it was only mid-afternoon. Fans were exchanging various theories about Dion and Janine's mystery disappearance – and spoke of their doubts that the new front man could come anywhere close, performance-wise. He was, after all, trying to fill the shoes of two singers and had the audacity to think he could play lead guitar as well. He wasn't even blond, for goodness' sake. No, he was in for a rough ride.

"Glad I didn't eat that lunch," Jo-Dan said and he felt physically sick.

"You'll be great," Paul told him. "Seeing Victoria afterwards?"

"No. She ain't coming. I pissed her off big time going round to her house. She said she'll call the cops if I go there again, so I'll have to think of some other way to see her."

Lucas dropped Paul and Jo-Dan outside the stage door after passing the security checks, with Jo-Dan ducked down on the back seat out of sight of fans. They leapt out of the car and were guided to the main stage, where a sound check was due to take place.

Jo-Dan had performed at bigger venues in the USA, one with his own band and one with Son of Gabriel – both events at the invitation of Dion. But the last time he had performed with Dion's band, he had only had to pull off one song; this was a completely different league – two hours of extraordinary concentration and energy were required.

He had asked for bottles of vodka to be left for him in the dressing room as part of the rider. He had planned on celebrating after the gig, but now…looking at all these people, busying like worker bees getting the show together, he suddenly felt a huge responsibility. The weight of that responsibility almost drove him straight to the vodka bottle, but he lit up a cigarette instead.

Paul and Lucas were there to join the crew setting up the equipment.

Jo-Dan was relieved to see his L.A. mates already busy. They shouted across the hall to him, which gave him some familiarity and comfort, but they were too tied up in what they were doing to come over.

Tommy was supervising his kit being set up but he left the stage for a moment to join Jo-Dan for a cigarette.

"You OK?" Tommy said. "Impressive huh? And you'll be the one carrying all this."

"Thanks for reminding me," Jo-Dan said. "I was fine until I got here."

"Can I give you some advice?" Tommy said.

Jo-Dan nodded and wondered what was to come.

"Lay off the booze. It was obvious why you were in such a state the other day at rehearsal. You've got your vodka, as requested, but don't touch it until after the show. I don't care what you do in your own time or who you do it with – but I won't have anything affecting your performance."

"I'll be drinking water," Jo-Dan said. And he meant it. He had to have all his wits about him tonight.

"Hey, what's the crack after the show?" Jo-Dan said. "I hear you're the one who gets all the women. Fancy sharing some?"

Tommy laughed. "You'll have plenty of your own, trust me," he said. "There are two dressing rooms: one for the girls and one for us. There'll be a bit of an after show party – so let's hope we have something to celebrate. I know we don't always see eye to eye but you're good at what you do. You'll be great. Enjoy."

Those words meant the world to a shaky Jo-Dan. This was it, the moment of truth. He could be booed off stage and back on a plane to America.

He watched the technicians for a while as they set up the stage lights, which were spectacular enough, but nothing extra, no special effects. He felt momentarily peeved. After all, Dion and Janine had special effects at every show and he wanted this first night to be spectacular.

All the time, he was going over and over lyrics in his head, his breathing getting more and more laboured. He found his way to the dressing room and ripped through some of the songs on his guitar, but his fingers were trembling and he could feel his heart pounding.

The vodka called to him, but he didn't answer.

As the afternoon wore into early evening, everything was in place. The support band had arrived and they were offered a quick sound check. The twins appeared, looking stunning in new sexy black leather outfits.

Jo-Dan had been in and out of the dressing room, getting more and more uptight with every passing minute. It seemed such a massive undertaking that at one point he seriously considered doing a runner.

The auditorium was filling up. There was a first floor balcony area all around the hall and fans were in good spirits. The sense of expectation was palpable.

Miles had turned up and would be watching from the side of the stage.

"You're quiet for once," he said to Jo-Dan backstage. Nervous?"

"Shit scared if I'm honest."

"You'll be great once you get out there, you'll see. You OK with the backdrop at the end of the first song?"

"Yea. Perfect. Hey Miles, I lost my playing card. Can you do one of your shit magic tricks and give me another. Could do with something to calm my nerves."

Miles looked around him, rolled up his shirt sleeves, showed Jo-Dan his empty hands back and front and held his right hand in front of their eyes.

"Let's just see what comes, eh?" he said.

And a card appeared from nowhere in his hand.

"You are completely fuckin' scary, you know that?" Jo-Dan said.

"Ace of hearts. One heart, Jo-Dan. You're gonna have to work harder to make that two."

"Nice aura colours, green and gold," Jo-Dan said. "A good combination for a businessman."

"And you think I'm the one who's scary," Miles answered, handing him the card.

Jo-Dan put it in his pocket, keeping his hand on it for comfort, as often as he could, until the band met for a pre-concert confab.

The band members stood in a circle backstage, as the noise grew ever louder from out front. They stood with their arms around each other's shoulders, something they had always done with Dion and Janine.

"Good luck, everyone," Tommy said. "This is our comeback. It has to be good. Jo-Dan, I know you're gonna give one helluva show. We all believe in you."

The vote of confidence was a much-needed boost and Jo-Dan was genuinely touched when every member of the band shook his hand, hugged him, said "good luck" – and the girls even kissed him.

The intro tape had started. Jo-Dan felt as if he needed an oxygen mask right now. He was breathing out repeatedly and rapidly, trying to bounce on the spot like a boxer to psyche himself up. They had rehearsed this over and over and over – but there is no substitute for a live performance.

He could hear chants of "Di-on, Di-on, Di-on" over and over which did nothing to help calm his nerves.

"Oh my God," Charlotte squealed to Victoria in the audience. "How exciting is this? And you know the new lead singer, you lucky cow. "

"Charlotte, I nearly didn't come. He is the most infuriating specimen you could ever meet. I only agreed because I didn't want to let you down. We'll see the show, then that's it."

"You're not using the backstage pass? How can you not do that? I was hoping to meet Tommy; he's gorgeous."

They joined in a Mexican wave and Victoria glared at her best friend as she joined in the "Di-on" chant.

"Sorry," Charlotte said. "Where did you tell your mum and dad you were going?"

"For a meal – with you."

"Oh. Dressed like that?"

"I put a thick jumper over my T-shirt when I left the house."

"You look stunning," Charlotte whispered to her. "Don't think your mum and dad would approve of that skimpy top though……"

Victoria looked every inch the rock chick, wearing tight jeans and a very revealing short black top. Her hair was roughed up and tumbling around her shoulders. She had already attracted admiring looks, so she felt good about herself tonight. And she was glad she had come, after all; the atmosphere was so exciting. Charlotte, all hair and boobs, was the only friend she knew who enjoyed rock music.

The lights went down. There were whistles and cheers from the audience. Charlotte squealed and Victoria's heart was beating fast. He was annoying, yes, but she wanted the performance to go well for him. She had never once seen him perform and couldn't imagine how such an imbecile would pull this off in front of so many people. That thought made her nervous. The last thing she wanted for him, however moronic he was, was for the show to be an embarrassing disaster.

Tommy's drum pounded, the crowd were on their feet straining for their first view of Dion's replacement but apart from lights flashing on the drummer in time with the beat, the stage was still in darkness.

Then the twins appeared looking stunning. Victoria felt a pang of jealousy but could not understand why. After all, she didn't want him but she knew she wasn't a patch on those girls when it came to the beauty stakes. The guys in the audience whistled as the twins took up their place – front of stage – as Dion wanted.

The bass player joined the drummer with a driving beat, so loud and powerful that the audience could feel it in their chest. The rhythm guitar player joined in, there was a blinding flash of light along the front of the stage and Jo-Dan was there, centre stage, already ripping through the opening bars of *Thank You for the Ride* – the very song he had ached to perform last time he shared the stage with this band. For him, this was a special moment indeed.

There was a measure of disappointment from the crowd, used to seeing a mesmerising front man with flowing long blond hair. This guy was the opposite: tanned with black hair, but there was no denying the guitar work already – and he had the moves to go with it.

And then his vocals came across clear, tuneful, hard-edged rock style. Every word was enunciated and every facial expression, picked up on the giant screens either side of the stage, was like an actor, living the words of the song.

He was wearing tight light blue jeans and a simple cutaway black T-shirt which emphasised his muscular upper arms. Although of average height, he looked small and vulnerable in the vast auditorium Victoria thought.

The crowd was ready to hate him instantly, but this opening number was good. He was singing it true to the original and reached every high note with ease. *Thank You For the Ride* was a demanding song vocally because of the range required, but not only did he reach the notes, there was a sense that he had even more in reserve.

When there was a break in between the vocals, Jo-Dan was off like a rocket, looking supremely confident, aiming his guitar at the audience, playing up to the front rows in the crowd and gyrating suggestively at the twins. The lights threw different shades on to his glossy, long hair which seemed to bounce and flow in all directions, following his every move.

"Oh my God, Victoria he's fantastic," Charlotte shouted at her. "And he's really beautiful."

Victoria could not take her eyes off him, largely because she was so shocked.

This was only the first song and already he had stampeded on to the set, taken complete control of the stage and oozed confidence. He couldn't have given that song any more.

She prayed the audience felt the same way she did about him, at least about his performance.

There was an absolute roar of a welcome at the end of the song, but Victoria wasn't sure if it was for the return of Son of Gabriel, excluding Jo-Dan.

And then the massive backdrop fell at the rear of the stage.

Dion was there in charismatic, cheeky pose, blond hair tumbling around his shoulders, jeans slung low on one side, showing his bare behind emblazoned with a "kiss my ass" tattoo, ice blue eyes, fist raised defiantly in the air and an expression that said 'fuck it'.

Jo-Dan placed his guitar against one of the amplifiers, turned towards the backdrop, dropped to his knees, raised his arms and performed an exaggerated "I'm not worthy" bow to Dion, leaving his hands to rest palm down on the stage.

And there he stayed, hunched over, while the audience decibel level went even higher and went on and on for several minutes. The cheers, claps, shouts and whistles all said, 'We miss Dion. There will never be another icon to match him and we want him back'. But the applause was also intended for Jo-Dan. It said 'Well done. That was the right thing to do. We respect you for that and we're prepared to give you a chance'.

When Jo-Dan instinctively felt the time was right, he stood up and took centre stage. Tommy held his breath. The band was expecting to launch into the second song straight away, but it looked to him as if Jo-Dan was going to speak. On past experience, this was where it could all go horribly wrong, he thought.

Every band member tensed up.

"Hello Wolver-hamp-ton," he said, but not in rock-star style; it was more like an introduction. And the word "Wolverhampton" had never sounded so sexy as when Jo-Dan said it.

There was a roar from the crowd, including screams from Victoria and Charlotte.

And then he paused with his eyes closed.

Oh no, he's doing his get-my-head-together pause thing, Tommy thought. That might work in a rehearsal studio, but not here, with thousands of people watching.

Victoria felt a knot in the pit of her stomach. She knew more than anyone that Jo-Dan had a gift for saying the wrong thing.

The crowd was starting to whistle, not expecting this lull so early on into the show.

The big screens picked up Jo-Dan's eyes opening slowly and there was a hush.

"He's got beautiful eyes," Charlotte whispered to Victoria whose nails were digging into the palms of her hands with dread.

"Hi. I'm American with black hair; quite a disappointment for you I should imagine," Jo-Dan said.

"But Dion is my icon."

There were cheers from the crowd.

"I am here thanks to him. It was his idea to land you with this crazy fuckin' American. And I won't let him down."

Jo-Dan's voice was coming across crystal clear on the mic and everyone was now entranced, wondering what was coming next.

"I know you guys are here because you want to see an amazing show – but I have something I need to say."

Victoria was so anxious she gripped Charlotte's arm.

"Dion will be back," Jo-Dan said. "I feel it in my heart, he will be back. I promise you. And if we find Dion, we find Janine."

And he punched his chest with his fist where he imagined his heart would be.

There were cheers in response.

Just shut up and get on with the show, Tommy was praying, with his head down.

"But I need to ask something of you," Jo-Dan continued. "The most important thing in life to Dion was his music, so we need to keep his music alive. I need you – and he needs you – to believe: to believe in his music and to believe he will return.

"We need to *make* him return.

"Can you do that?"

There were cheers from the crowd.

"Can you do that?" Jo-Dan shouted again.

There were louder cheers from the crowd.

"Can you really do that?"

The crowd was in uproar.

"Let's go in search of Dion," he yelled as loud as he could – then picking up his guitar launched into the new up tempo version of *Magic of Rock*.

The crowd went wild.

Victoria stood with her mouth and eyes wide open in astonishment. Who was this eloquent person in front of her, who could command the attention of thousands of people and order them to do exactly as he wanted? And she suddenly felt ashamed for thinking he was an idiot.

She now realised all the things he had said about his ability at the press conference had not just been boastful claims, they were all true.

A strobe light flickered for the final chorus, making Jo-Dan appear as if he was performing in slow motion.

God, how he hated strobe lights, even though they looked effective. He was already struggling with the haze of colours emanating from individual audience members and the stage lights. Now he had to cope with a strobe light as well.

The band smashed through their well rehearsed set, Jo-Dan doing his best to make it sound raw and rough round the edges. He introduced several changes, which the others had to stumble their way through as best they could.

About half way through the set Jo-Dan was dripping with sweat. He frequently mopped his face and hair with a towel which he left at the base of the mic and he drank several bottles of water on stage to keep hydrated. Some of them he just poured over himself, drenching his hair even more.

Victoria watched him on the big screen. He looked so tired, yet at the same time more alive than she had ever seen him, she thought. He gave a big smile to the twins, captured on screen, and that was the first time she had noticed his perfect white teeth.

"Victoria, how could you have turned him away?" Charlotte hissed, now quite annoyed with her friend. Charlotte was besotted, even if Victoria wasn't.

Jo-Dan took the mic. Since his first "chat" to the audience he had stuck to merely introducing the song titles, but he needed a short break – and this was the ideal opportunity to pause for a minute.

"I have a gift for you," he said clearly. Then looking down at a buxom rock fan on the front row he added, "Looks like she's got a gift for you as well, mate."

The cameras swooped on the girl's ample chest, which was magnified big time on the screens. There were cheers, whistles and laughter from the audience.

"Seriously, this next song is really special to me. I found it in Dion's studio and this is the first time an audience has heard it. You" (and he paused) "are the only people to hear his brand new song, which is about to be released as a single… featuring pre-recorded vocals by Dion."

There were excited cheers and applause.

"You all remember those eyes of his which could kill you at ten paces?"

(Cheers).

"This is – *Ice Blue*."

The band crashed into the song and the audience got it straight away. After just one chorus they joined in, loving it so much that the band repeated the chorus several times, louder and louder.

You laughed as I cried
Tortured me inside
My blood ran cold right through
Ice blue

Jo-Dan was surrounded by pink and blue – his own aura visible to the entire audience – who assumed it was stage effects. He was not even aware of the phenomenon as he normally saw it anyway, but what a spectacle it made for the audience. He could just about see another pink and blue in the crowd, but could not make out any individuals in the seething mass of people and colours.

The audience response at the end of the song was ecstatic.

Jo-Dan took to the mic and gestured for a stool to be brought over to him.

"OK. I need a rest now, if you don't mind, I'm fuckin' knackered."

Cheers.

The lights went down and there was a sense that something special was about to happen.

'I know you're here for the classic Son of Gabriel songs," Jo-Dan said wiping himself with the towel and swigging water, "but we have one more new song for you before we crack on with the rest of the set. I'm takin' things down a notch – if you don't mind."

There were cheers of approval. It was as if he already had a natural rapport with the audience, something Victoria was still in awe of.

"This is one of my own songs. Hope you like it. It's for Victoria. She don't like me much, but…anyway…it's called *Someone Out There Somewhere.*"

There were a few expectant cheers and whistles from the crowd then it went deathly quiet. They were listening intently. This was Jo-Dan now. Let's see what he's made of…

Charlotte looked at Victoria in astonishment. "Oh my God, he's dedicated a song to you – and he thinks you're not even here."

"Sssssh," Victoria said, her heart pounding. She had no idea there was going to be a dedication to her – and anyway it might have lyrics that were insulting, knowing Jo-Dan.

Somewhere out there is a special girl

Living life so aimlessly

Searching for someone throughout the world

She just doesn't know it's me

It was performed beautifully, every word was sung with expression and meaning, Jo-Dan's soulful brown eyes opening and closing gently with lyrics on the big screen.

Jo-Dan sat on that stage with one lone spotlight on him and gave the performance of a lifetime. He looked lonely and sad. Victoria now realised she had never seen the real Jo-Dan; this was who he was.

Does she feel the same way that I do?

Is she waiting to be mine?

I promise faithfully I'll find you

Somehow, somewhere, some day, some time

The last line was delivered with characteristic, dramatic pauses to emphasise the lyrics.

Victoria felt a lump in her throat and her eyes welled up with tears for the beautiful soul inside the crazy guy she had dismissed so readily.

The applause was genuine and went on for several minutes, as Victoria openly cried while Charlotte gave her the biggest hugs.

"You have to see him after the show," Charlotte said.

The band stormed into the rest of the set, working the crowd into a complete frenzy. Sparkles fizzed over the crowd, just out of reach, a sight that terrified Jo-Dan and he had to work really hard to ignore them. Some audience members climbed on to each other's shoulders to catch them, but they would disappear as soon as they were touched in the darkness.

The concert was a triumph. Victoria could not have been more proud and the journalists were already writing their headlines:

Jo-Dan Smashed It

and

Jo-Dan Rocks

Chapter Twenty-Nine

After two encores, every band member was well and truly exhausted. They lined up for their final bow at the end of the evening. Before they left the stage, Lou and Eva shoved Jo-Dan forward. He stood alone, blowing kisses, punching his heart and bowing to every part of the vast auditorium, including to those on the balcony. He had earned the applause; he knew it and the audience knew it. He had sung and played his heart out, giving his all to the point of exhaustion.

The applause for him was rapturous; there was a thunderous noise of the crowd stamping their feet in appreciation, mixed with a chant of "Jo-Dan, Jo-Dan, Jo-Dan" reverberating around the hall. He could not have been more on a high as far as the concert was concerned.

The band left the stage and tried to make their way back to the dressing rooms, with the sound of the crowd still ringing in their ears. But the corridors were lined with hordes of people, all wanting to shake hands, slap them on the back, congratulate them, touch them. For Jo-Dan this was a completely new experience and whilst he lapped it up and tried to be appreciative, he was drenched in sweat, exhausted, light-headed as he had not eaten and was now actually shaking with a delayed reaction to all the stress which he had felt in the run-up to the show. All he could think of was: shower, vodka.

"Well done, mate," Tommy shouted as they pushed their way through the crowds.

"Thanks. I'm so glad the first one's over," Jo-Dan said. He now felt so dizzy, he felt only the swell of the crowd was keeping him upright.

As they neared the dressing room the crowds were even more tightly formed. There were dozens of girls screaming band members' names as they approached. Jo-Dan was surprised to hear his name being called out with the rest.

"See, I told you you'd have your own groupies," Tommy laughed, dragging him into the dressing room as girls surged forward trying to grab their clothing.

Joey and Rick crammed into the dressing room after them and shut the door – and they were immediately plunged into a strange world. From having thousands of people in front of them with noise, lights and mayhem they were now just four guys in a room with the din contained outside.

"Oh my God, vodka," Jo-Dan said and collapsed into a chair with one of his precious bottles, drinking half of it in one go. The effect on him was almost immediate due to his empty stomach; his anxiety remained, but it was lessened. He staggered to the bathroom and splashed his face with cold water, pausing to look long and hard in the mirror.

His brown eyes looked exhausted, he was drenched with water and sweat and his T-shirt was stuck to him with moisture. His long hair had lost its shine and bounce and as he stepped into the shower, he had the sudden realisation that this was how life was going to be. This was only the first night of a long tour and he suddenly felt a deep respect for the rest of the band who had kept up this pace, and worse, for years.

As he got out of the shower and wrapped himself in a towel, Tommy walked into the bathroom and plunged his face into a sink full of cold water. He ran his hands over his shaved head and leant over the sink for a moment, relieved at feeling cooler.

"Tight security tonight, did you notice?" Tommy said.

"Yea, what was that all about with the men in suits?"

"I asked a security guard and he said extra staff from some special unit are gonna cover all the concerts, just in case of any 'funny business'."

"Better hope they're rock fans then, or they're gonna suffer," Jo-Dan said. "I could've done without the strobe light. Makes me feel really sick."

"We didn't order any strobe light," Tommy said. "We never use strobe lights."

"Oh," Jo-Dan said, knowingly. "Well, don't look at me. Nothin' to do with me."

"I suppose those pink and blue lights all around you had nothing to do with you either?"

"Oh those; they're always there."

Tommy gave him a look in the mirror and was just about to say "you're weird, mate" when - Dion stood behind them. Both let out a startled gasp at the same time and turned around. The contrast between their bedraggled appearance, and Dion's smooth complexion and cascading mane of blond hair, could not have been more extreme.

Tommy felt his legs wobble beneath him, so Jo-Dan grabbed his arm to support his weight.

"The band was great," Dion said, his trademark blue eyes fixing from one to the other.

"I love you, Tommy. Great job, Jo-Dan, see you both again," and he was gone.

Tommy leaned back on the sink to hold himself up.

"Did you…? Am I going crazy? Did I just see…?"

"We saw Dion," Jo-Dan confirmed. "Tommy, we need to have a talk. Not tonight, but once we've had chance to rest."

Tommy looked visibly shaken and kept staring at the spot where Dion had appeared.

"I need a bottle of your vodka," Tommy said. "You need to tell me what's going on."

Someone had opened the dressing room door and the din from outside intruded and cut their conversation short.

Rick stuck his head round the door.

"Joey's gone to the cellar bar for the after show party; I'm off there now. You joining us?"

"Be with you later," Tommy said, distracted and still staring.

"You O.K. mate?" Rick asked him.

"Yea, just tired, *really* tired…"

For the first time, Jo-Dan felt a closeness to Tommy. They had shared something incredible, if only for a few seconds and Jo-Dan resolved to tell Tommy the truth, but not now, with all this chaos around them.

Jo-Dan suddenly became aware of feeling absolutely starving, but he was still too uptight to eat, especially after the split-second appearance of Dion, so he downed the other half of the vodka bottle. One of their security staff opened the door of the dressing room and the din outside hit them again.

"Guys, they sure are getting restless out here."

"OK, comin'," Tommy said, and still reeling from what he had seen, he gave a look at Jo-Dan as if to say "what the f…"?

"I'll tell you everything when we have some quiet time," Jo-Dan said.

Tommy nodded in agreement and wondered what the hell Jo-Dan could possibly tell him to explain what had happened – and what more he could explain that he didn't already know.

The minder was by now struggling to keep the door closed, so he gave it a hefty knock and called, "Need some help here."

"We better 'meet and greet' before there's a riot," Tommy replied, throwing a felt tip pen at Jo-Dan. "Here, be prepared to sign anything – and I mean *anything.*"

The vodka had now really hit home and Jo-Dan had started on the second bottle when the girls poured in a few at a time, a screaming mass of semi clad women who wanted autographs on their bellies, their bums, their boobs and other places.

The girls stole kisses, they sat on their laps, they pressed against them, they shoved boobs in their faces – they were up for it.

Tommy disappeared into the bathroom area with a couple of girls leaving Jo-Dan way out of his comfort zone. He was used to having women throwing themselves at him, but this was on another level; so he downed more vodka and started to enjoy the attention.

A stunning girl, about eighteen, all legs and straight blonde hair was all over him. His head was now swimming in a fog of alcohol and as she deliberately pressed her thighs against him he felt a surge of desire.

Tommy came out of the bathroom.

"Your turn, mate," he said. "I'll hold them back."

Jo-Dan offered no objection. He stood up unsteadily and put his arm over the girl's shoulders to support himself as he staggered into the bathroom. He leaned up against the wall and was tingling with anticipation, as she knelt on the ground before him and unzipped his jeans. Finally all the tension started to leave him as he pulled her on to him – and Jo-Dan let go of everything.

Charlotte squealed as she entered the dressing room and saw Tommy. It had been a long wait, in a hot, crowded corridor but now it was worth it. She launched at him. "I'm Charlotte," she said breathlessly. "I think you are *so* gorgeous."

"Well, you're not so bad yourself, Harlot," Tommy said pulling her into him.

"I'm here to see Jo-Dan," Victoria said to him quietly.

"He's in there," Tommy indicated with his head, "but hey, I wouldn't go in there for a…"

Victoria opened the door.

Jo-Dan was standing in front of her, his back up the wall, gripping the sink to hold himself up, his eyes closed in ecstasy. He was naked from the waist up and his hair was still wet. The girl had finished, his eyes opened slowly and he let go of her hair.

The look of hurt in Victoria's eyes was the worst thing he had seen in his entire life.

The look of shock in Jo-Dan's eyes was the guiltiest expression Victoria had ever seen in her entire life.

Jo-Dan shoved the girl off him so hard she fell to the floor and Victoria fled. He zipped up his flies, tried to follow her, but was mobbed by the girls waiting in the corridor. He was shouting "Victoria" over and over, but the girls' screams were louder and he lost sight of her as she squeezed through the crowd and ran to the exit doors.

Jo-Dan made his way back to the dressing room and had a massive tantrum, clearing everything off the shelves with his right arm, throwing chairs and ordering the girls out while Tommy looked at him as if he had gone completely mad.

“I’ll leave you to it, mate,” Tommy said, seriously concerned for his own safety. “See you in the cellar bar.”

Jo-Dan went into one of the toilet cubicles, locked the door and kicked and punched it repeatedly until it broke, then continued a relentless assault on the other cubicle walls around him.

A security guy, who had by now sent all the girls to the cellar bar, was alerted by the noise and came to investigate what was going on. He stood outside the cubicle door watching it shake violently.

All he could hear from inside the cubicle was the crashing and banging of fists and feet and anguished cries of, “fuck, fuck, fuck, fuck, fuck.”

Chapter Thirty

There was no celebratory party for Jo-Dan after the Wolverhampton concert. He asked Paul and Lucas to bring their car to the stage door, threw himself on the back seat, lay down and returned to Cannock Wood, angry and upset with himself. He had two days to recover before the next part of the tour – two sold-out nights at Birmingham NEC.

Jo-Dan was uncharacteristically quiet at Cannock Wood: partially because he was nursing the mother of all hangovers; partially because he felt exhausted and ill due to a combination of anxiety and not eating; but mostly because he was utterly miserable.

He rang Victoria's office several times, under different names, but the staff had obviously been primed and he was told she was 'unavailable'. Finally he asked Paul to ring her claiming to be someone with a query about one of her press releases. As soon as she answered Paul gave the phone to Jo-Dan.

"Hello?" Victoria said, as Jo-Dan fought for the right words to say.

"Hello?" she tried again.

Jo-Dan's heart lurched even at the sound of her voice. Even that one word sounded ridiculously English to him.

"Hi. It's me. Don't put the phone down – please."

There was an icy silence at the other end of the phone.

"I'm phoning to apologise. Please talk to me."

"I have absolutely *nothing* to say to you," she replied – and the phone clicked as she placed it back on the receiver.

The boys drove Jo-Dan to the Garrick Theatre, where he waited in the multi storey car park for five p.m. They watched as the assistant manager fetched Victoria's car and drove it to the rear doors so she could jump straight in. Jo-Dan realised what was happening, leapt out of Lucas's car and ran to the rear doors of the theatre, arriving just as she came out of the back door. She caught sight of him, looking ridiculously out of place in his tight white jeans and white T-shirt which contrasted with his jet black hair.

She looked startled and was clearly shaking as she tried to bundle herself into the driver's seat. She just about managed to close the driver's door as Jo-Dan arrived at her car, breathless, already attracting attention from passers-by.

Victoria looked straight ahead, ignoring Jo-Dan who had his hands on the driver's window, and she crunched the gears as she tried to put the car into first.

"Victoria, I only want to talk for a few minutes," he shouted through the pane of glass.

"She doesn't want to talk to you, mate," the assistant manager said. "Leave her or I'm calling the police."

Jo-Dan totally ignored him and leapt to the front of the car, leaning on the bonnet as she tried again to pull away. Now it was impossible for her to move the car without hurting him. He stood upright, hands palm down on the bonnet, his hair flowing forward over his shoulders and down his chest.

The assistant manager ran back into the building and Jo-Dan knew he was now in serious danger of being arrested.

Tommy's words rang in his head. "I don't care what you do, but don't let it affect the band."

He raised his hands as if to say "OK, you win," and stepped aside.

Victoria looked him full in the face as she drove by and his heart ached at the sight of her expression, one that said she was still very hurt. And her heart also ached when she saw the sadness in those brown eyes.

"I'll dedicate the song to you every time I perform it," he shouted to her as she pulled away; then he fled back to Lucas's car, in case the police arrived.

Victoria could not understand two things: one, why on earth he would be interested in her at all when there was an auditorium full of women prepared to throw themselves at him; two, why was she so upset by the sight of him that she cried all the way home?

The band members were due to meet in a hotel suite near to Birmingham NEC on the afternoon of the first performance, as Tommy had called for a band meeting prior to going for the sound check.

Tommy and Jo-Dan arrived first and sprawled in the comfortable VIP lounge which had been made available for them.

Tommy took one look at Jo-Dan and could see something was troubling him, at a stage when he should have been having the time of his life. Part of Tommy wondered whether he should enjoy the peace, as Jo-Dan wasn't prattling on as usual; but another part of him realised this was not the usual perky, cocky Jo-Dan.

"Want a beer?" Tommy asked.

"No thanks. Just water," he said sadly.

"Wanna talk?"

Jo-Dan sat up straight, took a deep breath and launched into an exasperated, "How did Dion do it? How did he find that right balance between living the dream and being a husband?"

"That Victoria chick. She's 'the one' is she?" Tommy asked quietly.

"Dunno. Never found 'the one'. Maybe this is what it feels like."

"And she caught you with your pants down – literally."

"I didn't know she was gonna be there that night, otherwise I'd have…"

"What?"

"Waited for her."

"Want some more 'Tommy advice'?

"Yea, I could do with it."

"Dion found that balance by never, ever letting anyone into the dressing room. Sure, he flirted outrageously with women – and men – but it was all part of the game to him. He would do pretty much anything, with anyone, so long as it stopped short of being unfaithful to Janine.

"He loved the rock 'n' roll lifestyle – but he loved Janine. If she's the one, then you've got a tough choice to make. You have the world at your feet now, women literally at your feet. You have to decide what you want."

"I've been thinkin'," Jo-Dan said. "I'll give it four months without goin' with any other women, to try and get her back. If that doesn't work, I'll admit defeat – and fuck it – I'll take whatever I'm offered."

"What, four months without – and it'll be there for you on a plate all that time? You'll crack, I'm tellin' ya. You'll never make it."

"Dunno what else to do to convince her; I know it's gonna drive me crazy, but, with any luck, I won't have to go that long; she'll come back before then."

"But how's she gonna know you're going without?"

"I got a plan..." Jo-Dan said.

The rest of the band arrived all together at that point, so Tommy called them over for their meeting and he wasted no time as soon as everyone had fetched a drink.

"This is something deadly serious," he said. "You are not going to believe what we are about to tell you, but it's the truth. Me and Jo-Dan saw Dion – only for a few seconds – and I get the feeling there's stuff we all need to know."

Everyone looked absolutely stunned. The girls had already started saying "Where? How? When was this?" Joey and Rick leaned forward eager for any tiniest shred of news.

"Jo-Dan?" Tommy said – and the floor was his.

After swearing every band member to secrecy, he told them absolutely everything he knew, everything that Dion's mum had told him – except the part about him taking Janine against her will. After all, Dion was still his icon and he didn't want any of the band to think he was capable of murder – and after all, he had no proof. If he was quizzed on that part of the story, he would have to plead ignorance, he decided.

The last thing he told them was how Dion had appeared and had spoken to him and Tommy after the opening night of the tour.

"Absolute bollocks" was how Joey and Rick responded. Eva and Lou looked freaked out and upset. Tommy, as Dion's best mate, was dumbstruck.

"*If* any of this shit is true, surely any of us could be in danger," Tommy said. "This is all connected – this disappearance of Dion and Janine and the phenomena that take place. Those bloody sparkly things for a start – did you see they are back? And the strobe light: that was nothing arranged by the band or the technicians."

"And what's with that pink and blue light that keeps appearing around you?" Eva asked Jo-Dan. "I don't mind admitting, I'm scared. And what if anything happens to the audience?"

"Don't worry about the pink and blue thing; that's just me," Jo-Dan said, as if that explained anything. "But you're right. I think we really have to be on our guard. There's extra security been drafted in apparently, just in case of a problem."

"What, the men in suits?" Rick asked.

"Yeah, they're gonna be at every gig; maybe not the same guys, but the same organisation, whoever they are," Jo-Dan said.

Everyone looked a bit uncomfortable at that revelation.

"Dion chose you because you have something that attracts this stuff, don't you?" Tommy said.

"No," Jo-Dan replied. "He chose me because I'm brilliant at what I do."

And everyone laughed at his total lack of modesty.

"But seriously," Jo-Dan added. "Dion will be back; I know it. I don't know when or for how long, but he will be back on that stage. I will promise that to every audience – and with all those people willing him to return, he will. And I know he *wants* to come back. I've had that feeling now of thousands of people all on your side. He had that and more; they adored him. He's not dead; he *can* come back, we've seen that, but for how long is up to him."

"And Janine?" Eva asked.

Jo-Dan tried not to change his expression, so as to conceal his worst fears.

"I don't have the same strong feeling about Janine, so I don't know," Jo-Dan said. "But I know this – he will bring her back with him if he can."

The atmosphere in the suite felt supercharged, tense; no one spoke for a few minutes.

"We better go," Tommy said. "Make of it what you like. We've told you the truth."

As everyone started to make a move, Tommy turned to Jo-Dan.

"Well mate – day one of being celibate. I'll have yours as well as mine then."

"Fuck off," Jo-Dan replied, then found himself feeling so angry he could have punched someone. 'But no' he thought, "I'll channel this anger into my performance. I'm gonna show 'em what Jo-Dan Rox can really do."

Chapter Thirty-One

For two packed-out nights at the NEC, the band gave performances that the audiences would talk about for years to come. At every show the Dion backdrop appeared, to tumultuous cheers and Jo-Dan would talk to each audience, varying what he said at each show, but basically assuring everyone that Dion would be back – but only if they willed it and kept the faith.

"There can be miracles, when you believe," he told them before slicing into the opening bars of the next up-tempo number.

Jo-Dan's reputation had already gone before him, so, rather than give him a hard time, the audiences were fully behind him. And he was angry, so angry. He was aware that life could have been perfect and he had messed it up. In fact he felt as if he would be angry for the rest of his life, a feeling he used to good effect for hard-edged rock songs. He had a bad ass attitude on stage, even worse than when he had first appeared on the scene - but if anything it served to *enhance* his image for the diehard rock fans.

He was also acutely aware that the press were hanging on his every word and he was determined to use that to his advantage.

The phenomena were building: the sparkles were increasing in numbers, something that alarmed all the band members who tried to carry on regardless, as if it was part of the show, mindful of what had happened to Dion and Janine.

A kind of strange fog had also descended on the audience, which sent security into a panic, until it started to lift and disappear as quickly as it had come. Jo-Dan's aura would appear more often throughout the performance and strange dancing white lights spontaneously lit the aisles in the auditorium. Occasionally, the strobe light would flicker throughout a section of a song, as if it knew where to enhance it. At such times, Jo-Dan would try to focus on his precious guitar, to diffuse the effect it had on his brain.

Every night, Jo-Dan sang *Someone Out There Somewhe*re – and every night, he dedicated the song to Victoria. His words were carefully chosen:

Night one, NEC: "This one's for Victoria: she hates me."

Night two, NEC: "This one's for Victoria: she still hates me."

Inevitably, the journalists took note of every word and questions started to be asked. Headlines began to appear in the local press.

Who is Victoria?

and

Victoria – Give Him a Break

On the first two nights after the show, Jo-Dan locked himself in the dressing room, refusing all groupies, after he had signed boobs, bums and whatever in the corridors. Then, being close enough to home, he would return to Cannock Wood, after Paul and Lucas had finished work with the crew, sober and celibate, a new concept for Jo-Dan, and something he hated with every fibre of his being.

Night 1, Coventry Arena: "This one's for Victoria: Hope she will forgive me one day."

Night 2, Coventry Arena: "This one's for Victoria: She won't return my calls."

Night 1, Sheffield Arena: "This one's for Victoria: I miss her."

Night 2 Sheffield Arena: "This one's for Victoria: Celibate for two weeks waiting for her."

Night 1, Manchester Stadium: "This one's for Victoria: Still not heard from her."

Night 2, Manchester Stadium: "This one's for Victoria: Celibate for three weeks waiting for her."

Night 1, Cardiff Arena: "This one's for Victoria: I'm sorry I'm such a twat."

Night 2, Cardiff Arena: "This one's for Victoria: I never even made love to her."

Night 1, Liverpool Arena: "This one's for Victoria: Celibate for thirty days and going out of my head."

Night 2, Liverpool Arena: "This one's for Victoria: Celibate for thirty-one days and struggling."

Night 1, Nottingham Arena: "This one's for Victoria: Celibate and sober for forty days and desperate."

Night 2, Nottingham Arena: "This one's for Victoria: Celibate and sober for forty-one days. Have lost the will to live."

Night 1, Dublin Arena: "This one's for Victoria: I need her.

Night 2: Dublin Arena: "This one's for Victoria: celibate for fifty days – aarrrggghhhh."

Not once did Jo-Dan break the vow to himself that he would wait for her.

By this time, the national press had now picked up the story. The audience hung on his every word as he announced the song and there was even a disappointed "Aahh" when Jo-Dan gave his latest revelation. Each audience hoped theirs would be the gig when he could announce "This one's for Victoria: we're back together."

By making enquiries in Lichfield the press narrowed the search down to a certain Victoria Kennedy.

The press reported:

Victoria's step-mother, Lichfield District Council Leader Councillor Dorothy Huff, said: "Any suggestion that my step-daughter could possibly have been in a relationship with this loathsome individual are completely untrue. Victoria is a respectable young woman with a good moral upbringing and fine reputation. I demand the rumours cease forthwith."

The publicity generated by the ongoing saga launched the heart-rending song straight into the charts, where it remained for weeks, even topping *Ice Blue*. Victoria, as instructed by Mummy, had to deny any connection with Jo-Dan, but she had to contend with hearing the damn song on her car radio every time she switched it on and it always had the same effect – it made her cry.

The national press screamed headlines such as:

Come on Victoria: He's Sorry

and

Victoria: Save Jo-Dan from himself

She wondered, just wondered, whether his claims of being faithful to her were true.

His latest dedication had been "'This one's for Victoria: Celibate for over two months and I just want to talk to you" - and she was starting to lose her resolve, hating herself for letting him get to her. She still felt so humiliated and angry, but could not stop herself from reading about the latest dedications, which appeared regularly in the national tabloids. And every time she looked at the latest photo of him she saw only the soulful eyes.

She wondered: what if his claims are really true and how would she really know? If she talked to him, could she trust that he would tell her the truth?

Jo-Dan was keeping an eye on the press reports, so he knew his tactic was working, but he still wasn't getting the result he wanted.

Step-mother, he thought. What was that all about? And a councillor? It just gets worse.

But there was one thought about Victoria being a step daughter that cheered him up.

"At least, as she gets older, V won't grow to look like she's got a stick up her ass," he told Lucas.

Christmas had come and gone at Cannock Wood and there had been no word from Victoria; January went into February and his pleas had been relentless at every performance. He prayed his next dedications would work – last throws of the dice.

Night 1, Leeds Arena: "This one's for Victoria: I never told her I loved her."

Night 2, Leeds Arena: "This one's for Victoria: Saturday March 30th is my thirtieth birthday. Please put me out of my misery and come to my party at home. I'm now seriously demented."

The night before Jo-Dan's birthday, Tommy rang him. They had become closer of late and now actually even enjoyed each other's company at times. Tommy appreciated that Jo-Dan was at least making an effort to get along with everyone, even though he was still irritated by his constant, inane chatter.

"You heard from her?" Tommy said.

"Not a thing."

"Oh. Plan B then?"

"Don't wanna do that. If I do, I blow my chances completely."

"You drinkin' tomorrow, being as it's your birthday?"

"Some wine maybe; I'll see."

"OK. See you tomorrow. Security all arranged? Shot yourself in the foot announcing your birthday party to the world."

"All sorted. Only those with invitations will be allowed in."

"Great. See ya."

"Bye."

Tommy looked thoughtful for a moment, rummaged in his leather-bound address book, took out a slip of paper and made another phone call.

"Hi. Is that Charlotte?"

"It is. Who is that?"

"It's Tommy here from Son of Gabriel. You gave me your number."

There was a shocked silence at the other end of the phone.

"Oh. How lovely to hear from you," Charlotte managed eventually.

"Listen, you've probably seen it in the press, but tomorrow's Jo-Dan's birthday. He's hoping Victoria will come but he's not heard from her. Would you like to come with her?"

"I'd love to," Charlotte said breathlessly.

"And please tell her – and this is important - everything Jo-Dan has been saying is true. I can vouch for that."

"I will."

"The party's at Cannock Wood. Victoria knows where it is. See you about nine? Let the security guys know who you are when you get to the gate. I'll give them your names beforehand to make sure they let you in."

"Brilliant. Thank you. See you tomorrow," Charlotte said as calmly as she could. She screamed out loud in the office as she put the phone down, leapt up and shrieked, "Yes! Yes!"

Charlotte drove straight to Victoria's house after work to give her the news and she thought that Victoria looked really upset when she told her that Jo-Dan had been telling the truth every time he dedicated the song to her.

"At least that's what Tommy said…", Charlotte told her, as Cllr Huff came into the room with a cup of tea in her best china.

"What's that about, dear?" Cllr Huff said.

"Nothing, Mummy. Charlotte was just telling me about this funny little boy and the daft things he says."

"Oh, would you girls like a biscuit?"

"No, thank you, Mrs Huff," Charlotte said. "I have to be going. I'll see you tomorrow, then, Vicky?"

"I'll let you know," Victoria replied. "I'll see you out."

"What have you got to lose?" Charlotte whispered as she went out of the door. "If you still think he's a dick, we can just leave early. Victoria, this is huge. The press will be there and everything. You don't realise how lucky we are to be invited. What are you afraid of?"

"That I'll get hurt all over again."

"Give him one more chance; let him show you he cares. I'll meet you at the City Frog at eight thirty. No excuses."

Charlotte gave a little hushed squeal and added, "Oh my God! Tommy, from Son of Gabriel!"

The following day's tabloid carried the headline:

Tonight's the Night Victoria

Cllr Huff tossed the paper into the bin as she sat in the council chamber that afternoon. One of the administrative staff had pointed it out to her and Cllr Huff was not amused.

Her mood darkened even more when she returned home to find Victoria getting herself ready to go out for the evening.

"Where are you off to, Victoria?" she asked.

"I'm going out with Charlotte."

"And where to, may I ask?"

"Oh just to a local restaurant. I shan't need any dinner, thank you."

"Your father wants a word with you, dear."

Mr Kennedy obeyed as his wife beckoned him into the front room. He cleared his throat and began with, "Now ,Victoria…We are aware from the newspapers that this certain young man has a birthday party tonight. Mummy and I think you would be ill-advised to attend, if that is what you are planning. I have assured Mummy that you have been brought up to have more sense than to throw yourself at some undesirable, but we are aware of the rumours and we are trying to protect you, sweetheart."

"Daddy, you needn't worry about me. I'm a big girl," she said and gave him a kiss on the cheek.

"But we do worry, dear," Mummy said. "And I'm rather concerned that you haven't categorically told your father you won't be going to that dreadful party."

"Mummy, I don't want to tell lies to you. I knew you would be upset if I told you. But I like him. I know you disapprove but you haven't seen how funny and open he can be. I would like to at least celebrate his birthday with him. He's thirty, Mummy. It's a big thing being thirty."

"Victoria," Mummy said, her tone getting more like a school teacher's, "If I were you, I'd telephone Charlotte and tell her you have a headache."

"I'm going, Mummy. I'm sorry."

"Victoria!" Now the tone was dictatorial. "I forbid you to go anywhere near that scruffy, no good, repulsive individual. I don't know what on earth you see in him. He's foul mouthed, dirty and doesn't have two brain cells, beneath that repulsive head of hair."

Victoria felt anger rise inside her. Jo-Dan was all kinds of things, but he certainly wasn't dirty and stupid.

"And what does he do for a living?" Mummy sneered. "Really! You call that 'singing'?"

Victoria could picture the concert in her head: Jo-Dan sitting on stage in the spotlight, thousands of fans hanging on his every word, his voice soaring into the silence and darkness as he performed *Someone Out There Somewhere* – for her.

"You know what Mummy? Jo-Dan was right: you *do* have a stick up your arse."

Mummy almost choked on her biscuit and, unable to speak properly, she gestured to her husband to say something as Victoria grabbed her bag and left the house.

"Have a good time, dear," Mr Kennedy said, trying to stifle the laugh which was welling up inside him.

Chapter Thirty-Two

Jo-Dan got out of the shower and lay on the bed, soaking the duvet in the process. He had discovered a grey hair; not only was he thirty, but he had his first grey hair and that really made him think.

He was lucky and he knew it. He had one almighty career, a Lamborghini in the driveway and the best friends ever. Paul and Lucas had even offered to throw their house open for his party; his band from L.A. would be performing in the outdoor marquee; Son of Gabriel would be guest spotting on stage and the night was unusually warm and pleasant for March 30th.

And he was horny as hell.

"I'll give her until nine p.m., then fuck it," he made a pact with himself, but he already knew he wouldn't be able to stick to it. If she wasn't there by nine p.m., chances were his Lamborghini would be on its way to her house, whether she called the police or not.

Cannock Wood was a hive of activity. The press were crawling all over the walls, like an army of ants. Every car arriving was photographed as it was waved through by security and Jo-Dan actually felt sorry for the chaos he was inflicting on his generous hosts.

'Time to move out,' he thought. 'This really is not fair on them for much longer.'

The caterers had prepared a lavish buffet in the marquee; even Rolo was wearing a big red bow for the occasion.

He could hear screams from girls at the gate, so presumed Tommy, Rick or Joey had arrived.

Jo-Dan took a deep breath. He would have to be cheerful if it killed him, for the sake of his hosts and guests; but he would be at his own party surrounded by beautiful women and gallons of booze and suffering this ridiculous self-imposed state of sobriety and celibacy. But not for much longer, no more; if she didn't turn up, or if she refused him if he drove to her house, then it would mean excess in all areas and making up for lost time.

He chose to wear tight blue jeans with a wide, buckled leather belt and a white T-shirt with the word 'Anarchy' across it. His hair (apart from the one grey one) was jet black and kind of bouncy thanks to all the conditioner.

"Looking good," he told himself in the mirror moodily and struck an arrogant rock pose before going downstairs.

The house was heaving and there were spontaneous shouts of "happy birthday" as he came down the stairs. There were hugs with breasts thrust at him, man hugs and matey slaps on the back.

"Got a grey hair," he said to Lucas as he poured a soda and glanced at the kitchen clock: eight p.m.

"Poor old bugger," Lucas said laughing and bent down to stroke an over-excited Rolo.

"Thank you for being the best friends ever," Jo-Dan said, joining in with the Rolo fuss.

"You're welcome. Hope you have a good night."

"So do I," Jo-Dan said, looking at the clock again: 8.01 p.m.

"Hey, Jo-Dan!" A crowd of roadies surged forward and their good humour was infectious. Jo-Dan actually managed to laugh and joke with them, forgetting his misery for a while. 8.51 p.m.

He could hear spontaneous singing of 'happy birthday' by the crowds outside the gates.

"You know what? I'll go and see them," Jo-Dan said. "They've stood there for hours. Least I can do is say "Hi" for a few minutes.

The security guards looked alarmed as the lead singer approached them.

"You sure about this?" they asked.

"It'll be fine. I'll do a quick meet and greet."

The screams went up to a crescendo as Jo-Dan appeared, flanked by security. He jumped on to a small brick wall outside the gates and held his hands up commanding the crowd to hush. It was as if he was in an arena again, fully in charge of his audience.

He jumped down and high-fived as many people as he could and autographed anything shoved in front of him.

"Thank you!" he shouted. "I love you, now bugger off and let me enjoy my party."

The security guards hustled him back into the grounds and Jo-Dan made his way to the marquee.

"What time is it?" he asked Paul as he walked by, busy, being sociable to everyone.

"Ten past nine," he said looking at his watch. "Want a drink?"

Jo-Dan looked anxiously toward the entrance gates.

"Fuck it. Get me a vodka. Make that two, no triple."

"Hey Lou," he said sidling up to the twin. "What you gonna give me for my birthday? You know you can't hold it back any longer. At least give me a birthday kiss."

Tommy came to Lou's rescue and looked over her shoulder. "Someone's just walked through the gates you might wanna see," he said.

Jo-Dan turned round, not even considering it would be Victoria, as he had resigned himself to giving up hope.

Paul was just about to place the giant vodka into Jo-Dan's hand but changed his mind as he saw his shocked expression. Victoria was wearing a long red dress with a slit up the side and high heels; her hair was loose and she clutched a small red handbag.

Charlotte had already fled towards Tommy.

Jo-Dan could not utter a word. He could not believe how beautiful she looked and he savoured every minute watching her as she walked towards him.

"Happy birthday," she said and kissed him on the cheek.

"You look stunning," he whispered.

"So do you."

Jo-Dan took her hand and it was as if everything moved slowly around them. The chatter sounded as if it was far away; people's faces came in and out of his vision; he led her into the house; he took her upstairs without saying a word until he opened his bedroom door.

"I promise you, like I did before…" he said. "We can lie on top of the duvet together. But you left me a kiss and I never got to collect it."

He pulled her little note from out of his top drawer.

V - x

"You kept that for all this time?"

"It's all I had of you."

They lay on top of the duvet face to face and Jo-Dan tentatively put an arm around her waist.

"I have missed you so much," he said.

"And all those things you said on stage are true?"

"I promise you, with all my heart," he said seriously then more playfully, "Now can I have my kiss?"

He moved forward, expecting a rejection, but his lips touched hers gently and she did not pull away. Jo-Dan felt desire completely overwhelm him and he was shaking.

Victoria put her arm round him and traced the length of his hair down his back. She marvelled how soft his hair was, as she ran her fingers through it over and over again. She kissed his nose, his cheeks and his eyelids then held him close round his skinny waist.

Jo-Dan changed position slightly on the bed, aware that he was fully aroused and desperate to disguise it in case she freaked.

His kiss became more passionate and to his surprise she was responding as she lay on her side. His hand moved slowly down her body and came to rest on the slit in her dress. Unsure, he left it there, thinking it best not to go any further.

Her hand slid under his T-shirt and she shuddered at the feel of his warm skin and pulled him close to her. Unable to disguise his bursting jeans any longer he glanced down, shrugged and said, "Sorry; been a long time."

"It's OK," she whispered smiling and she stroked his face.

"I love you, Victoria," he said quietly. "I should have told you a long time ago."

Victoria's eyes welled with tears.

"I love you, Jo-Dan, you crazy rock star."

"You do?" he said, his beautiful brown eyes wide, incredulous; and he was now shaking even more.

"You're trembling," she said. "Come here."

She wrapped her arms completely round him, savouring the smell of his hair as he buried his head into her. She kissed the top of his head, his eyelids, his fingers and his flat stomach.

"You are all I want for my birthday," Jo-Dan said, moving on top of her, his hand sliding into the slit in her dress. "You are all I want for the rest of my life."

He could feel the pink and blue of their auras mingling and was now kissing her passionately, aching to have her completely. He breathed in hard as her hand wandered down his body, undid the button at the top of his jeans and took hold of him inside.

Frantic now, he removed her knickers and pulled her dress up over her head. She was not wearing a bra, so Jo-Dan held his breath at the sight of her naked body for the first time, savouring every inch of her. He gently ran his fingers over her breasts and kissed every part of them making her sigh and arch her back with pleasure. She gently lifted his T-shirt over his head, pulled his jeans down and moaned in ecstasy as she felt his taut body move inside her.

They pulled the duvet over themselves and for the next four hours were totally lost in each other, until they fell asleep in the darkness. Despite having had sex with hundreds of women, Jo-Dan had never once in his life made love to any of them, until now. He missed his party, but had the best birthday ever.

Chapter Thirty-Three

Victoria stirred, felt the warm body next to her and nestled into his back, running her hand down his body. He was already aroused, though barely awake; as she touched him his desire went into overdrive, so he took full advantage of the situation.

They showered together, lay on the duvet together and talked in hushed tones, all the time touching every part of each other, wanting to know every last intimate detail.

Jo-Dan's stomach rumbled loudly and Victoria laughed.

"Don't you ever eat enough?" she said.

"You look good enough to eat," he said, lifting her hair and kissing her neck.

"You missed your party," she said. "I bet there was a banquet yet you had nothing."

"I had everything," he said with a smile.

They were silent for a moment, looking into each other's eyes.

"Marry me," he said. "I'm not letting you go now."

Victoria's eyes widened.

"You hardly know me," she said.

"Oh I do. Marry me. Say yes – but please don't tell me you want a big white wedding and all that shit. Let's just do it as simply as possible."

"Well that was romantic," she said with a smile.

"Say yes. I go away in two weeks for the European tour. I'll be away for months."

Victoria's heart lurched at the thought of that prospect.

"Come with me Mrs Jo-Dan."

"Are you serious? I never know when you are serious."

"I am deadly serious; can't say I'll be too fond of the in-laws though. Look, you'll say yes eventually, anyway, because you'll get sick of me asking, so you may as well say it now. And when we have our kids I'm sure your stick-up-the-ass mum would prefer we were married."

Victoria laughed at the very thought of introducing Jo-Dan to Mummy dearest as her son-in-law.

"Say yes, say yes, say yes," he kept on and on kissing every inch of her and making her moan with pleasure.

"But you could never be faithful, Jo-Dan; you don't want to be a husband. The very word 'husband' doesn't suit you. Look at you – all hair and energy. You don't want to be tied with one person forever. I'm trying to do you a favour here by not answering."

"Then what is this?" he said. "You don't strike me as the sort of person who would sleep with someone lightly. You love me – even if you don't want to. I know we will have three kids; I already know it and they will have pretty pink auras. I already see them – so you see you may as well say yes."

"Priddy pink?" she mocked.

"Priddy pink," he repeated seriously without the slightest flicker of doubt in his unblinking brown eyes.

"Oh well, I suppose we could always get divorced."

"That's the most romantic acceptance I ever heard," Jo-Dan said and jumped on top of her making her squeal as he squashed her playfully, held her down and made celebratory love.

When they eventually emerged at mid-day, all the tidying up from the night before had almost finished.

Paul and Lucas were in the kitchen loading the dishwasher when they walked in.

"Great party," Paul said, as if to confirm that everything went OK.

"Yes it was," Jo-Dan replied, with a wink. "Don't think you've met properly. This is Victoria, my fiancée."

Paul and Lucas looked at Jo-Dan to see if he was joking, but he didn't flinch or say anything inane.

They looked at Victoria who smiled and shrugged her shoulders as if to say 'I was battered into submission'.

When the penny finally dropped, the boys were genuinely pleased and they were quick to share the news with the stragglers who will still hanging around.

"Any food left? I'm starvin'," Jo-Dan said.

"We packaged a load of it for you," Lucas told him. "We figured you wouldn't eat as usual. You two go in the lounge, we'll bring you lunch."

"They are so lovely," Victoria said.

"The best," Jo-Dan replied. "I love those guys."

"Hey, where's Tommy?" Jo-Dan shouted to them.

"Left this morning; took someone called Charlotte with him."

Jo-Dan and Victoria exchanged a smile and snuggled together on the sofa.

Victoria looked at the huge framed photo of Dion and Janine on the wall.

"What's going on with the investigation into their disappearance?" Victoria asked.

"Oh, I have so much to tell you," Jo-Dan said, sliding his hand up her dress, after checking the boys weren't standing behind them. "You probably won't believe me, but I'll tell you later."

"He's beautiful," she said.

"Hey, who's got the wandering eye already?" Jo-Dan replied and felt a pang of jealousy as he watched her take in every detail of the picture – and it wasn't Janine she was looking at.

After lunch they went back to Jo-Dan's room for more antics when Victoria suddenly announced, "Oh, I forgot. I have something to show you."

And she produced a postcard from her bag.

"I thought you might like to see this," she said, mischievously. "Dion sent it to my Mum years ago. Mummy was mortified, almost had a heart attack with shock. Me and Daddy calmed her down, but we had to go into another room after we read it because we laughed so much. I hid the postcard and kept it ever since."

She handed the postcard to Jo-Dan. It had a quaint seaside picture on the front and he turned it over, intrigued.

"Mummy had been quoted in the paper several times, slagging off Dion and his band. It wasn't until he became rich that she was quoted as saying he was 'a fine young man'."

Jo-Dan read the postcard:

Hi Cllr Huff

Having a lovely time. Saw the newspaper article. Glad to hear you now think I am a fine young man.

Thought you looked a bit uptight on your photo.

If you ever fancy a fuck give me a call.

Love Dion

There it was, in the handwriting which he now knew so well.

Jo-Dan laughed and laughed and laughed, so much that he fell off the bed. Victoria had never heard his ridiculous infectious laugh before, only his constant chatter, so before long she was on the floor too, clutching her stomach because it hurt so much. Every now and then they would stop to get their breath, then would start laughing all over again until tears ran down their cheeks and their faces hurt.

"Oh God, I'm really gonna have to frame that," Jo-Dan said, when he could eventually get his breath. "I can just imagine the expression on her fat face reading that." And he started to chuckle to himself, then it turned into laughter, then it got louder and became infectious. Lucas walked by their bedroom door and all he could hear was two people laughing so hard they sounded as if they were about to wet themselves.

Chapter Thirty-Four

Paul and Lucas were shattered. They had really worked hard on that party, the party that Jo-Dan did not even attend. But they were happy for him; pleased that his melancholy mood had lifted. Over the past few months they had actually missed his nonsense chatter, his mischief and his humour. It was good to have the real Jo-Dan back and they couldn't have been happier for him that he intended to marry Victoria.

It was about eleven p.m. and the girls had already gone to bed as they had worked hard on that party too. Victoria and Jo-Dan had gone out for a celebratory meal with Tommy and Charlotte.

"I'd love to see her step-mum's face when she breaks the news tomorrow," Paul laughed.

"God, so would I," Lucas said. "D'you think she'll come round to the idea?"

"Not a chance."

They could hear the sound of Rolo chasing his ball around in the long hallway.

"At least someone's got some energy left," Paul said, groaning as he stood up.

They could hear the ball bouncing around, but now Rolo was barking excitedly. The boys took no notice at first, as this was

Rolo's usual 'mad hour' as they called it; but tonight it was going on longer than usual and he didn't always bark as much as this.

"The girls are shattered, we'd better shut him up," Lucas said. "You lock up and I'll calm Rolo down."

They walked into the hallway and Rolo skidded towards them on the shiny floor. He had caught the ball and looked pleased with himself; then he bounced back excitedly along the hall straight into Dion's arms.

Dion was kneeling down, his hair falling forwards over his shoulders, as he fussed and fussed his dog, kissing the top of his head and rubbing his fur playfully. Rolo was positively ecstatic, licking him and bounding around him, so pleased to see his master again.

Paul and Lucas practically bumped into each other, as they stopped in their tracks.

They had not seen Dion for more than two years, and here he was in the hallway as if it was the most natural thing in the world. He looked exactly as he had the night they last saw him and he was clearly happy spending time with his precious dog.

Dion looked up as they stood in the doorway and smiled. He loved these boys; he had brought them up, taken them all over the word, taught them to be polite and kind, just like their mum. There was no icy stare from those blue eyes, only a look of fondness and pride.

So, was he back for good? Where was Mum?

Their first instincts were to run towards him, but something made them stay put.

Dion stood up after giving Rolo one almighty cuddle.

"I am so proud of you boys," he said. "You've turned into beautiful young men and I really like the girls."

"Where's mum?" Paul said.

"I'm going to bring mum to see you, but I need you to do something. Get married, both of you. You love your girls and they are so good at looking after you two, this house and Rolo. Get married. Your mum misses you and sends her love. I can't stay long; each visit brings me nearer forty and that's not gonna happen, so I have to choose my times carefully. I need to see my fans and feel that adulation one more time; I'll bring your mum to a concert with me. Trust me - and tell Jo-Dan I'm really happy for him."

And he was gone.

Lucas screamed Dion's name in frustration. It was the first time they had witnessed him appear and they had so many questions.

"We did both see Dion, didn't we?" Paul said. "Tell me I'm not going mad."

"We did. He said he'll bring mum to one of the concerts. How will we know when? Which one: next week, next month, next year? Why can't he just spell it out?"

"If he can bring mum back, she must be alive," Lucas said. "Remember what Dion's mum said? But why couldn't she have come home with him here tonight?"

"And why would he tell us to get married?"

Rolo was charging up and down the hall, barking, confused and desperately trying to find where his beloved Dion had done.

"What the hell is going on?" Stacy called from the top of the stairs. "We're trying to get to sleep."

The boys exchanged glances as if to say, "Shall we tell them?" but Paul shook his head as if to say "No", not wishing to freak the girls out. After all, they had to live at the house and living with "ghosts" was not something that would appeal to them. The girls were often on their own here when the band was away, so the boys had never told them their real fears about their mum's disappearance.

"We're celebrating," Paul shouted back up the stairs. "We have decided we're gonna marry you girls – as soon as possible. You better go and wake Lucas's fiancée, give her the good news."

Chapter Thirty-Five

Jo-Dan and Victoria slept in late the morning after their celebratory meal.

With less than two weeks to go before the European tour, they had a lot to discuss. Tommy had already jumped at the chance of using Victoria's skills for the publicity side of the band. Victoria, meanwhile, was still trying to get her head around agreeing to be married and being swept off to Europe.

Her best friend had spent another night with Tommy but there was no request for Charlotte to join him on the tour; that would have really cramped his style. It was this thought that bothered Victoria: if Tommy didn't want a girlfriend coming along, why would Jo-Dan want that? She needed some assurances; she loved him, sure, but she had already told him she had no desire to change him, otherwise he would not be the person she loved.

So, snuggled together under the duvet, Victoria broached the question.

"Are you sure you want me to come on the tour with you?"

"I am so sure that, if you don't come, I'll quit and they'll have to find a new singer," he said, tracing his fingers around her body.

"Well, that's answered that one," Victoria said, tracing her fingers down his body.

"Jo-Dan: exactly how many girls have you slept with?"

"Slept with?"

"You know what I mean."

"You really want to know that?"

"I know the answer is not going to be single figures, but I'd like to have some idea."

"So, how many have you slept with?" he asked, sliding his hand between her legs.

"Two, including you." She caught her breath as he played with her, sending spasms throughout her body.

"So?" she said, grabbing his hand and stopping him for a moment.

Jo-Dan exhaled and lay on his back with his arms over his head.

"How good is your maths?" he said.

Victoria looked at him in disbelief.

"There have been so many that you can't even add them up in your head? Oh my God, Jo-Dan. See, this is what bothers me; how are you going to change the habit of a lifetime? Am I being a fool?"

"Never been in love before," he said simply and gave her a soulful brown-eyed look, knowing full well that would diffuse the situation.

"OK, numbers," she said determinedly. "I'll do the maths."

"Well, let's see… say you start from when I was sixteen… say an average of two or three a week… sometimes I'd see one or two girls again, most often not… then if you multiply that by fifty-two weeks in a year… times that by…"

Victoria sat up in bed and leant across the bedside table for a pen and paper.

"Hold on, hold on," she was saying while she scribbled. "Three times fifty-two, that's a hundred and fifty-six…"

"And I'm thirty now, so let's say two different girls a week rather than three so it don't sound so bad… so from age sixteen to thirty… that's what, fourteen years…?"

Victoria continued scribbling and thinking aloud, "So one hundred and fifty-six times fourteen…" she said. "Oh my God, that's 2,184!"

"You're wrong," he said smiling broadly.

"No I'm not. You check these figures, look…"

"You can take more than four months off that while I went without because of waiting for you. So what's that…? Round it off to four months, so that's at least two a week that I *didn't* have, so that's eight a month I didn't have…times that by four months equals thirty-two. So you can take thirty-two off.

Victoria did some more scribbling and showed him the new total 2,152. "It's still atrocious and I suspect the figure is probably higher," she said.

"It is," Jo-Dan said and noted her shocked expression. "It's 2,153; you forgot to add yourself."

Victoria looked mortified.

Jo-Dan slid down the bed kissing her from her belly button down and down and down.

"Ask me how many girls I have made love to," he said, looking up at her for a moment with huge puppy eyes.

"How many girls have you made love to?" she said, caught out by his determined downward assault.

"One," he said, then sent her into ecstasy.

Lying together an hour later Victoria watched his face as he dozed. "What *am* I doing?" she said to herself then gently kissed his eyelids.

Jo-Dan stirred and smiled as he opened his eyes. He still wondered whether he was dreaming sometimes. "Hello, Mrs Jo-Dan," he whispered and kissed her hand.

"I wonder that thing's not worn out," she said glancing down his body.

"Oh, Little Jo?" he said.

"Little Jo? Is that what you call it?"

"Depends if he's tired. Little Jo or Big Dan. Uh-oh, here comes Big Dan!" he said leaping on top of her for a mock fight.

Not for the first time Paul and Lucas could hear a fit of giggles coming from the bedroom.

Later that morning Jo-Dan and Victoria finally emerged for a late breakfast and sat talking in the kitchen with Paul and Lucas.

"Is it today you break the news to Victoria's Mum?" Lucas asked.

"Break the news?" Jo-Dan said. "You make it sound like it's a bad thing."

Victoria looked at him sideways and refrained from confirming the obvious.

"Hey, I'm gonna need a house when we get back from the tour. Can't keep imposing on you guys. But look, you're not gonna get rid of me that easy; I need somewhere near here where I can still see y'all.

"You know the area. Can you start looking for me? Don't need anything pretentious, but would love somewhere secure with a garden and a studio."

"Sure, I'll take a look," Paul said. "We'd love it if you lived nearby."

"We can all still go to the Park Gate sometimes," Jo-Dan said. "Long as we stay away from that creepy 'Ring' place."

"Castle Ring?" Paul asked.

"Castle Ring. Don't get me a house near Castle Ring; I'd never sleep at night. Oh yeah, and when we go to the Park Gate, our five kids can play in the beer garden."

"Five kids? What five kids? Jesus, I've only just got engaged," Paul yelled.

"Oh, don't worry, three of 'em are ours."

"Just ignore him," Victoria said. "He talks like this all the time – as you know. You've put up with him for much longer than I have."

"Just sayin'…", Jo-Dan replied, shrugging his shoulders.

"You gonna get changed before you meet Victoria's Mum?" Lucas asked.

"Why?" Jo-Dan said and he paraded in his tight black leather trousers and black T-shirt, his hair flouncing around him with every movement. "Never know. I might turn her on."

The neighbours' twitching curtains went into overdrive as Jo-Dan parked the Lamborghini in Cllr Huff's driveway. Neighbours watched in fascination as the leather legs eased themselves out of the car. They called other family members to the window just in time to see Jo-Dan lean forward to straighten his hair, then toss it back until it fell into an organised mess.

Victoria slid out of the passenger door, still in her red dress and Jo-Dan took her hand. The twitching curtains caught his eye, so he gave a rock salute to the neighbours (index finger up, middle fingers down, little finger up, thumb in) which came as naturally as breathing to him.

Cllr Huff was already standing in the doorway, calling for her husband to, "come quickly."

"Bet you say that to him all the time," Jo-Dan said as he stood facing her in the doorway, but the joke was lost on her.

Victoria visibly winced and kicked the back of his shins as they walked into the hallway. "Take your boots off and try not to swear," she hissed, kicking off her shoes.

Cllr Huff watched unimpressed as Jo-Dan sat on the stairs, his leather trousers squeaking, going through the long process of unbuckling three straps on each boot in order to remove them.

"Sorry about last time I was here, Mrs H. Wasn't very well."

"It's Cllr Huff to you," she said. "Victoria, what is the meaning of this? I thought I had made my views perfectly clear."

Daddy gave a self-conscious cough and said, "Nice car."

"Gorgeous, ain't she? Like your daughter," Jo-Dan said.

Victoria had a bad feeling about this.

"Shall we go into the lounge, Mummy? We have something we'd like to tell you."

Mummy and Victoria sat down on the comfortable pink suite, as Jo-Dan paced around the lounge.

"Tea?" Daddy asked.

"Got a beer?" Jo-Dan said.

"Erm, think so," Daddy said, darting a look at his wife who was sitting bolt upright on the armchair.

"Jo-Dan, why don't you sit down for a moment?" Victoria said. She could see he was already irritating Mummy by looking at photos and ornaments and she knew he wouldn't be able to stop himself picking them up any minute now.

"No thanks," he said. "Don't like sittin' about. "Nice photo," he said, picking up the framed photo of Victoria as a child. "This you? Yea, you still look just as cute."

"Jo-Dan, come and sit here a minute," Victoria said indicating to the arm rest of the sofa, hoping he would at least manage that. He agreed, but only because it gave him the chance to drape his arm over Victoria's shoulder.

"One beer," Daddy said as he came back in and handed the glass to Jo-Dan. "Now then, (throat clearance noise) what's all this? You have something important to tell us?"

"We're gonna get married," Jo-Dan blurted out and added, "As soon as possible."

The effect on Mummy was immediate and she went a kind of purple colour.

"You OK?" Jo-Dan said seriously. "Look like you're havin' some kind of fit or summat."

"Get married? Over my dead body," she said in a voice that was an octave higher than usual. "And what's the rush? Oh my goodness Victoria please tell me you're not pregnant."

"She's gonna have three kids," Jo-Dan interjected, "three girls."

Mummy was now looking very hot and flustered and even Daddy looked on in disbelief.

"You're pregnant with triplets?" Mummy screeched, followed by lots of 'oh, oh, oh' sounds.

Jo-Dan was in full flow about how 'priddy' they would be and how he thought she should know and how he had already thought of the names and how V would make a great 'Marmy'.

Victoria repeatedly tried to get a word in, but it wasn't until Jo-Dan paused for a swig of his beer that she managed.

"Jo-Dan, shut up for a minute," she said firmly. "Mummy, I'm not pregnant. Take no notice of him. He often says things like this. Jo-Dan's a bit, erm...different."

Mummy was still in the "Oh, oh, oh" phase.

"Your aura's real deep purple," Jo-Dan told Mummy, which earned him a death stare from Victoria.

"Victoria, why on earth would you want to marry this…this madman? I'm not happy about this at all, not at all. Daddy, say something."

"I love him, Mummy," Victoria said. "I've loved him for a long time, but I couldn't admit it, even to myself."

"Aaah, hon'," Jo-Dan said affectionately. "I always knew. Remember that first night we slept together and…?"

Another death stare from Victoria.

"Anyways," Jo-Dan continued. "It'd be really cool if you could be happy for us an' all and I know you don't like me much, but I can make you some real cute grand-daughters."

Mummy fled the room and huffed and puffed her way upstairs as fast as her fat legs could carry her. To say they had reached an impasse would be an understatement; time to finish the beer and leave.

Jo-Dan's trousers squeaked as he went into battle with the buckles on his boots then he stood in the doorway, chain-smoking and throwing nub ends over the neat lawn while he waited for Victoria.

She was upstairs hastily throwing clothes and other belongings into a suitcase and bags.

Mummy was crying and shrieking at the same time pointing out how she had "brought up that child from the age of six as if she was her own."

"Ungrateful girl; taken leave of her senses; and what about her job? She's got a very respectable job; she'll rue the day; what will the neighbours say? What will they say in the council chamber? I'll be a laughing stock; grandchildren – what, with that moron?"

Daddy was doing his best to calm his wife, encouraging her to 'have a lie down'.

He carried his daughter's suitcase down the stairs and to the car. Word of Jo-Dan's visit had already got round and a small gaggle of giggling, screaming girls had already started to gather at the end of the driveway shouting "Jo-Dan, Jo-Dan" and there were more on the way.

"Look after my daughter," he said to Jo-Dan and he gave Victoria a hug. "Don't mind Mummy; she'll come round."

"I don't think she will," Victoria said. "Love you, Daddy."

"I will look after her," Jo-Dan said seriously. "I love your daughter. She's comin' on tour to Europe with me week after next. Tell her ladyship indoors we'll be in touch about the weddin'. It'll be low key or it'll end up being a media circus." He nodded towards the girls, as if to make his point, and they screamed as he looked in their direction.

"Her ladyship needs her blood pressure checked out," Jo-Dan said. "I can see it in her aura."

Victoria shrugged and gave her father a look as if to say, "See what I mean?"

"Better do as he suggests," she said. "He's usually right."

They got into the car and Daddy went round to Jo-Dan's side. "By the way," he said secretively and looking furtively up at the bedroom window, "I love your music."

Jo-Dan beamed and gave him a "high five", then drove away tentatively, weaving around the excited girls at the top of the driveway.

"I like your dad," he said as they drove away. "He's an OK dude."

"OK dude?"

"Doesn't sound right when you say it," Jo-Dan said, throwing her back into the seat with G force.

"Everything will be fine," he added. "You'll see. Her ladyship will be dead proud of her son-in-law."

Chapter Thirty-Six

The smoke swirled around the capsule and it was so dense that it was impossible to breathe.

Jo-Dan smashed at the glass walls with his fists but it was impossible to break. He could hear Janine screaming in the background and he was conscious of his heart pounding in his chest.

Dion was there, his red aura now even more vivid, laughing as he took a long draw on the cigarette.

"Remember how you blew smoke into my face when we first met?" he said. "You thought it was funny. Not funny now, is it?"

And then there was another scream and it was Victoria.

Jo-Dan's fists hammered into the capsule but the walls were now made of plastic and they were cracking. Victoria was on the outside screaming at him to, "breathe, breathe."

But try as he might, there was no air and his lungs were hurting with the effort. He was above his body now, watching as his pink and blue aura began to fade. They had almost lost their colour completely when he felt a pounding on his chest and a searing light blinded him, hurting his eyes.

"Jo-Dan!" Victoria screamed.

He was exhausted, drenched in sweat, shielding his eyes and shaking uncontrollably.

Victoria took him into her arms; she could see where his damp hair had left a wet patch on his pillow. She was sitting up in bed, rocking him and shushing him.

"It's OK, just a bad dream, just a bad dream; breathe, breathe."

She handed him a glass of water, but had to support it, as his hand was still shaking. "Same dream again?" she said.

"I'm haunted by his return," Jo-Dan managed to say. "I am the one calling for him to return; yet the thought also terrifies me – and I don't even know why."

"Go back to sleep; I'll leave the lamp on. It's two o'clock and we have to be up early for the tour. We'll talk about it tomorrow."

They never did get to talk about it, as their new life took over.

Son of Gabriel was back on the road, this time for a year in Europe and it felt as if everything had gone up a gear.

At the first concert in Europe, Jo-Dan announced, "This one's for Victoria. We are back together and we are going to be married," to absolutely thunderous applause. The news was widely reported in the UK press and a collective "Yes!" could be heard across the nation.

Victoria made herself indispensable. She struck the right balance of staying in the background but being there whenever she was needed. She looked after everything for Jo-Dan, so he could concentrate on the job at hand; and she never failed to marvel how he seemed to turn on a switch and become the arrogant, hard rock persona the instant he walked out on stage.

She never missed a single show, watching in the wings as her fiancé enthralled the hardest of rock fans from all over the world. She didn't have a ring, only a promise. They were to marry at

Lichfield Register Office as soon as they had a break in the schedule.

Victoria felt proud of Jo-Dan being able to command the attention of thousands of fans with his personality and sheer talent. She gave him freedom, standing out of the way while he flirted outrageously with women and men. But true to his word, he kept them all at arm's length. She took care of his every need: his laundry, his catering, his paperwork and his sexual appetite. She was there whenever he needed a towel or a drink on stage; she loved him unconditionally. In addition to this, she took care of the band's publicity, something that came naturally to her.

Jo-Dan never once let up on his absolute belief that Dion would return; he included him in every single concert in one way or another. The Dion backdrop remained; he dedicated songs to him, he encouraged the fans to use "mind power" to bring him back and he promised them that he absolutely knew that he would return.

The police still maintained a presence at the concerts, under the guise of security and public protection, but they had scaled back on manpower. Unknown to the band, the arrangement was: any sight of Dion, immediately ring for back-up.

Miles turned up at a gig in Barcelona and even he was impressed by the ever-increasing incidents of phenomena. He made a big show of producing a new playing card out of thin air for Jo-Dan to keep, proudly presenting him with the poignant two of hearts.

Victoria, now being put fully in the picture about the stage phenomena by Jo-Dan, insisted in her press releases that the band had become "masters of creating unfathomable special effects"; but there were times when she feared for the band's safety, Jo-Dan's in particular.

She knew, from his recurring nightmares, that he was genuinely terrified of the sparkle effects, which grew in intensity with every show.

Fans were in awe of the "Northern Lights" effect, which now regularly formed part of the show. It was truly beautiful, spanning right across arenas, but being unable to explain the source of the lights was also un-nerving. Jo-Dan emanated a pink and blue aura for all to see. It surrounded him and his microphone for most of the show; following him around as he bounded across the stage.

The popular *Second Coming*, written by Jo-Dan, went down particularly well at the concerts, largely due to his playfulness and suggestive moves.

Second Coming

The first time you came
Didn't even know your name
You meant nothin' to me

We met up once again
And I really felt ashamed
You said we were meant to be

Chorus

Second time around
Ain't all that it sounds
Come again? Jesus Christ
No, I won't stay here tonight

So here we go once more
On the table, on the floor
Wonderin' how long we can last

But how you did complain
When I forgot your name
So I checked out again - real fast

Chorus

When they weren't performing, the band members took part in endless interviews, recordings, photo shoots, video shoots. Every concert was a complete sell-out, their albums were riding high in the charts and they were rich, very rich – something that was not wasted on Cllr Huff.

When they eventually returned to Lichfield, during a break in the tour, the wedding took place at the Register Office as planned, Jo-Dan in tight white jeans and white T-shirt, Victoria in a simple white dress with a delicate, pretty tiara. The tiara was at Jo-Dan's insistence. She was, after all, his Queen Victoria, he said.

News of the wedding had been leaked to the press, so it did turn into the media circus which Jo-Dan had hoped to avoid. But he was happy, very happy.

"He's very rich, you know," Cllr Huff was heard to say proudly to one of her cronies at the wedding. "Victoria will want for nothing. He's a bit rough round the edges, but we're working on that…"

"Good luck with that then," was the sarcastic reply from her colleague, as she watched Jo-Dan sweep Victoria up in his arms and twirl her around the gardens until they fell onto the lawn in ungainly fashion, laughing in a heap.

Paul and Lucas had found the couple a property, a similar size to theirs, in the neighbouring quiet, leafy village of Gentleshaw.

"Gentle Shore?" Jo-Dan had said. "Ain't very rock 'n' roll, is it? So where do you live, hard-ass rock star?" he asked himself. "Oh, Gentle Shaw," he replied to himself, in a mock English accent.

"It's Gentleshaw, Jo-Dan," Lucas told him.

"OK, whatever. It ain't too close to Creepy Ring is it?"

"Far enough away so the creeps can't get you," he was assured.

Housekeepers looked after the properties while they were away and Rolo had his paws well and truly under the table at the Park Gate Inn until they returned.

The tours rolled on and the following year took them to the States, where Jo-Dan at last felt as if he wasn't constantly the odd one out. He revelled in performing to American audiences, feeling at home and loving being surrounded in his own accent. Bonuses were: he was returning to his own country in triumph and he still had the company of his crew, his former band mates and Paul and Lucas.

Victoria was leafing through a magazine in a hotel one day and she came across a description of the Aries male, which made her laugh. There was Jo-Dan on the page, spelt out for her and it comforted her to realise she already knew him so well – and was on the right track to keep him.

It read*: the Aries male has raw masculinity. He is a dominant, natural born leader who thrives on challenge and confrontation. Governed by a fiery force, he can be aggressive and unbalanced, hard to tame and suffers a lack of self-restraint.*

They are immature and admired by women and men alike.

The Aries male gets along with other men, until he's challenged. Any man who steps in his way will quickly feel his wrath.

The mention of *his love of sports cars and martial arts* made her smile, especially considering he was named after "a kick-ass karate move", as he called it.

In business, war or love, Aries is always up to the challenge. He is highly competitive in every area of his life. She laughed at the part that said *he even competes with himself.*

His career is a benchmark of accomplishment.

And of his love life: *He is drawn to the most desirable partner. He enjoys the competition to win the object of his desire, since he's certain he'll be the victor. He is demanding and needs to be number one in your life.*

Victoria made a mental note of*: If he ever feels he isn't your number one, he'll find someone else to give him that first place. He needs validation. Cut him some slack, if you feel he's too demanding; give him the loving kiss or reassuring hug. He needs this more than other sun signs.*

He needs praise. He is a special man.

The article advised being *physically demonstrative and sincere.*

He needs loving words and has built-in radar for insincerity. If he suspects you're playing him, he will take off in his sports car.

The Aries man has a difficult time finding an ideal mate (understatement, she thought) *but he is a leader who thrives on challenging projects.*

Commitment is not in his nature. He has a hard time settling down. It will take a remarkable woman to keep him. An equally passionate mate, who is direct yet mysterious, may have a chance of keeping his interest long-term.

The last thing you want to do is chase him. He prefers to be the hunter. He enjoys flirting. Enjoy the attention and don't give in too soon. The harder he tries to win your attention the greater he'll consider his win.

He's number one and deserves only the best.

She read how he is *tempted to stray, unless his mate rekindles his imagination. He wants true love, but is a romantic and wants a partner who can be a pal, someone who can shift in and out of the role of lover and friend.*

Don't try and restrain him. Allow him to thrive. The world has developed by the drive of Aries individuals.

Victoria felt the article described everything about Jo-Dan and their journey. Now all she had to do was keep him…

It seemed as if the weddings came in thick and fast. The twins married, Paul and Lucas married – Tommy saw Charlotte now and then

The USA tour finished on a high and Jo-Dan allowed himself copious amounts of vodka, eventually falling into a heap and having to be gently put to bed by Victoria.

Only one thing marred his celebration: Dion had still not returned. The "Dion Found" reports kept coming, but none were ever validated.

Chapter Thirty-Seven

"I have an idea," Jo-Dan said as he burst into the kitchen in Gentleshaw, covered in sweat and grass.

"What on earth have you been doing?" Victoria said, totally ignoring his enthusiastic announcement.

"Oh the usual, romping round the garden with the dog like a mad person. Did you hear what I said?"

"Christ, Jo-Dan, I even have to clean you up when you're not on stage," she said, grabbing a towel, running it under the tap and wiping the dirt off his arms and face.

"What was the point in having a white dog? Thanks to you, it's constantly covered in mud. Now you're getting grass everywhere; get those boots off."

She tried to pretend to be angry with him but the brown eyes captivated her, even now. He was thirty-five, but still behaved like a petulant child, still had too much energy, still prattled on endlessly and was still full of mischief.

"I'm being serious," he said, sliding his hand up her T-shirt.

"Jo-Dan, anyone could walk in right this minute."

"They're all in the garden. Paul, Lucas and the girls are playing piggy in the middle with Polo Sweet." They could hear the dog barking and shrieks of laughter from outside.

"I could take you across that table right now," he whispered at her mischievously, "but I need to run something by you first."

"Go on then," Victoria said and shrieked as he lifted her off the floor. "No, I didn't mean take me on the table, I meant go on then, I'm listening."

She watched his face change from mischief to focus: something she was now very familiar with. It was the expression she saw, standing in the wings, minutes before every single performance.

The focus face stared back at her, brown eyes fixed as he hunched forward on the stool.

"I've been thinking. Every time I appeal for Dion to come back, there is a moment when the entire audience joins me; you know, when we get to that part where I ask everyone to join their thoughts together?"

"Yes and I'm sure they think you're completely mad."

"Yeah, maybe; but they do it, don't they? They all stand in silence, willing him to come back."

That much was true. Victoria never ceased to be amazed that this crazy force of nature could persuade even one person to stand quietly for two minutes, least of all thousands of people.

"So, what if I command fans across the country, across the world to focus their energy on one thought all at the same time?"

"Jo-Dan…"

"No. Listen to me. It will work; I know it will. If we all concentrate hard on the same words, 'Dion. come back'…"

"Jo-Dan, you're driving yourself round the bend with this obsession. It's been six years. No one is going to blame you if Dion never returns. He's where he wants to be."

"But he promised. He said he would bring Janine to see the boys. He said he would make it right."

"Stop it. Stop it now," she said kindly. "For your own sake, leave it."

"I can't, V, I'm gonna do this. You can issue the press release. We'll do it at Bir-ming-ham NEC next month, January 31st for two minutes, dead on nine o'clock – all across the world. It's his birthday on that day; he'd be forty-five. If it fails, I'll look a dick. So what? I often look a dick."

Victoria smiled and touched his cheek gently.

"What's funny, hon'?"

"You still can't say 'Birmingham'."

Jo-Dan and Victoria were savvy; they knew the media loved something different, a new angle to write about and they were right. The media went to town on the story and it went international.

The tabloids carried front page headlines such as

Dion: the Return

Dion: Now or Never

and

Has Jo-Dan Finally Lost It?

Fans were asked, wherever they were in the world at nine p.m. British time, to take a quiet two minutes out from whatever they were doing, to concentrate and repeat the words "Dion, come back."

"The fans really need to feel the words," Jo-Dan was quoted as saying. "I am asking everyone to come together at the same time and picture Dion in their mind standing on that stage. We are going to *make* him return – and if he comes back, he will bring Janine with him."

The papers and TV reports all carried photos of Dion, Janine, Jo-Dan and the band.

"Always was a strange individual," Cllr Huff said when approached by one of her colleagues at the council chamber about the headlines; then she whispered conspiratorially, "I think our Joseph has a knack for self promotion."

"Joseph?" her colleague interrupted.

"Well, I'm sure that must be his proper name," Cllr Huff replied sniffing into a handkerchief. "Anyway all this nonsense in the newspapers is not such a bad thing; all this publicity makes him very rich indeed. Of course they could do with an even bigger house really, but the one in Gentleshaw just about suits their needs; doesn't do to be too ostentatious. It was our Victoria who issued all the information to the press, you know. She's such a clever girl; yes, I think we made quite a good job of raising her; couldn't be more proud."

The significance of the headlines was also not lost on the police, who arranged to step up their presence at the concert "just in case."

"All nonsense of course," the lead officer said at the briefing. "But if he does show up tonight, we'll be there and we will be armed.

"We will be in plain clothes and in touch via ear pieces to co-ordinate the operation.

"If we don't see Janine, our priority is to arrest him and he'll be doing thirty years, like he deserves. If he resists arrest we'll take him, dead or alive.

"If, like that idiot Jo-Dan says, he brings Janine with him, fine. We immediately call a halt to the investigation, we all stand down and go home, but only if we see her with our own eyes."

Dion's parents, Miles and Dion's former boss all decided to attend the show, just in case. Miles would watch the show as usual from out front, enjoying the spectacle, even if Dion was a no-show.

After setting up the concert, Paul and Lucas would join the girls and watch from the wings.

Also in the wings would be Jo-Dan's former L.A. band mates and Victoria.

The hype around the concert was so out of control that legions of fans had turned up outside the venue, even though they had no tickets. If this worked, they wanted to be part of history; they wanted to say in years to come, "I was there on the night Dion returned."

Extra police had to be drafted in to cope with crowd control and the sense of anticipation was palpable.

"You nervous?" Victoria asked her husband, as he jumped up and down on the spot, shadow boxing and breathing hard.

"No. I'm never nervous," he said. "Always excited; just wanna get out there, even with what's at stake."

The roar from the crowd was tremendous as the intro tape started and Victoria watched her husband in awe as he changed focus. She knew that now was the time to step back and leave him in the zone.

The band did their usual group hug and there were final words from Tommy.

"We'll believe," he said. "Join the fans and do as Jo-Dan asks. Keep the faith."

The "Northern Lights" swept across the arena, sparkles fizzed and darted everywhere and the special police force took up their positions, doing their best to look inconspicuous inside the auditorium.

Victoria's heart was pounding. Life was good; she and her husband had everything they could wish for; and she suddenly felt very afraid at the realisation that this night could ruin everything. Whether Dion returned or not, she feared for her husband's safety and sanity that night.

The reception from the crowd could not have been more enthusiastic. Jo-Dan was the Son of Gabriel front man; he had long since put his own stamp on that and he loved being "back home", as he called it, in Bir-ming-ham.

He even introduced a new song, *Party Like There's No Tomorrow* which went down a storm.

Miles watched in fascination as Jo-Dan's vivid pink and blue followed him around the stage. He remembered the irritating twenty-nine-year-old who arrived in England and now felt a kind of fatherly pride listening to his vocals and wailing guitar. He smiled to himself at the mock arrogance of Jo-Dan's confident performance. He had the crowd in his hands.

Jo-Dan glanced at his expensive watch: 8.55 p.m. and he suddenly felt as if he would descend into a total panic attack.

"Ice Blue", he announced and his heart pounded as he watched the sparkles gather momentum and swoop like birds just as they had before. He knew in his heart what was to come. The police were on heightened alert and so were the fans across the world.

As the song finished, it was 8.59 p.m. Victoria's nails dug into the palms of her hands as she watched her husband try to keep his composure. She knew, from the many nightmares he suffered, how he feared those sparkles and tonight they were out in force.

One of the crew brought a stool on to the stage and Jo-Dan sat in the spotlight, breathing hard and shifting his focus and the audience hushed without even being told to, waiting for the command.

"Believe," Jo-Dan suddenly said and his voice reverberated around the arena. "Focus on the backdrop; it's time. Dion, come back. Say it in your head; say it aloud, say it in your hearts. Dion, come back."

Jo-Dan sat absolutely still, watching over the audience and he prayed like he had never prayed in his life. The band members stayed in their positions and repeated the words over and over. They had been in this position before and they had willed Dion out of a coma; so they had to trust and try.

Victoria sat on the floor because her legs were shaking so much. She could hear her husband over the microphone quietly repeating "Dion, come back; Dion, come back; Dion come back" and she could feel the tension in the arena.

Jo-Dan pictured the crowds outside and the fans at home or at work or on the street or in a bar. He pictured them in England, in America, in Europe and across the world – all at this very moment repeating "Dion, come back; Dion come back", for two full, long minutes.

Caught up in the moment, Jo-Dan did not look at his watch. It was 9.03 p.m.

He heard the distant screams of some girls in the audience but could not make out whether they were screams of fear or excitement. The electricity in the air was now tangible and there was heat coming from the rear of the stage.

He didn't see the men in dark suits talking into their jackets.

It was only when Jo-Dan slowly turned round that he could see the sparkles had amassed and had started to form a solid shape; silver, sparkling, open yet closed.

The audience watched entranced as the solid mass of light almost filled the right hand side of the stage. Paul, Lucas and Jo-Dan's mates darted on to the stage, to move some of the equipment a few feet out of the way.

Tommy leapt from his drum kit and joined the rest of the band at the front of the stage. They stood with their backs to the audience, watching the lights as if this had all been rehearsed.

But in truth they had no more idea than the rest of the audience whether the spectacle would continue or fade.

The "Northern Lights" swept in front of the sparkle formation, making a curtain of colour.

The technician's hand shook as he tried to keep the spotlight steady.

The curtain of light opened and Dion stepped onto the stage, moving forward, arms outstretched, in total control, yet extremely vulnerable. The men in suits went into overdrive, speaking into their jackets and they slowly started to move forward.

They went unnoticed by the crowd who shouted, whistled, screamed, clapped and stamped their feet – anything to make a noise. The audience was drinking in every inch of the iconic vision in front of them.

Dion stepped forward to the front of the stage and absorbed the love, as if he could not take in enough.

Jo-Dan dropped to his knees behind him and said a silent "thank you" prayer; then, like everyone else, he turned to watch the extraordinary sight that was Dion.

Tommy and the twins rushed to him, but stopped at the last minute, unsure if he was real. Eva touched his face and felt his smooth, flawless skin; Lou put her hands to her mouth and cried. Tommy almost crushed Dion he hugged him so hard – and all the time the crowd cried and laughed with them.

The extra crinkles on his band members' faces, their dyed hair and fuller figures had not gone un-noticed by Dion and he felt a wave of validation that he had done what was right for him.

Dion turned to Jo-Dan and knelt close beside him.

"I was going to come anyway," he said softly.

Paul and Lucas could stand it no more. They left the wings of the stage and threw themselves at their step-dad and they all hugged as if their lives depended on it.

"Your mum's waiting for you," Dion told them. "Behind the curtain of light."

The "boys", now "men", did not need to be told twice; they ran to that wall of light and walked right through it.

The men in suits were closer to the stage.

Dion glanced behind him and saw the backdrop and he imitated it precisely, fist in the air and dropping his jeans just enough to reveal his "kiss my ass" tattoo.

The crowd roared in approval then fell into absolute silence as Dion moved to the microphone.

"God, how I've missed this amazing feeling," he said.

(Roar of approval from the crowd)

"I wanna thank Jo-Dan and the band for keeping Son of Gabriel going. This band still means everything to me."

(Roar from the crowd).

"Janine wants to spend time with her boys, so please be patient. She won't be performing, but you will see her soon," he said.

(Huge roar from the crowd).

"Can we trust him? Should we move in now?" the men in suits were debating.

Dion turned to Jo-Dan and said out of earshot of the crowd, "OK if I use your guitar? Had time to fine-tune my skills where I've been."

Jo-Dan handed it to him gladly and left the stage fully intending to take a back seat and just enjoy the moment. Victoria wrapped her arms around him.

"I told you," he said and they both watched in awe as Dion owned the stage and the band took up their positions.

"Look at him," Victoria said. "He looks exactly the same as the day he left – and that was six years ago."

"That's what he wanted," Jo-Dan said. "He'll be counting every minute that goes by."

"This one's a favourite of mine and it's appropriate," Dion said. "*Thank You For the Ride.*"

The crowd went crazy as Dion launched into the lead, which even took Jo-Dan by surprise. He had always considered himself the better guitarist, but this was making him take notice.

The vocals were word perfect and effortless and word was already leaking out of the stadium and around the world that Dion was back on stage.

The big screens at the side of the stage emphasised his stunning youthful looks and perfect body. He was every bit as beautiful, as the day he left, something that had not escaped his parents and former boss who were next in line for a hug.

The applause was going on for too long; Dion had limited time and he knew it, so he raised his hands for them to stop.

"I have time for one more," he said. "This is my version of *Ice Blue*."

The men in suits conferred as he performed and inched their way forward. They would give him his moment, then would move in at the end of the song. They realised that if they stopped him now they would have a riot on their hands.

At the end of the song, which Jo-Dan had to concede was better than his interpretation, the applause was ecstatic and the crowd then burst into a spontaneous '*Happy Birthday*'. Dion looked genuinely touched and was gracious, but inside he was thinking, "I haven't got time for this."

No one was happier than Jo-Dan and Victoria – until one of the security guys approached Jo-Dan and whispered something that made his blood run cold.

"See the men in suits," he whispered urgently. "They're here for Dion. They're gonna arrest him. I'm not supposed to know, but I got a colleague who's one of them. Look, I shouldn't say, but they're gonna do him for murder. And unless we see Janine, he's gonna be doing thirty years inside. I'm a Dion fan. I don't wanna see that happen. Also, they are armed but I haven't told you this."

Jo-Dan darted a look into the arena, and, yes, the men in suits were moving in. He hadn't realised until now just how many there were of them, having assumed they were ordinary security guys. They were trying to be subtle, but he could tell by their demeanour this guy was telling the truth – and they were now near the stage.

Jo-Dan could picture this beautiful performer languishing in a cell. He could see insanity creep up on his icon if he was denied his calling, which was to create and perform.

Despite his outward display of dislike towards Dion in the early days, he had always admired him for his no-compromise attitude. He loved that he did things his way; he loved everything he stood for; his determination to succeed; his arrogant stance, his talent and flowing hair.

Whatever he might or might not have done, being responsible for Dion holed up in a cell, growing old and fat, was a thought that made Jo-Dan feel sick. He would never know whether Dion really would have returned of his own accord, but Jo-Dan knew he could never live with himself if he had influenced his return and it ended with him in a prison cell. He absolutely knew that the incredibly vain, lively and funny Dion would rather die.

Dion was winding up the song and receiving rapturous applause, so Jo-Dan bounded back on stage and, on the pretext of hugging him, whispered frantically, "The guys in suits. They're coming for you unless you show Janine."

Dion nodded calmly and took the mic, seemingly completely unfazed by his predicament.

"I have to go," he said, showering kisses and was met with collective distraught cries of 'No'. "I will leave you with this extraordinary band and I will remember this day forever. Thank you for keeping me in your hearts; I love you; but before I go, Janine is desperate to see you."

Dion ran to the curtain of lights and the men in suits now started to lose their composure.

"Do we wait or do we move in?" they were asking.

"Move in. If you don't find her, we take him," came the command.

Jo-Dan grabbed the mic and shouted to the crowd, "See the men in suits? They're here to take Dion. Don't let this happen. There are about fifty of them and thousands of us."

There was a buzz around the arena as the audience honed in on the suits.

"Oh shit," one of the suits said into his jacket. "Back up; we need back up, now."

One of the suits was making his way on to the stage, so Jo-Dan blocked his way and the rest of the band joined him. It was mayhem in the auditorium – until a collective gasp told them something extraordinary was happening.

Everyone stopped at the sight on the big screens. Janine was there: beautiful, ageless, arms in the air, hand in hand with Dion, blowing kisses, touching her heart, looking ecstatic. The curtain of light had moved aside and she was inside the sparkles, but they had separated, become spaced out, so that she could be seen clearly.

On the big screens there was no mistake. This was Janine and she looked blissfully happy.

The roar from the crowd was one of absolute affection.

Janine's boys joined her from behind and they hugged her and waved to the crowd.

"Stand down, stand down," the call came from one of the suits.

"We've been had," he said. "She was alive all the time. This is one elaborate publicity stunt. We were wrong. Thank God; at least I never have to attend another Son of Gabriel concert as long as I live. We've been conned and so have the audience. This is the work of some clever-dick illusionist. Let's go home." And they didn't need telling twice.

They left to the sound of the fans shouting "Fuck off" over and over again in unison.

Dion's parents and ex-boss took advantage of the chaos and ran onto the stage. Dion stepped out of the sphere and swept his mum up into his arms and she took in every perfect detail of her son and cupped his face in her hands. She kissed his face and told him she understood he had to go back and she was happy for him.

Dion gave a final wave at the crowd, struck up a defiant rock pose and stepped back into the curtain of light as the applause went on and on.

"This next song features the girls," Tommy said over the sound system and a wall of enthusiastic whistles greeted the twins as they took up their place. Everyone was in the greatest mood and ready to party.

The big screens flicked between the twins and Dion, saying his final goodbye to Jo-Dan through the colourful curtain.

"Come inside," Dion said to Jo-Dan. "It's OK. Time means nothing in there; they won't even know how long you are gone."

Jo-Dan was intrigued, but this was his worst nightmare. The damned sparkles had tormented him in his sleep for years, ever since he had first met Dion. He was about to decline, not ashamed to admit he was too scared, when something caught his eye inside.

Dion looked momentarily as if he had been caught out – and Jo-Dan was too perceptive to have missed the expression. All his senses were now heightened and every instinct told him that something was very wrong.

Security had all but disappeared in the stadium and as Dion spoke through the curtain of light he said matter of factly, "I'm taking the boys. I promised I would make it right. I can't watch her cry for them ever again."

Jo-Dan's heart dropped like a stone as his eyes tried to make sense of what he could just about make out from the broken image inside the sphere. He knew what he thought he could see but now Dion's words had confirmed the very situation he dreaded most.

Dion never lied; he chose his words carefully and he also chose what to omit. When he said he would 'make it right', he had his own interpretation of what was 'right'. He had never once mentioned killing the boys, least of all to Janine.

There was an inner chamber where Paul and Lucas looked as if they were struggling. Their backs were against the sphere and they were sliding down onto the floor, a white floor made of a material Jo-Dan did not understand.

"I told Janine she had to wait for the boys inside," Dion said. "She always does as I say; she trusts me and I didn't want her to see…"

"Dion, they're gasping for air," Jo-Dan said. "For God's sake get them out. This is not what Janine wants."

"They can't go voluntarily," Dion said, his steely eyes looking completely unconcerned. "They aren't gifted. Janine won't know I took them this way. Don't worry, they won't feel any pain; it will be just like passing out.

"She doesn't even know I killed her. All she knows is she felt pulled towards our world and the boys will feel the same; we can all be together; we'll be a family again. Even if you told the boys I killed her, they wouldn't believe you. How could I have killed her if she is standing in front of them, looking alive and happy?"

Jo-Dan's heart was thumping so hard he could feel it in his chest and he found it excruciating that Dion could talk about taking lives in such a calm and controlled manner.

Lucas was thumping the walls of the sphere, trying to break it, but his efforts were weak and Jo-Dan could see his beautiful orange aura fading.

"Come with us, Jo-Dan. You'll love it. I can't wait to be back. I can already feel the pull – and you feel it too, I know. You will stay the same age you are now, forever. Do it, Jo-Dan; you belong there."

It was true. Even touching the sphere, Jo-Dan could feel a wave of euphoria come over him and he felt compelled to give in to this incredible force that tugged at his creative soul.

"You are an evil bastard, you know that?" Jo-Dan shouted, his voice getting more desperate as he watched the boys losing consciousness. "Let the boys go. They have a life. They got married. You told them to get married."

"I do what I need to do," Dion said dispassionately, lighting up a cigarette. "I do what I think is best at the time. I told them to get married to protect my house and the girls. They will inherit the house and the boys' money; they will take care of the house and Rolo. Sure, they will be sad, but they'll get over it; I've given them a mansion and a fortune."

Jo-Dan's brain went into overdrive, desperately trying to think what he could say to get through to him, but he was struggling to think at all – and that sensation was surging through his body; and it was so beautiful that he could already see the place and he wanted to be there.

He could see Victoria standing in the wings, looking puzzled, watching her husband leaning against the sphere, his arms raised with palms down on the circle of lights. She presumed he was saying his final goodbye, but there was something about his body language that scared her.

Jo-Dan's heart lurched at the very thought of leaving his life behind and he took his hands off the sphere.

"I have everything I need right here," Jo-Dan said. "You know, my life is beautiful. I saved you from getting arrested, you mad bastard," he shouted, but no one else heard him above the noise of the band. "If the cops had asked Janine to step out of the sphere they would have known something was wrong. She can't get out, can she? If she does, she is dead and there's no going back for her. Don't do that to the boys. Let the boys go."

The contrast between the two stars could not have been more extreme in appearance and mannerisms. Dion was standing perfectly still, apart from drawing hard on a cigarette and blowing smoke into the capsule. He was absolutely composed, his clean blond hair tumbling perfectly into place, like a fallen angel. His eyes were fixed and cold, the lack of oxygen having no effect on him.

Jo-Dan was fidgeting nervously, his eyes darting from Dion to the boys and all around him desperate to find some way of saving his friends. His long black hair, wet with sweat, flounced as he moved this way and that and he was now pacing in front of the capsule with wild arm gestures. Victoria knew something was wrong.

Dion, standing in the absolute peace of the capsule entrance, could hear the faint sound of the twins performing and the thump of the bass and drums but they sounded distant, distorted and other worldly. He took another draw on his cigarette and blew the smoke nonchalantly behind him.

"Look at her boys, you callous bastard," Jo-Dan screamed. "You can't even look at them. They are dying and all you can do is fill what little air is left with cigarette smoke."

Ice blue eyes fixed on him. Dion was in control as usual and there was a flicker of smug amusement in his eyes, which angered Jo-Dan even more.

This is what Dion had planned all along; this is what he wanted for Janine. He would have done it sooner, but time meant nothing in their world.

Jo-Dan's recurring dream was right there in front of him, his biggest fear; but it was now clear to him that the warning had not been for his own safety, it had been for his dear friends who were now seriously struggling to find any air in the smoke-filled capsule. To watch their distress was torture, as he knew exactly how they felt; he had experienced it in his nightmares.

Jo-Dan felt as if he had been used and it infuriated him. He pounded on the capsule with his fists in frustration; and with each strike sparks of light flew from the structure, creating a strobe-like effect.

The twins had reached the end of their song and the applause was deafening. As well as being for the girls, it was also for the spectacular scene on the big screens, showing Jo-Dan pounding on the sphere, sparks flying past him, Dion standing unmoved, unaffected by his pleas.

"He's taking the boys!" Jo-Dan screamed. His words were lost in the huge stadium, but the band heard them – and so did Janine and the girls.

Jo-Dan grabbed the first thing at hand to try and smash the structure. It was his precious guitar. He slammed the guitar into the walls of the sphere, sending sparks flying into the air, creating a real spectacle for the fans who roared in approval at the finale. Dion did not even flinch.

What a show. What a great way to end the concert.

Tommy did a flying leap from his drum kit and the rest of the band ran to Jo-Dan's aid as he screamed and smashed his guitar repeatedly into the sphere.

"The boys are dying in there," he screamed. "Help me. Help me. We have to get them out."

Only now appreciating the seriousness of the situation they were all there for him, even the twins finding whatever they could to break into the structure.

Miles was on the stage, smashing at the sphere with one of the guitars as the crowd went wild with excitement. Sparks flew everywhere as the capsule slowly started to rise and only then did Victoria and the girls really realise what was going on.

Jo-Dan's guitar was in pieces – and so was he. He grabbed a microphone stand and smashed it into the capsule with all his might, but it didn't even make a mark.

The last thing he saw was Dion, with a self-satisfied look, blowing smoke towards him as the capsule started to fade.

"They are pregnant!" Jo-Dan screamed at him. "The girls are pregnant. I saw it in their colours. The boys don't know. Even the girls don't know. Please, don't do this."

And suddenly there was a revelation. Jo-Dan had always pictured five kids playing in the Park Gate beer garden – but he had never seen Paul and Lucas with them in his vision.

He looked up at Dion, his brown eyes pleading for a last minute stay of execution. He thought he detected one flicker of regret in Dion's expression as the capsule faded and was gone, its disappearance resulting in rapturous applause.

Jo-Dan was inconsolable and there were thousands of people still watching.

Small lights fizzed high above Jo-Dan in the auditorium but he wasn't sure if they were really there, since no one else seemed to see them.

"Let's take a final bow without him," Tommy said. "The audience will think that it's part of the act."

They lined up at the front of the stage, with the dramatic scene of Jo-Dan hunched over on the floor where the capsule had been, head in hands, still screaming. It was like a stage set from a West End musical. What a finale, the audience thought.

Tommy made a sign for the technical crew to cut the lights. A backing track of music was played as the exhausted audience gradually and reluctantly started to file out of the building, talking animatedly about one extraordinary night.

Victoria ran on to the stage which was now in almost complete black-out. A few technicians, including Jo-Dan's former USA band mates, were standing awkwardly, not sure whether to start work or not. Jo-Dan was sobbing uncontrollably; the girls were screaming for Paul and Lucas and no one could give them any answers; and Victoria's worst fears about Jo-Dan's mental health had come true. He was truly broken.

"I could have saved them," he wailed to her. "I should have stopped them from going in the capsule. I could have had him arrested; I knew what he had done; I could have told the police. I called for Dion to come back, for Christ's sake. All of this is my fault. I have killed my best friends."

Victoria tried to comfort him, but she knew that although he could not have foreseen the consequences, what he was saying was actually true. Tommy tried to approach Jo-Dan; Miles knelt next to him; Eva, Lou, Joey and Rick all tried to reach him, but he was inconsolable.

Dion's parents and ex-boss took the decision to keep well away and they quietly left the building.

Jo-Dan could still hear the girls screaming backstage and it knifed his heart.

Victoria put her hand on his shoulder. "Come on. You can't stay here," she said gently.

Jo-Dan had never once in his life raised his voice to Victoria, his soul mate, but he screamed, "Leave me! Leave me alone!" and stayed hunched over on the floor, rocking forward, his head in his hands.

She stepped back, figuring it was best to give him some time.

"Please keep an eye on him," she said to one of the technicians. "I'll come back in a while."

The technicians slowly and quietly started to work around Jo-Dan, saying nothing, until they finally left him with a dim light on the stage, still in absolute distress. He lay there for hours, small lights still fizzing above him.

It was five a.m. when one of the management approached him, at the request of Victoria.

"Sir, are you OK? Can I get you anything?" he said, but got no response, so quietly moved away.

Jo-Dan had stopped crying, but he was mentally and physically exhausted. He knelt on the ground, staring ahead, thinking of the years of support Paul and Lucas had given him and how they had put up with his nonsense, loving him all the same. He thought he could not possibly have any more tears left, but they started to flow again and he sobbed uncontrollably in the darkness.

He looked up at the lights, still fizzing in the air, feeling absolutely beaten. He thought of all the iconic artists the world had lost too soon and wondered where they were, and whether Dion had found them.

"Dion's right," he said to himself. "There should be a special place where we can go. We don't have a choice to be born, but we should have a choice whether to die; and if you have a creative soul, what is the point of having a gift for it to be taken away?"

Then waves of anger washed over him. Dion was right to go; that was his choice, he thought. But he denied that choice to Janine and the boys. How could he ever redeem himself? How could he live with taking them away from those they loved?

There was a distinct crackle in the air and Jo-Dan could feel the electricity around him. The lights above him had lowered and they were becoming organised, fizzing and sparking, lighting up the dark, cold arena. Jo-Dan could barely breathe; he felt he could take no more, whatever this was about to throw at him.

The capsule emerged slowly from the lights and descended to the empty stage. A swirling "Northern Lights" formation surrounded the capsule and swished to and fro until it formed a colourful curtain. A very bleary-eyed Paul and Lucas emerged from behind the curtain.

Jo-Dan, still hunched on the stage, breathed in hard. If they stepped out from that capsule he had no idea what would become of them. Dion and Janine were standing behind them and they hugged her boys long and hard before they stepped out of the capsule.

"What you doin' there all on your own?" Lucas said.

"How did it go?" Paul asked as he approached the sorry-looking sight in front of him. "We missed the end of the concert. Jesus, was it that bad? You look a wreck mate."

"Was hot in there; we passed out," Paul added. "Dion looked after us while we recovered; feels like we've been in there ages; where's the girls?"

Jo-Dan would not believe they were back until he physically felt them, even though he could see their vivid orange auras.

"The girls really need to see you. Go find them, but give me a big hug first," Jo-Dan said – and they obliged, still a bit puzzled why he was sitting there in the semi-darkness.

"Yuk, you're all sweaty and disgusting," Lucas said. "Think you need a shower mate."

"I do. You're right. I'm so pleased to see you both."

"You're weird, you know that?" Paul told him, as they went off to find their wives, and Jo-Dan had never been so pleased to hear his friend's insult.

Still sitting in a heap, Jo-Dan looked up at Dion and their eyes met.

"I couldn't do it," Dion said simply. "I would know if you weren't telling me the truth."

"I saw flecks of pink in the girls' auras," Jo-Dan said. "It's not my place to tell them, but I remember smiling to myself when I saw it a few days ago."

"This is Janine's decision, to bring the boys back," Dion said.

"She loves her boys as much as me; but we've been away for a long time and you forget how everyone else grows up and moves on. All she wants is for her boys to be happy."

"They're not my boys now," Janine said, sliding an arm around Dion's waist. "They are grown men; and knowing that they are about to become parents, they need to be back here. We haven't told them; that's for their wives to do.

"It's time for me to let go. No more tears for Dion to contend with. I'm happy for them and even happier to think I will be a grandmother."

Dion moved behind her, put his arms round her waist and looked at Jo-Dan, as if to make a point he was still staking his claim on her.

She leaned back and kissed him affectionately.

"Dion saved them," she said, as if he was some hero. "He took them into an area where they would get oxygen. He saved my boys."

Dion's eye bore into his, but Jo-Dan's expression did not waver. He gave nothing away, but he was about to get his own back in style.

"You're the hottest grandmother I've ever seen," he blurted out, not only being deliberately provocative but meaning every word.

"I always fancied you," Janine replied, with a wicked expression on her face that Dion could not see. "I always fancied having a toy boy."

Jo-Dan realised from her expression that she was playing with him and he loved her for that mischievous streak; but the reaction on Dion's face was priceless; that livid expression was something he would treasure forever.

The effect was immediate; all down to Dion, Jo-Dan presumed. The sparkles quickly condensed, the capsule rose slightly and faded into obscurity. For once, Dion did not get the final word.

Jo-Dan lay on his back staring at the ceiling. The lights above him had gone. All that remained was the dim light left by the technician and it was starting to get light outside.

He played that final scene over and over in his head and started to chuckle.

Jo-Dan revelled in the irony of Dion's obsession about staying young, and his then having to contend with his wife admitting that she fancied someone even younger.

Dion was absolutely fuming and that alone made the last few hours' trauma well worth it. Jo-Dan had pissed him off big time and he could not stop laughing. He lay on the dusty stage and laughed until he hurt, then cried tears of relief. Exhausted, he spent time collecting his thoughts and it must have been about seven a.m. by the time he eventually sat up, wiped his tired eyes and stared into the half light of the empty auditorium.

Jo-Dan did not hear the little footsteps approaching from the wings of the stage but he felt the little arms go round his neck.

"Are you sad, daddy?" his little girl said.

Jo-Dan's heart melted as he sat his daughter on his lap and hugged her close, while Victoria watched off-stage. His wife had returned home in the night, but had rushed back to the stadium as soon as she could.

"No honey, I'm not sad now."

"Marmie said a naughty man made you cry," she said, her big brown eyes looking into his soul.

"He did, sweetheart, but he's gone now."

"Is he an asshole, daddy?"

Jo-Dan laughed out loud. "You know you're not supposed to say that," he told her gently.

"It makes Marmie cross," she said seriously then giggled.

"Yes, it does," her daddy told her. "It makes Marmie cross with *me*," and he giggled too.

She was just four years old, with long, black, messy hair, way smarter than her age.

Jo-Dan rocked her in his lap. This mini-version of himself was someone who never minded how much he prattled. He made her laugh with the silly things he said and she had his accent because of all the time he spent with her.

"Unca Miles gave me a present for you," she said.

"You mean *Uncle* Miles," Jo-Dan told her.

"Whatever," she said, cheekily, Jo-Dan's own words coming back at him.

"Unca Miles is magic, you know," she whispered seriously as if it was a big secret.

"I know he is," Jo-Dan said. "Do you have my present?"

"Uh huh, right here."

Jo-Ann reached into her coat pocket and pulled out a playing card.

"Wow. How many hearts does that have?" her daddy asked and she counted carefully.

"One, two, three, four, five."

"Very good," he said and looked across at Victoria, struggling to hold the wriggling twins. She knew this would be the best way to reach Jo-Dan: bring his children to him.

"Your colours are priddy today," Jo-Ann told her daddy.

"Priddy?" he said.

"Yes, she said decisively; *very* pink and blue, like Marmie's."

"That's right," he said, "and yours are priddy pink."

Victoria walked over to join them, allowing the twins to totter as she held their hands.

She bent down and whispered to the two-year-olds, "Daddy needs lots and lots of love today. Do you think you could give him lots of great big cuddles?"

Jo-Dan moved his four-year-old to sit on his right leg and put a protective arm around her, as she amused herself twirling the playing card in her hand and trying, but failing, to make it disappear and reappear like Miles did for her. Her daddy held his left arm out and snuggled the twins into his lap on the other side.

He kissed the toddlers on top of their heads, breathing in their smell and burying his head in their pink auras.

"You OK now?" Victoria said, stroking his face. "Paul and Lucas are at our house with the girls. Everyone's fine."

"I'm great," Jo-Dan told her. "I have you and my kids. Dion came back. Everything's perfect."

"Can we go home now?" Jo-Ann whined. "I want to play in the garden."

"In a minute sweetheart," Victoria said. "But daddy's tired; he needs to go home and rest, not play in the garden."

"But I want to play piggy in the middle again with Polo Sweet," she insisted.

Jo-Dan moved her messy hair from her eyes and said, "We'll play piggy in the middle with Polo Sweet, I promise. But we'll have to wrap up warm, won't we? Then, after we've played, I need to go to bed. Is that a deal?"

Victoria gave him her usual look that said, "You spoil her; you never say 'no' to her," but she loved him all the more for that.

"Deal," Jo-Ann said emphatically.

"Show Marmie what Uncle Miles gave you," Jo-Dan said gently.

Jo-Ann twirled the card in the air. "Five hearts, Marmie. I counted them," she said proudly.

"Did you? You are clever," Victoria said.

Jo-Dan pulled his daughter close and whispered to her, "That's one heart for me, one for Marmie, one for you, one for Aura and one for Angel Rox."

Before I Am Old
by Dion

If I choose to remain
I'll be old and grey
With aches and pains

So I choose another way
And I'm not afraid
Don't care what people will say

'A cruel streak' they'll say
For taking her away
But tomorrow's not another day – for us

There's a place she can be
To live life with me
I set us both free in a new reality

She's the love of my life
My soul mate, my wife
I can't let her cry for the rest of her life

I'll visit many times
And I've made up my mind
Being selfish ain't a crime

Yes, I am vain
Don't wanna remain
So call me insane – if you want

I always knew,
Thirty nine – and I'm through
Your life's up to you

Party Like There's No Tomorrow

(Words and music by Jo-Dan)

No one on their death bed, ever said
"I should've done more chores"
Oh what a bore
No one on their death bed, ever said
"I should watch more TV"
Obviously

CHORUS
Party like there's no tomorrow
Live life, have fun
Don't look at life through a window
Your time has just begun

No one on their death bed, ever said
"Should've saved more money"
That right honey?
No one on their death bed, ever said
"I should've ate more greens"
Know what I mean?

No one on their death bed, ever said
"I should've lived life less"
Let go the stress

No one on their death bed, ever said
"Should not have loved so much"
It's good to touch

So - party like there's no tomorrow
Live life, have fun
Don't look at life through a window
Your time has just begun

Previous Books by Janet Lee

Mistress Magic (Olympia Publishers)
Saturday Rock Dog (Apex Publishing)
Living with BDD (Apex Publishing)
From Sixpences to Dollars (Apex Publishing)
Kissed by Angels (Apex Publishing)